THEY SETTLED IN SITKA

Cheryle Coapstick

First paperback edition November 2023

Paperback: ISBN 978-1-7366706-4-4
eBook: ISBN 978-1-7366706-5-1

Cover design and interior formatting by Andy Towler
www.aplusscreative.com

Published by Biorka Books
chercoaps@gmail.com

Acknowledgments

First and foremost, forever and always, my deepest heartfelt gratitude to the Lord Jesus, who puts these stories into my soul.

Encouraging the characters to leave my heart and enter the manuscript is sometimes tricky. Arranging them on the pages is time-consuming and often challenging. When I need a bit of encouragement to continue, I think of all of you and am grateful.

To my readers: I'm thankful to those who have read the previous books in MY MAMA'S MAMA series:

ALASKA'S FIRY,
ABOUT MISS RUTH,
ALASKA'S MAMA

I enjoy your comments and feedback on my Facebook author page, and of course, I love meeting you in person and talking face to face. Those dear readers who have taken it a step further and left star ratings and reviews on Amazon, Goodreads, and their social media have my heartfelt thanks. I cannot stress how important it is. The more ratings and reviews, the more algorithms, especially Amazon's, are activated, and the more people will see the books.

To Pond and Parchment Writer's Guild: Thank you for your consistent encouragement and enthusiasm. A special thanks to Amy Jury for hosting our meetings and feeding us.

To my developmental editor, Patty Huey, my line editor, Maureen Harlan, and my accuracy and fact-checking editor, Vicki Karlsson: Your dedication to my novels and the hours you have contributed to the work are priceless. No words can describe the gratitude I have for each of you.

To Denise Phillips: You were there from the beginning—my first encourager and the photographer for my author photograph. Many thanks.

To my cover designer and interior formatter Andy Towler of Aplusscreative: I'm grateful for the visual depth and interest your cover designs add to the books.

Please visit my author page for more information about Alaska, my books, and my writing journey.

Facebook.com/cheryle coapstick author

"Those who
Settled in Sitka
looked
for
a person
and a place."

—*The Professor's wife*

PROLOGUE
New Archangel, Russian America
October 1867

"What is it, Tasha?" Princess Maria Maksutov, petite, dark-haired, and beautiful, let the lace curtain drop and turned to face the teenage Creole—a person with a Russian father and a Native mother.

Tasha, taller than her mistress and ten years younger, smiled as she said, "It's time, Madam." With her oval face, high cheekbones, and straight nose, she looked as aristocratic as the Princess she served.

"Did you see the ships?" The melancholy Princess turned her gaze back to the harbor.

Tasha threw up the sash and leaned out the window. "I'm glad they built the castle on top of the hill. We can see everything! So many ships! The John L. Stephens, the Ossipee, the Resaca, and the Jamestown. Those English letters are so hard to read."

"You are such a bright child. Your command of English is excellent."

"You are a good teacher, Madam, but I wish you would teach me French." Tasha grinned—she had been secretly learning that language from the Princess's children.

Princess Maria wandered away from the window and leaned against the four-poster bed. The dark gray morning dress that lay there suited her mood. The October weather necessitated a wool coat, which was as dark as her thoughts. "You do not need to learn French."

"Everyone speaks French when they attend your dinners and receptions. Everyone except the Americans."

"Those Americans! The only language they speak is English. How uncivilized! French is the language of princes and palaces."

"And more important—it is the court's language in St. Petersburg, Madam," Tasha added.

"I have told you many times you are not coming with me!" The words were emphatic, the Princess's tone sharp. She chewed on her bottom lip, gently pulled on one of Tasha's long braids, and softened her voice, "This is a journey you can have no part in."

Not wanting to argue with her mistress, Tasha gazed out the window again. "Look! Pavel is flying between the ships. I count four skiffs bringing the American soldiers ashore. Do you think they will all come to the ceremony?"

"I hope not; they are uncouth. Dimitri and I opposed the cession of Russian America but did not have enough influence with the Tsar. This is a sad day for Mother Russia and for us."

"Surely, Madam, Bozhe is in control; does He not lead the Tsar?"

Princess Maria handed her young servant a silver-backed hairbrush and sat at the dressing table. Their eyes met in the mirror, and the Princess smiled sadly. "I think the Tsar has other advisors who are not as wise as your Bozhe."

Tasha artfully arranged the Princess's hair into a complicated chignon. "He is everyone's Bozhe, Princess."

The Princess picked up a diamond earring. She held it to her ear and then scowled, "Has Pavel brought back the one he stole?"

"Even though you leave bread crumbs and glossy gold paper scraps for him every morning, he will not bring back your trinket. He eats the bread and takes the paper. Ravens love shiny things."

"Trinket? That earring is worth more than many of the buildings in New Archangel. I thought that bird liked me. I named him. I fed him. What more does he want?"

Tasha laughed. Last month one of the children found his father's gold cufflinks on his desk. They played catch with them in the courtyard, and Pavel caught one of the precious links in his beak. The offender confessed to his father and was punished, but the Princess did not need to be informed that her favorite bird was a thief—a fact she had soon learned.

"I will ask Bozhe to tell Pavel to return your trinket."

"How easy life would be if we all had your faith, sweet Tasha. But now we must do our duty."

"May I accompany you to the ceremony, Madam?"

"Why do you want to see the glorious Russian double-eagle lowered and the ugly American flag raised? I do not understand, but I will be glad for your company."

A grim-faced Prince Dimitri and his equally somber aide met the Princess and her servant in the reception room. "We will do our duty, my dear," he said as he kissed his wife's cheek and offered her his arm.

She tucked her hand into the crook of his elbow as they left the sizeable Victorian mansion known as Baranof's Castle. The aide and Tasha followed. The little group stood on the veranda momentarily and observed the officials gathered in the small courtyard, then joined the American Generals Rousseau and Davis near the cannons in front of the flagpole.

About a hundred soldiers of the Siberian Line Battalion had assembled before the one-hundred-foot-high flagstaff. A battalion of American troops led by Brevet Major C.O. Wood, Ninth Infantry, stood on the other side of it. An honor guard of perhaps twenty brought the American flag and stood at attention in front of the battalion.

The Americans were boisterous, and General Davis signaled to Major Wood to control his men. The embarrassed Major hastened to do so. The Russians stood at attention, stiff and stoic, rigid and somber.

The transaction and legal paperwork had occurred thousands of miles away in Washington D.C. and St. Petersburg. Today's short ceremony proclaimed the official transfer of Russian America to the United States. A land the Americans called Alaska.

Pavel sat atop the flagpole; his black eyes flitted from official to official as greetings and salutes were exchanged. He screeched and flew away when the cannons fired.

"Even Pavel does not wish to witness this," Princess Maria whispered.

Captain Peshchurov stepped toward the flagstaff, and the Princess closed her eyes. Tasha stared as the Captain released the Russian flag, and its vibrant colors fluttered in the breeze. A moment later, she gasped and clutched the Princess's arm.

The double-eagle had caught on a yardarm halfway down the flagpole. Several titters from the American soldiers were silenced by a savage look from their officer. Captain Peshchurov released the pulley, and the flag continued its downward journey but was snagged by a Russian bayonet. The embarrassed soldier ripped it free. He quickly folded the torn flag and shame-faced presented it to the Prince.

Princess Maria Maksutov faded and would have stumbled if Tasha had not held her firmly. Ashen-faced, tears hanging on her lashes, she stared at Tasha and whispered, "It is an evil omen. Russia will be torn as I am."

Prince Dimitri stepped closer to his wife but stopped when he heard Tasha say, "It's almost over, Madam, and we can go inside."

"It will never be over. I am forever exiled." She hung her head and refused to look.

The United States Commissioner, General Rousseau, oversaw the raising of his country's flag. The American ships fired their cannons when the stars and stripes reached the top of the flagstaff. Its military cheered. The Russians were again silent, and the soldiers of both countries were dismissed.

The Americans raced down the hill, whooping and hollering, anxious to see what entertainment Sitka could offer. The Russian soldiers dragged themselves back to their barracks.

Prince Dimitri and the two American Generals retired to the reception room and shared a glass of champagne. Princess Maria and Tasha went directly upstairs.

"Help me, Tasha, these corset stays are too tight."

"Shall I choose a dress for the reception, Madam?"

"I am indisposed, a raging headache."

"You are the hostess, Madam."

"This house now belongs to the Americans. I have no place here."

"But, Madam..."

"Never again will New Archangel be called the Paris of the Pacific. I shall no longer hold court or preside over official dinners, receptions, or theatricals." Princess Maria, released from her corset, breathed deeply and threw it across the room. "What will happen to my home—my beloved New Archangel?"

"Bozhe knows, Madam. You will be all right if you lean on Him."

"I brought culture and gaiety to my miniature Russian court. Every ship that anchored here vied for an invitation. My husband and I represented the Russian Imperial Crown! We stood in place of the Tsar!"

"Yes, Princess, all the ships' captains, dignitaries, and other important persons looked forward to your welcome," Tasha spoke soothingly and hastened to pick up the offending undergarment.

"In Russia, I shall be one of many." The Princess sighed, opened the wardrobe door, and pulled out an elegant black dress.

"Black, Madam? Black is for mourning."

"Yes, it is," Princess Maria gave Tasha a wan smile. "Ask your Bozhe to help me do my duty one last time."

Tasha laced the Princess into the corset.

As the wet October days turned into a cold November, fifteen-year-old Natasha Petronova Bravebird had great difficulty encouraging her mistress. She talked to the Aunties—the matriarchs of the clan house—and visited the priest. She spoke to her parents and grandfather. No one had any advice for comforting their beloved Princess. They would miss her when she returned to Russia.

"What will life be like in St Petersburg, Princess?" Tasha asked as she folded another pillowcase and placed it in the large steamer trunk in the center of the room.

"Colder in winter, not much warmer in summer, but it's not the weather that frightens me."

"I thought you were sad, not frightened."

The Princess's countenance matched New Archangel's dismal weather. "Sitka, what kind of a name is Sitka?" She grumbled as she oversaw packing the family's belongings. "Stupid."

"This island you call Baranoff, we call Shee. Sitka means on the outside of Shee because it faces the ocean."

"I'm sorry, Tasha. I shouldn't sound so harsh."

"You are grieving, Princess."

"This is my home. My babies were born here, and now we are banished to a land they have never seen."

"Surely you have good memories of Russia."

Princess Maria sat back on her heels. "Sit beside me, Tasha." She moved a pile of linen and patted the floor. "As soon as I married the Prince, we embarked on his mission to Russian America. I have never been to the court in St. Petersburg. Dimitri says it is full of minor princes and aristocrats vying for favor and position. Lies, rumors, intrigues, and scandals. I know I will hate all the backbiting and manipulation."

"But your family?"

"Everyone I love is here." The Princess swiped at her eyes with a linen handkerchief. "I will do what must be done once ensconced in the Tsar's court: charm and flatter unworthy royals, bribe and cajole courtiers to further Dimitri's career. I feel weak thinking about it."

"Can you not help your husband's career with kindness, truth, and decorum?"

The Princess rubbed her forehead and gave Tasha a look of disdain. The young Creole ignored it and patted the Princess's hand.

"Bozhe says the joy of His Great Son is our strength."

"I will miss you, dear Tasha." Princess Maria hugged her.

"You do not need to miss me. I will come with you."

"Do not make such childish statements." The Princess shook Tasha's shoulders. "I will not take you to Russia! You would long for Shee." Princess Maria almost smiled, "Did I pronounce it correctly?"

"Bozhe will go with me, and I will have His joy."

"I will not change my mind! Now help me pack." The Princess turned away and held a handkerchief to her eyes.

"Oui, Madam." Tasha took no notice of the other woman's harsh tone and grinned as she answered in French.

It had taken slightly over two months to pack the family's belongings and arrange for passage to Russia. Prince Dimitri, now appointed Russian Consul by the Tsar, was to stay and facilitate the emigration of Alaska's Russians. Most were returning to their homeland.

Prince Dimitri Matsukov knew January was not the best time to sail these northern seas. "The ship is stout and the captain competent. Have no fears, my dear." Dimitri kissed each of his five children and sent them scuttling up the gangplank along with their governess. He held his wife in a long embrace.

As Princess Maria hid her face in her husband's shoulder, the Prince looked over her head, nodded, and winked at Tasha. She raced after the children and hid behind a lifeboat.

Dimitri removed his scarf and tied it gently around his wife's neck. "The time will pass quickly, and we will soon be together."

"I'd rather stay, even if it's only for a few more months."

"Too many corrupt scallywags and opportunists are coming into Sitka with every ship. It's becoming quite lawless and dangerous. I want your memories of Russian America to be happy ones."

The day was cold and unusually sunny for this time of year. The winter water was almost as blue as the canopy above. Wind rising. Ropes creaking. Sails filling. The Princess stood at the rail with her children as they waved and yelled repeated farewells to their father. She drew a shaky breath as the distance between the ship and New Archangel widened. When she could no longer see Prince Dimitri, she told the governess to take the children below.

Once alone, the Princess sagged against the rail. The forlorn figure tore at Tasha's heart. The shaking shoulders gave evidence to the woman's silent sobs. Tasha crept across the deck and stood beside the Princess, who felt her presence after a moment.

"Natasha Petronova Bravebird—what are you doing here? You belong in New Archangel. Oh, why are you here?"

"I am here for you, Princess. Where you go, I will go. Your family will be my family."

"I should be angry, but I—I—" The Princess enveloped the young Creole in a fierce hug.

"I will bring Bozhe's joy and peace with me." They turned for one last look at the place that meant so much to them.

Pavel, who watched from a high spar on the mast, swooped down and dropped a shiny earring at the Princess's feet. He flew back to Shee with a loud squawk.

ONE

He tugged on his ear, a nervous habit from his childhood.

The rain spattered on the window and crawled down the glass. It was warm, almost stuffy inside the small office. The woman behind the desk seemed immune, although she was clothed from neck to ankles in a black outfit that seemed to belong in another century.

He looked proper and professional in a buttoned-down white shirt. Black framed glasses. Polished shoes. Well-worn leather briefcase. Young, with the beginnings of a scruffy beard. He tugged at his collar, discreetly loosened his tie, and hoped she didn't notice the perspiration on his upper lip. "I agree with you, Miss Ruth. This needs to be done; I'm not sure I'm the one to do it. I am not an archivist or a historian. Not yet, anyway." He pulled on his earlobe.

"You have the necessary qualifications."

"I'm still in grad school and have no experience with this sort of thing. I'm not good with people."

"You have a keen interest in history coupled with analytical skills, and according to your father, you are extremely curious."

"How do you know my father?"

"You have changed your major two times. It's time to leave the classroom and see what life is all about."

He didn't know how to respond to that. He definitely wouldn't tell her he was thinking of adding another degree, which would mean another three years in school after completing his master's. "I'm no journalist. I don't know how to conduct an interview."

"I agree you're a bit reserved. I'm sure you will loosen up as the project moves along. Let your curiosity lead you."

He scratched his head and grinned, "Dad always said I've killed too many cats with more questions than he could count."

Miss Ruth smiled and set aside her spectacles. "We've watched you over the last few years and agreed you are the man for the job."

"We?"

"Members of the Territory of Alaska's Society for the Collection and Preservation of the History of its Multi-Cultural Peoples."

"That's a mouthful and rather intimidating." He began to sweat in more places, and his glasses fogged. He shook a handkerchief out of his pocket and carefully wiped the lenses. "It will take a great deal of time away from my studies—and the pay? I would have to tighten my belt."

"For a very worthy cause, my boy." Miss Ruth offered him another cup of tea, which he didn't want but accepted anyway.

"Yes, but..." He could feel the warmth flooding his earlobe as he continued to tug.

"I'm sure you can find ways to tighten that belt, and I will see what I can do to enhance things along the way."

"Yes, but..."

"We will include travel expenses, of course. Father Alexi has retired to Kodiak. All the others are in Sitka."

He picked up the list, which was several pages long. "There are scores of names on this list, and they come from all over the Territory."

"The ones I'm overseeing are from Sitka." She tapped the sheaf of papers in his hand. "They are underlined in red. Other members of the Society will cover different areas of the Territory. Some are conducting interviews, some checking the Territorial census, others are scouring old newspapers, journals, diaries, and letters of people who have passed and can't be interviewed."

"If I accepted this job, wouldn't I be better suited to interview people here in Fairbanks?"

"My goodness, no. And for the same reason I'm not interviewing anyone from Sitka. We want these interviews to be completely unbiased."

"I don't think you would be biased, nor would I."

"The Society deemed it unacceptable to have the interviews conducted by friends or acquaintances, so Sitka is the place for you. It's much smaller than Fairbanks, but I'm sure you will enjoy it."

"Yes, but I haven't actually accepted..."

"I will make the arrangements for your trip to Kodiak, and who knows, I might even go with you. I have a yen to enjoy one more Selaviq."

He gulped down his tea, and his temple throbbed. He now had a job he didn't consider himself qualified for and apparently was taking a trip to Kodiak with this formidable, old woman so she could take part in a Selaviq, something he had never heard of. Even though curious, he wouldn't ask; he was entangled enough. "Miss Ruth, I beg you..."

She patted his knee and then handed him his coat. "Alaska will become a state in a few short years, and we want this project finished before then."

"A few years—" he gulped, "I'm beginning my master's program, and I don't see how I could..."

"Yes, isn't this a wonderful research project? Perhaps you

will find your thesis. Why else would your professor have sent you to me?"

Why, indeed? It seemed his future had been mapped out for him, and although he felt nervous, unqualified, and out of control, it did intrigue him. "Why does the project need to be finished before we become a state—if we become a state?"

"Did you know I attended the Constitutional Convention in Fairbanks last year?"

"That was cool, fifty-five delegates in 1955." He laid his hands in his lap and gave his earlobes a rest.

"It was decided to have fifty-five delegates to echo the fifty-five at the Constitutional Convention in Philadelphia."

"Were you one of them?"

"In 1787? I'm not that old," Miss Ruth chuckled at her own joke and shook her head at the young man's embarrassment. She cleaned her spectacles and perched them on the end of her nose. "I was the Society's representative—more of a lobbyist—sent to the Convention to garner support for this project. We intend to present these historical accounts at the first session of the Alaska State Legislature and have them read into the official record."

"You can do that?" He shrugged into his coat and picked up his notebook.

"Young man, I have been in Alaska more than twice as long as you have been alive. You would be surprised at what I can do; just ask your father."

His curiosity was piqued, and he raised his eyebrows. "Perhaps I should start my interviews with you."

"Or with him." Miss Ruth laughed and practically pushed him through the door. "I'm just an ordinary old woman. There are so

4

many others you need to question."

The young graduate student closed the door and mentally put Miss Ruth at the top of that list. While on this project, he would do all he could to investigate her, and he would definitely have a conversation with his father.

TWO

"I don't have time for you."

"I can come back when the Café is closed."

"I will be too tired." Agrefena Evans grabbed the coffee pot and left him staring after her.

He watched her chat with the diners, refill their coffee, and yell orders to her staff. This was the third time he had tried to make an appointment. "Please, Mrs. Evans, this is important." He followed her from table to table, tugging his ear with one hand and holding his briefcase with the other. "I am trying to interview people who settled in Sitka. Can you at least tell me how you came to be here?"

Agrefena banged the coffee pot on its burner and whirled to face him, "I have been here for ten thousand years. That is all you need to know." She waved her wooden spoon in his face. "Do not put me in your book."

"It's not a book," He rubbed his earlobe and wondered if it could be. Universities liked their professors to publish, and he was determined to be a professor one day. He retreated to the counter and ordered a cup of coffee. He shook his head when Mike offered cream and sugar.

"That is one stubborn Indian, I mean Native; that's what they want to be called now, or is it Inuit? I can't keep track."

Mike leaned his elbow on the counter, his face a few inches from the frustrated would-be interviewer. "And that's precisely why my wife, Agrefena, won't talk to you. She doesn't believe you will get it right."

"Get what right?"

Mike scowled as he filled the glass containers with paper straws.

"I meant no disrespect."

"So, you were just clumsy, careless with your words?" Mike glanced at Agrefena, and his expression softened.

The young man gulped his coffee and muttered to himself, "I told Miss Ruth I wasn't qualified for this job, that I didn't know how to talk to people."

"Did you say Miss Ruth?" Mike scratched at the beard he was growing for the upcoming Alaska Day celebrations. "Agrefena won't change her mind, and I won't go against her by talking to you." Mike chewed on the end of his drooping mustache and stared at the frustrated young man, "Miss Ruth must see something in you." He motioned to Ade Bunderson, made the introductions, and explained the situation while keeping half an eye on his wife.

Ade slid onto the stool beside the graduate student and whispered, "We can't be seen together, Professor. I don't want Agrefena to know I'm talking to you."

"I'm no professor, just a grad student."

"Good enough for me, but keep your voice down." Ade looked over his shoulder and breathed a little easier. Apparently, Agrefena was back in the kitchen.

The intense young man pulled a piece of paper from his vest pocket. "You are on the list, too. Can we meet tomorrow? You can tell me about yourself and Mrs. Evans as well."

"Well, Professor, I'm not that interesting unless you want to hear some great fishing stories."

Mike laughed, "Don't let him get started, Professor. Nobody believes Ade's fish tales."

"I told you I'm no professor."

"You are now." Mike laughed, grabbed the coffee pot, and made the rounds to his thirsty customers.

The notepads, pens, and small tape recorder bulged from the Professor's briefcase. He set it on the counter, stuffed everything back into it, and forced it closed. "I've been commissioned to learn how and why the people on this list settled in Sitka. I don't think that includes the fish."

Mike put the aluminum coffee pot back on the burner as Ade leaned on the counter and motioned for him to refill the cup. Mike snatched the pot and banged it back on the burner when Ade rubbed his burning stomach and shook his head. "Make up your mind." Mike groused.

"Mike and Agrefena were some of the first people I met when I arrived here." Ade scratched his head. "Summer of 1922, it was."

"Just a snot-nosed kid, unsure of himself," Mike laughed.

Ade reached over and punched Mike on the arm while the young man Miss Ruth had hired whispered, "I'll meet you tomorrow afternoon at the library. Agrefena Evans is first on my list, and I don't want to return to Miss Ruth empty-handed. We'll schedule another time for me to get your story."

Ade slapped him on the shoulder, "Sure, Professor, I'll tell you about Agrefena, but I have some great fish stories, and they are all true."

Mike snorted.

"I just want to know the whys and wherefores that caused you to settle in Sitka," The young man said as they shook hands.

THREE

**Territory of Alaska's Society
for the Collection and Preservation
of the History of its Multi-Cultural Peoples**

<u>Subject: Agrefena Evans</u>

"Agrefena, where are you, girl? We need to pack for Fish Camp."

Instead of answering her mother, the newly graduated eighteen-year-old closed her book and raced to the third floor of the clan house. "Auntie, ask Mother if I may stay with you during the season," she said.

Agrefena's toothless great-aunt chuckled, "Do not stand in the doorway." She patted the sofa cushions. "I will answer the question you did not ask. My old bones ache, but I am well. You want to avoid Fish Camp?"

"I am sick of fish."

"It is the way of our people. We catch in summer to eat in winter."

"It's work from sunup to sundown, and the sun won't go down." Agrefena pushed out her lip and pouted like a child, and her Auntie chuckled again.

"Life is work," she said, "If you don't work, Bozhe, our good God, says you don't eat. I am disappointed in my old bones. They will not tolerate the canoe trip to Fish Camp; I will do my part by weaving baskets for fish, clams, and berries."

"So I can stay?"

"You need more discipline, Agrefena, a better work ethic. Go to Fish Camp."

A better work ethic? Agrefena fumed internally. When she wasn't in school, all she did was work. There were numerous chores and jobs to perform for her mother, Auntie, and other elders in the clan house. She could rarely steal away and read.

"I could gather Devil's Club and other things, and we could make medicine." Agrefena knew one of her Auntie's favorite pastimes was making curative salves and ointments.

"It is summer. I gather Devil's Club in the fall. Besides, you were careless last time. The spines broke when you handled them. They pierced your skin."

"I will be more careful."

"Always you say that, but you move too fast."

Agrefena knelt beside her Auntie and rested her head on the old woman's lap. "Everyone listens to the Aunties of the clan house, to you most of all."

Agrefena's great-aunt smoothed the girl's unruly hair with her gnarled hand. "I will take you to the woods and show you once more how to gather summer's medicinal plants. We will go again when the Devil's Club is ready. You must be slow and careful."

Agrefena bit the inside of her cheek and tried to think of a reason to go alone. "But, Auntie..."

"Agrefena, it will be as I say, or it will not be. You will also spend many hours weaving baskets. I have all the dried seagrass needed; the cedar bark is also prepared."

The girl jumped up and paced the room, hair flying.

"Put your hair in braids; it is as wild as you are," Auntie chided, but her tone was gentle, "While your family is at Fish Camp, you will not run wild in the white part of town. We will make the salves and weave the baskets," her Auntie said.

Basket making was tedious, and although Agrefena was skilled at weaving the designs, she did not enjoy it. After several hours, her fingers always cramped and hurt, but it was better than Fish Camp. She lowered her eyes. "Yes, Auntie."

"Send your father to me. I will tell him I need you."

Agrefena stared out the window and saw her little brother chasing his friends around the canoes pulled up on the beach. The boys' noisy play echoed into the room. She closed the window to silence their laughter.

Her home was the first of many clan houses stretched along Katlian, the only street of Indiantown, the Native neighborhood on the edge of Sitka. Most houses were large cedar structures, built close to each other and unpainted. Several extended families lived together. The houses were often chaotic and noisy, but Agrefena's parents' section was quiet today, quiet but tense.

"I must think of your future. You have finished school and are no longer a child," her mother said.

"You are Raven, so you must marry someone from Eagle. There will be men of Eagle at Fish Camp," her father spoke in his usual quiet way. "I will watch how they work and conduct themselves."

"To make a good marriage, you must fully embrace our ways and tame your wildness," her mother spoke firmly as she sewed glass beads on a pair of sealskin slippers.

"Agrefena, pay attention!" Her father's aunt, called Auntie by everyone in the clan house and matriarch of their family, snapped.

Agrefena let the curtain fall back even as the words washed over her. She wondered why everyone thought she was wild, perhaps because she spoke her thoughts freely. She had already decided who she would marry; he was not Eagle, not even Tlingit.

"Mother, I know all the Tlingit ways, but they are of the past. This is the modern world—the Jazz Age. Automobiles, telephones, restaurants, and buying food at the market. It is much easier to buy than to gather." Agrefena tugged at her hair and wished she dared to get it bobbed. It was all the rage, and she wanted to look like a flapper. She tossed her thick braids over her shoulders and imagined she looked like Clara Bow.

"Bozhe, our good Lord, has given us food. All we have to do is go to the sea and the forest. We hunt. We fish. We trap. We gather. And where would you get money for such foolish things as telephones and restaurants?"

"I could get a job at the bakery, the Sitka Café, or maybe the new library."

"Work for the whites? No, you are too pretty."

At four feet, nine inches, Agrefena knew she was too short to be pretty. Many thought she was still a child; others thought her cursed because of her small stature. She was nothing like the willowy silent film stars she longed to see at Budnikov's theater.

She peeked at their photographs in the Photoplay and Screenland magazines when she stole into Wortman's Drugstore, ignoring the sign that said NO INDIANS OR DOGS ALLOWED. Because she was small, she could hide behind the displays and merchandise. For a while, anyway.

With every turn of the page, Agrefena compared herself to the glamorous Hollywood stars and found herself lacking. Her face was too flat, and her nose too broad. Her black hair, dark eyes, and brown skin were identical to every other girl in Indiantown. She was proud to be Tlingit but knew pale milky skin and long flaxen tresses or bobbed brown hair were needed to be beautiful. This would never happen, so how should she live?

Sometimes she lived aggressively, pushing herself forward and forcing a token acceptance. Other times, she faded and made herself docile, invisible. She often lived with a confusing discord in her soul, two natures—two minds.

Many in Indiantown were also of two minds. They held tight to the old ways and rejected anything considered white, including education. Others excelled in learning, striving to retain the ancient ways while incorporating the new. A few shed their Tlingit ways and pretended to be exclusively Russian and, therefore, white.

Across town, the Sheldon Jackson Boarding School housed Native children from all over Alaska. They were taught reading, writing, art, music, and math. They were provided vocational training, homemaking, and other skills to navigate the civilized white world. All good things—but given in exchange for Native language and culture, a stripping of traditional ways.

Children brought to the school from remote areas of Alaska when they were young lost their culture and were forced to forget their Native ways. Some were allowed to visit their families after five or more years. They often felt like strangers, returned to school to finish their education, and few went back to their villages. After graduating, many embraced white practices and lived in a small neighborhood close to the school called The Cottages.

Agrefena asked her Auntie about the divergent Native thought. Auntie shook her head and said, "Our culture is wounded, perhaps fatally. We practice the old ways. Others want to be white. Many are straddle people; they sit on the fence, one leg on the side of their ancestry and culture, the other dangling in the white world. It is not known if our wounds will heal or the fence will hold." She shook her head. "You also straddle the two worlds, Agrefena. Be careful which way you fall."

Agrefena pictured herself standing atop the seawall in Totem Square. From there, she could look into Indiantown, and with a slight turn of her head, she could gaze down Lincoln Street into the heart of Sitka. Would she keep her balance? Could she embrace the good of white ways and be true to her culture? Why did there have to be division?

She turned to her Auntie's favorite topic. "Auntie, I am not pretty enough for anyone in the Eagle moiety to marry, but I don't care."

"You are pleasant to the eye but read too many books. You search for something more, something beyond." She shrugged, "You are tiny, and I think many are put off by that. Besides, you have a mind that does not aim to please a man."

"I aim to please myself."

"That is not our people's way. You must put your family, house, and clan before yourself. I fear the men of Eagle will not accept you."

"I heard stories about your strong-willed ways, Auntie, yet you married."

"He was weak, and it was not a good match. But I had my children. I do not wish such a union for you. Consider your ways. Grow yourself up."

The petite Tlingit girl was determined to marry the white man with the blue eyes even though it was a betrayal of her clan and her people. Would her future children, half Tlingit, half white, be accepted by either world? What kind of difficulties and struggles would they have to endure? Could she prepare them for the trials they would face?

And this white man? She had never spoken to him; what would he think of her? How could she entice him to see her and care for her?

A few days later, sullen and surly, Agrefena, in the canoe with her family, was on her way to Fish Camp under her mother's watchful eye and her father's strict rules. She vowed to remain miserable all summer and not speak to any eligible men from Eagle.

Aunties of the clan were always respected and obeyed; why not this time? She knew her Father thought marriage was the answer. He was so wrong.

Paddling thirty miles up the coast of Baranoff Island caused tired and aching muscles. Why couldn't her father purchase a trawler or seiner? If not a boat, then an engine to attach to the canoe. Why did everything have to be the old way? Why couldn't he blend the old and the new?

Cleaning, gutting, filleting, and hanging strips of fish over wooden frames, long days filled with flies, mosquitoes, hot sun, cold rain, and hard work; fish scales and guts sticking to skin, hair, and clothes--sweat, woodsmoke, and fishy odors clinging to everyone. Throbbing muscles, numerous bug bites, itching and oozing--this was Fish Camp. For Agrefena, it was day after day of misery.

One hot afternoon, with mosquitoes swirling around her face, she raised the fish knife and hacked off her hair. She looked at the long braids in her hand and swung them at the attacking insects. She shook her head and felt her hair sashay around her face.

"Agrefena, what have you done?" her mother cried. The other women stopped working, clucked their tongues, then turned away and mumbled about Agrefena's wild ways.

"I wanted to look like a flapper."

"Ugly, like the little girls at Sheldon Jackson who have their hair cut off by the whites," her brother laughed and pointed.

She turned her back on her younger sibling, determined to hide the hurt his words caused. Her fingers itched, and she felt like beating him. He pointed and laughed until his mother slapped him and sent him and his jeering friends to gather driftwood for the fire.

Agrefena stared at the long braids dangling in her hand. She flung them into the fire, aghast yet thrilled that she had dared to cut her hair.

As the tide changed, she saw her father paddling toward shore and longed for the sea's cool breeze. She waited until the canoe slid into shallow water, helped him pull it onto the beach, and asked to accompany him next time.

For a long moment, he stared at her silently. Agrefena hung her head, and her hacked hair fell over her face.

"When you respect our people and let your hair be as it was, I will speak to you," he said without looking at her.

Agrefena sniffed and watched him gather the fish from the boat and take it to the piles ready to be cleaned. She followed him, determined to renew the conversation. The tension in his stance and the pain in her heart stopped her.

During summer's many hours of daylight, everyone worked—from the youngest child to the oldest elder. Agrefena joined the others and searched the mud flats at low tide for cockles and clams. The men fished from their boats, and the children used dip nets to catch the salmon racing up the nearby creek to spawn. The women picked blueberries, salmonberries, and nagoon berries as they came into season.

During fearly spring and summer, herring spawning season, they tramped along the seashore, laid lacy hemlock branches into the water, and the tiny eggs clung to the branches. The season was short, and herring eggs were such a delicacy that Agrefena didn't mind taking part.

At night, the elders told stories of how difficult things were when they were young and how easy the current generation's lives were. Agrefena did not want to believe them, although she knew they spoke the truth.

When the salmon stopped running, Fish Camp was dismantled, the contents of the caches packed, and everyone returned to Indiantown. The fish and other foodstuffs they had gathered were shared with the old, the infirm, and others unable to participate.

"I have heard Fish Camp did not go well for you, Agrefena." Auntie, nearly toothless yet determined, sucked on a piece of smoked salmon as if it were a lollipop.

Agrefena pushed her short hair behind her ears. "I hacked off my hair in anger, although I think it's pretty. I yelled at my brother all summer, even when he didn't do anything. I scratched my bug bites until they bled and became infected, then smeared them with all the Devil's Club we brought. I felt sorry for myself. Why do I act like that, Auntie? I don't want to."

"Ah," Auntie said as she handed Agrefena thin pieces of cedar to tear into strips. "The first step to maturity is recognizing you are out of control, like a child."

"When does it get easier?"

The older woman laughed, "Never. I start each day praying to Bozhe to help me hold my tongue and restrain my thoughts. You would be wise to do the same."

"I suppose." She pulled back the lace curtains and fixed her eyes on her favorite view, the mountain and the water.

"Agrefena, you have many talents and gifts. You see how things should be ordered and organized. It is useful, but no one listens when you do not display a proper attitude."

"If I know how things should be done, people should listen, attitude or not." Agrefena almost stomped her foot. She smiled, proud that she had restrained herself.

Auntie pointed to the cedar, "Come away from the window and finish making cedar strips. I want to start another basket soon." She finished the last stitch on a ceremonial blanket, bit the thread between her teeth, and handed the needle to Agrefena. "You must earn the right to tell people what to do. You must first love Bozhe, and then you will be able to do what's right."

"It is difficult to love someone you cannot see or hear."

"You will hear Him if you listen. Indeed, you cannot see Him, but you will know what He is like if you look at all He has made."

Agrefena threaded the needle and poked it into Auntie's pin cushion, ready for the next time. "But what shall I do with my life?"

Many of Agrefena's friends had already applied to work at Booth Fisheries or Pyramid Packing, but she refused. Several in her class went on to higher education. Although Agrefena had graduated from the government day school with the highest marks, further education was not an option for her. She accepted that but was determined to learn by reading as many books as possible.

FOUR

She dressed carefully on her first day of work and left the house without her mother knowing. When she returned that evening, Auntie was seated in the living area, as were her mother and father. Her brother was nowhere to be seen.

That was her first and last day working at the Pioneer's Home, a facility to care for old sourdoughs. The buildings once housed the United States Marines and were falling down around their current residents. There was talk of erecting a new modern facility for the old-timers. All of that was beside the point. Agrefena had dared to get a job in the white part of town without her parent's knowledge or consent.

"They hired me to cook, but all I did all day was mop the hallway floors."

"You are a good cook, Agrefena, the best in Indiantown," Auntie said.

Her mother demanded, "You must stay among your own kind. There is danger in white Sitka."

"She needs to be married; that will calm her impulsiveness," her father, grim and stern, said.

"I am sorry. I did not think things through." Agrefena sat next to her Auntie, but she spoke to her parents. "Auntie is teaching me to think before acting, but it is difficult. I fail often."

Agrefena's mother shook her head and frowned, "That is something you should have learned as a child. I am the one who has failed."

"I will do better." Agrefena's voice had faded to a whisper.

"You must find the best of yourself—who Bozhe created you to be. Keep your fiery spirit, but rid yourself of this recklessness," Auntie said.

"Hmmph!" her father snorted. "She is too much as you were at that age if all the stories about you are true."

Auntie stood and spoke with a matriarch's authority, "She will stay with me while you are at autumn Fish Camp. We will sell my baskets. The tourists will come for a few more weeks."

"I do not want her sitting on the sidewalk and meeting strangers—white strangers." Agrefena's mother glared at Auntie.

"She will be covered and silent. I will watch her," Auntie promised.

"Agree to this, or we will immediately marry you to old Bob Tom, a highly respected Eagle." Agrefena's father stood before her but would not meet her eyes.

Agrefena, grateful her father had broken his vow of not speaking to her, touched her still-short hair and sighed. Would she have cut it if she knew how hurt her father would be? She shrugged; it was done and could not be changed. It would take years for it to grow. She wondered if old Bob Tom had seen her cropped hair. "He's a widower and a grandfather," she cringed.

"He will strengthen our clan." Her father left the room.

"You will obey Auntie and stay away from the whites," her mother said, indicating the basket-making supplies at her feet.

It was a sunny day, and a tourist ship had arrived. Agrefena, staggering under a load of various-sized baskets, trailed behind her

Auntie, who stopped outside Wortman's Drugstore.

"Auntie, there are too many women selling here. We should go up the street."

Auntie nodded, and much to Agrefena's delight, Auntie stopped outside of the Sitka Café. They spread a blanket on the sidewalk and arranged their baskets. Auntie handed Agrefena another blanket. "Sit down and cover your face." Auntie pulled one over her head and drew it across her face like a veil as she leaned against the Café just below the front window.

"But why?"

"Some stare, and others take photographs like we are just one more wild animal from Alaska to show their friends."

The three other basket-makers had already covered themselves. Soon, a well-dressed man and woman stopped in front of them.

"Look, George, we could sell these baskets back in Los Angeles for a lot of money."

"Don't smile or gush. We don't want them to think we're interested."

"But we are, and look at the slippers; the beadwork is exquisite."

"They are too stupid to realize the value of what they have, which works in our favor." He picked up a large basket and held out a bit of change. Auntie reached for the money, but Agrefena shook her head and tried to take the basket back.

The man laughed and held it higher. "Here's a two-bit piece." He flipped it into the air, and it landed at Agrefena's feet.

She threw the blanket off, jumped to her feet, and grabbed for the basket.

He held it above his head, and his eyes darkened. "Dirty Indian," he snarled.

"Please, George, these are the best we have seen in the South-east. We will make a fortune even if we give them a dollar a basket."

"I'll not give these savages more than what I already offered. They are trying to cheat me."

Agrefena knocked the rest of the change from his hand. "Who is the cheater?" she screamed in English, "Do you know how long it takes to gather the seagrass and cedar? All the steps required to prepare them? How many hours it takes to weave even a small basket? How our hands ache and fingers swell! You are the cheater! You!"

She pushed him; the basket flew out of his hand and hit Auntie in the face. He raised his hand to strike Agrefena. While his arm was extended, Mike Evans opened the door, broom in hand. He surveyed the situation instantly and swung the broom in George's direction. George took a step back. Mike threw the broom down and shoved him. George stumbled and fell off the wooden sidewalk.

His wife cried and knelt beside him, "Are you all right?"

He brushed himself off and growled, "We're never coming back here. Dirty thieving Indians."

"Get lost," Mike growled.

"Indian lover! You're no better than they are," George spat at Mike's feet.

Mike Evans turned to Auntie and said something in very bad Tlingit. The three other women, who had huddled in fear, now giggled behind their blankets.

He looked at Agrefena and said, "I asked if she was hurt, but I guess I didn't say it right."

"You said you were sorry the man ate a sea lion."

He turned red but chuckled and said, "Tell them I hope he gets indigestion."

He bought three of Auntie's large baskets and a small one from each of the other sellers. He paid a fair price.

Agrefena watched him as he carried the baskets into his Café. She patted her hair and wondered if Mike thought she looked like a flapper or a film star. Mike Evans, as tall as she was short, as light as she was dark, as pleasing to the eye as a summer's day. He looked a good dozen years older than her, but that didn't matter. How long before he knew she was his woman?

She remembered the day several months ago when she had left the Russian Church. She had been harassed by several white boys. One knocked her prayer book to the ground, and another pulled her hair. They pushed her behind the church. Mike Evans chased them off, picked up the small book, and held it out. She took it and ran, but one look into his blue eyes told her they held her future.

Now, on the sidewalk outside the Sitka Café, those blue eyes showed her a soul that was faithful and true. But how could she get Mike Evans, the owner of the Sitka Café, to notice her not as a Tlingit but as a woman?

A few minutes later, Mike pulled a long table from the Café and placed it in front of the window. His waiter brought several chairs. "These will be available whenever you come, and please, make the Café the permanent place to sell your items."

Agrefena nodded and told him her name.

"Your name is as pretty as you are," he said.

That was one part of the conversation she did not translate.

Auntie and Agrefena spent the rest of the tourist season in front of the Café. The tourists saw the value of their products but not the women who produced them. Agrefena seldom translated what they said but usually replied to these disrespectful tourists in kind. They tended to walk away angrily without buying anything. Soon, the three other women took their wares and moved further down the street.

"I am sorry, Auntie. We haven't sold many baskets."

"I don't know what you say to them, but I know you say what you think. It is not always a good thing," Auntie said.

"Mike Evans buys something nearly every day," Agrefena said.

"Be careful of that blue-eyed man. I see the way he looks at you."

"Auntie!"

Auntie rearranged the baskets on the table, pulled a piece of salmon jerky from her pocket, and gnawed on it. "I am not so old that I do not remember what such a look means, and you look at him the same way. It will not end well."

Agrefena frowned and wanted to beg Auntie to keep silent about Mike Evans of the Sitka Café. The older woman patted her hand and smiled, letting the girl know her secret would be honored.

However, others noticed, and soon the rumors reached her parents. "Agrefena, what do we hear about you and a white man?"

"Nothing." Agrefena looked to her Auntie, who shook her head.

"There has been talk that this man gives you too much attention, and you respond in kind," Agrefena's mother frowned and laid her sewing aside, "I do not approve. If such talk continues, arranging a marriage for you will be more difficult."

Agrefena bowed her head and said, "I do not wish for a marriage to be arranged."

Her father and mother put their heads together, whispered, and then her mother said, "By this time next year, you will be married to someone from the Eagle moiety, perhaps from the Hawks Nest House of Wolf Clan, Bob Tom's clan."

"No! I will not!" Agrefena hung her head and chewed on the tip of her thumb. "I did not mean to be disrespectful."

"It is decided," her father put his hand on Agrefena's shoulder, "It is our people's way."

FIVE

Nothing was said over the next few weeks, and Agrefena pushed the distasteful subject of the marriage negotiations from her mind. She concentrated on Auntie's lessons in self-control and decorum while they wove basket after basket.

One day Mike Evans brought a middle-aged woman to their table. The elegantly dressed white woman smiled at the two weavers and examined their baskets.

"Mike, these are museum quality." She turned a small basket over and over.

"I told you these two were excellent artisans, the best I've ever seen." He hooked his thumb in his suspenders and rocked on his heels. His face beamed as if he had made the baskets himself.

"I have contacts in San Francisco and New York, as well as my own store in Seattle. I can sell as many as they can make. Do you think they will agree to sell to me exclusively?"

While Mike and Mrs. Grafton talked, Agrefena studied the woman. Her envy of movie stars was replaced with an admiration for this woman who had come from the United States. Mrs. Grafton was just over five feet tall, just a few inches taller than Agrefena. Her hair and clothes spoke of confidence and a self-assurance rarely seen in a woman. She talked to Mike as an equal and made decisions without consulting her husband. *If I were white, I could be her; I will be her.* Agrefena stood and determined she would learn from this woman.

I will be a businesswoman in Sitka and make a place for myself. At the same time, I will keep my place among my people.

Mike took Agrefena's arm and gently pulled her forward, introducing her. "She speaks English, Tlingit, and Russian."

"Mrs. Grafton, you can buy from others on the street at a much lower price. Why us?" Agrefena asked.

This no-nonsense businesswoman spoke to her as an equal. "Your items have the best workmanship, and your designs are the most artistic. Mike says you are dependable. I trust his judgment."

Auntie looked from Mike to the woman from Seattle, not understanding the English conversation. Out of respect, Agrefena asked Auntie to make the decision and translated her answer, "My bones are too old to sit outside all day, even though this Mike Evans has given me a chair. We will stay home next to our warm fire and weave for this woman."

"I told her to come inside anytime to rest and get warm." Mike smiled at Auntie.

Mrs. Grafton insisted on a written contract to protect both parties.

"Mike, will you sign for me?" Agrefena, red-faced, mumbled.

He protested, and Agrefena said, "You forget, I am Tlingit. I am not a citizen of the United States or the Territory of Alaska. I am unclear about the laws about Natives owning a business, but I know they are restrictive."

"You trust me?"

The young Tlingit woman felt her toes tingle and warmth cover her face. She nodded.

"Stupid laws," he muttered as he took the pen from Mrs. Grafton and signed.

As Mrs. Grafton signed the contract, she smiled at Agrefena. "Mike may have signed for you, but you and I are equal. We will decide things together."

Daily, Agrefena found reasons to see Mike. Sometimes delivering one basket at a time or asking his opinion about a particular design.

Agrefena assumed her parents thought she was in Auntie's small, curtained alcove on the third floor of the clan house. She did not tell them otherwise. Auntie waved her away each morning with a warning to keep her emotions in check.

❧

One day Mike said, "Mrs. Grafton thinks you are an astute woman and don't need me as a go-between."

Agrefena lowered her eyes and spoke softly, "I'm more comfortable letting you handle things." She knew she could handle the business herself but needed the excuse to see him.

He shook his head as he wiped the counter in front of her with a damp towel. "I enjoy your daily visits and don't mind doing the paperwork, but it's taking more time than I can afford."

She tossed her head and felt her bobbed hair swing around her ears. He followed the movement with his eyes. It made her heart flutter, and she hurriedly said, "Mike Evans, you are a kind and good man. You are not, that is, you do not know how to do things."

"What do you mean, Agrefena? Fena?"

"Fena?"

"Can I call you that?"

She nodded, suddenly shy. "Only when we are alone."

She explained several ways he could refine the flow of cleaning, clearing the tables, and improving the service to his customers.

"How do you know all that?"

"I grew up in a clan house, many people with many needs. I learned to do things quickly and efficiently, especially around mealtimes."

"I'll be." He scratched his head.

"Mr. Mike Evans. I propose a trade. You continue with the details and paperwork for the basket business, and I will run the Café." She knew she would soon be running his Café and her business.

He poured her a cup of coffee. "Agrefena, you just finished school. You have no job experience; I can't let you run my Café."

She looked at him over the cup's rim, "Try me for three months."

"I'm barely making it and can't afford to pay you."

"You will make it, and you will pay me."

"What about your Auntie and your parents? Don't you need their permission?"

"You leave them to me."

"You want this man," Auntie's mouth formed a grim line, "You love him?"

Agrefena lowered her lashes and whispered, "Yes."

"Raven marries Eagle. We do not marry for love but to create a stronger alliance with the opposite moiety, to strengthen our clan and improve our house." Auntie jerked the pile of cedar strips closer.

"What about love?"

"Love comes after if Bozhe wills."

"I will only marry for love."

"Do you know the pain it will create in your mother, the con-flict in your father?"

"I do not want to hurt them, Auntie, but I want to be happy." Agrefena bent over her small basket. She tied off the ends of the seagrass and put the finished product with the others.

"Your parents want you settled but will not see union with a white as good. Your father will be shamed."

"You know Mike Evans is a kind man. It should not matter that he is pale and I am dark."

"I do not think it matters to Bozhe," Auntie whispered, "but Mike Evans is not Eagle."

"It will be difficult, but I love him."

"He must be a dozen years older than you."

"I don't care."

"Agrefena, does he love you?"

"You see the way he looks at me."

Against her parent's unspoken wishes and with a heavy heart, Agrefena continued her daily visits to the Café. Once she pushed open its doors, she shed the guilt she carried from Indiantown and embraced the job and the joy of being near the man she loved.

Mike scratched his head when she added fry bread to the menu and served a complimentary basket at every table. "That's going to cost a lot. I thought you said you were going to turn this place around."

She patted his hand and lost her concentration when she gazed into those incredible blue eyes.

"Well?" he asked.

She felt the heat rush to her face, "Uh...they will eat the bread and not notice that the meal portions are smaller. They will be full and completely satisfied."

And they were. Agrefena attacked the kitchen, replacing the cook with herself. She streamlined the menu, eliminated waste, and incorporated Tlingit ingredients into the dishes. She paid her brother and his friends to gather them in the woods and along the shore.

Soon tourist season ended, and the Café depended on the townspeople to keep the business going. Agrefena introduced daily specials and fancy desserts. The locals fell in love with her French crullers.

As he had for over a week, Mike helped Agrefena into her coat. "Won't you let me walk you home?"

"It's not far." She didn't want anyone from Indiantown to see them together.

"It gets dark so early now, and I don't like the thought of you unescorted."

"This is your first winter in Alaska. Be glad you don't live farther north. You would never see the sun," she laughed.

"Fena, I'll feel better if you let me come with you."

She shook her head, stuffed her hair under her hat, and waved goodbye. Mike locked the doors of the Café and followed her at a discrete distance; this became his nightly routine throughout the winter.

One night, unseen by Agrefena, he intercepted two men who were obviously drunk and intent on having their way with the young Tlingit girl. He dragged them to the local lawman, who did nothing.

Mike fumed and went to the ANB hall the next day and asked to speak to the head of the Alaska Native Brotherhood. "I don't know what can be done to protect your women when the law seems unconcerned."

The Tlingit said nothing.

"There must be something you can do; we can do." Mike ran his fingers over his hair.

Again, the Tlingit remained silent.

"What about the tribal police?" Mike asked.

"They have no authority over the whites."

Mike paced and swore.

"You follow Agrefena home every night. It has been noticed."

"I do not want to see any harm come to her."

"It is enough."

Mike could not hold his frustration in check. "It's not enough. Perhaps I could join the ANB, and together we could find a solution."

"You will not be allowed to join, but I will speak to the clan heads. Perhaps we can consult with you and ask for your perspective as we work to eliminate segregation and injustice. We need as many interested whites as possible."

"I would like that."

"For your own sake, do not tell anyone you are sympathetic to us."

Mike shrugged and said, "I think everyone already knows how I feel." He shook hands with the older Tlingit. "You won't tell Agrefena I followed her, will you?"

The old man's leathery brown face wrinkled as he smiled, "That would not be wise."

SIX

Although Mike welcomed everyone to his place, few Tlingits came. Most did not have the money. If they did, they would not waste it eating at a restaurant. However, one evening a Native of average height, middle age, and a prominent brow stood in the doorway. After a few moments, he sat at the counter. Mike poured him a cup of coffee and handed him a menu. "I'll be back in a few minutes to take your order."

The Native held the menu but watched Mike wait on his customers and clear the tables. Agrefena peeked around the kitchen door, which she had cracked open just enough to see and hear everything.

When Mike returned, the Native laid the menu beside the untouched cup of coffee and stood to leave. He was bumped by two older white men, a fisherman and a logger. "Get out of the way, you dirty..." the fisherman said.

"They shouldn't be allowed in a place where decent people come to eat," the logger showed his tobacco-stained teeth.

The Tlingit said nothing, but Agrefena saw the tension in his clenched jaw and fists.

Mike came from behind the counter, all six feet two of him, and grabbed the logger and fisherman by their upper arms. He pulled them to the door and pushed them through. "You are absolutely right; this is a place for decent people to eat. I don't want to see either one of you here again."

After the Tlingit left, Agrefena said, "That was my father."

"Why didn't he tell me? Why didn't you come out of the kitchen?"

"I was trying to figure out why he came."

"He didn't say one word to me, not even to ask about you."

"I will talk to Auntie; she knows everything."

"Fena, do you think he will allow you to continue to work for me?"

"I do what I please." Agrefena swallowed and whispered, "I mean, I will try to find a way."

"I don't want to come between you and your family."

"You won't," she smiled, but he already had.

"Mike, a young man is at the back door. I have told him he can wash dishes for a meal."

"You have a kind heart." He smiled, which set his blue eyes dancing.

"He just arrived from the States and has no money, no place to sleep, and no prospects."

Mike opened a bottle of Coca-Cola and slid it across the counter to Agrefena. He poured himself a cup of coffee and leaned across the counter as she sat on the stool. "Now, why do I think this young man has a place to sleep and will soon have money and prospects."

"He will sleep in the storeroom and wash dishes for now. He wants to be a fisherman, but no one will take on a cheechako with no skills."

"And?"

"I will send Petrov Bravebird to you, and you will convince him to apprentice this young man."

"I don't know Petrov Bravebird. Why would he listen to me?"

"If you make a good case, he will listen."

Several days later, Petrov Bravebird entered the Café at closing time just as the last customers left. He seated himself at the counter and introduced himself to Mike. "Your window is without the sign that says NO INDIANS OR DOGS ALLOWED. That is good."

Mike poured the Tlingit a cup of coffee. "Agrefena tells me you have the biggest boat and are the best fisherman in the Southeast."

Petrov Bravebird said nothing.

"I mean, you have a modern boat." Mike wiped the same spot on the counter repeatedly.

"I have fished the waters of these islands since I was a boy. My family has used traditional and modern methods, but I do not think you want to discuss my fishing techniques."

"Yes, that is, no. There is a young man who wants to be a fisherman, and no one wants to hire or even apprentice a kid with no skills or experience."

"No one?"

"None of the white fishermen." Mike signaled Agrefena, and she pushed the young man through the kitchen door. He stumbled and stood at the end of the counter.

"Show me your hands," Petrov Bravcebird said.

The fresh-faced, blond-haired boy held out his large hands. One hand had a scar on the back, and thick calluses covered both palms.

"You may return to the kitchen," Petrov dismissed the boy and reached for his coffee.

Agrefena propelled the boy toward the sink and stepped back into the Café. She looked at the two men, "What do you think?"

Petrov Bravebird turned his attention to the Café owner, "Is he trustworthy?"

"He has been washing dishes and sleeping in the storeroom for several days. I do an inventory every morning, and nothing is missing," Agrefena grabbed a dishcloth and wiped the counters.

"What is his tribe?"

"His name is Ade Bunderson, age sixteen, Swedish," Mike said.

"Alone? No family?"

"He arrived at our back door by himself last week, although he said he came north with a buddy who is now working in the woods."

"Will he work for a Native?"

Ade burst through the door, wiping his hands on a dishtowel; his smile reached his ears. "Yes, sir. I worked with Indians and Mexicans throughout the Southwest before making my way to Alaska."

Petrov gave him a long look. "I said work for, not with."

Ade laughed and pointed to Agrefena. "She is the most demanding and toughest boss I've ever had. I can take it."

The old Native nodded, and his lips twitched as he held back a smile. "Be on the docks at four tomorrow morning. I will find you. We fish for crab."

Ade frowned, "Not salmon or halibut?"

"Fish for fish in summer. Fish for crab in winter."

Later, Mike asked Agrefena, "How will others in Indiantown feel about Petrov Bravebird taking on a white deckhand."

She shrugged and grabbed a broom. "Petrov Bravebird loves Bozhe and does what is right. He sees all colors as equal."

"I'll have to remember that," Mike whispered to himself.

SEVEN

Like the thick fog that camouflaged the mountains surrounding Sitka, Agrefena's soul was shrouded by a fog-like uncertainty. Auntie said negotiations for the marriage were slowly moving forward. Agrefena knew there was no use talking to her father, no way to stop his plans.

Her heart told her she could marry no one but Mike Evans. But how? And what would that do to her relationship with her family?

Early winter's cold, misty rain had given way to midwinter's ice and snow. Agrefena's heart felt as frozen as the snow on the mountains surrounding her island home. The sidewalks and streets of Sitka looked like donuts with a powdered sugar glaze.

Agrefena often fled to her sanctuary with Auntie and stared out the window. Across the sound, snow-covered Mount Edgecombe rose majestically as always. The mountains that encircled Sitka and the surrounding waters had been constant in her life, solid and stable. Now, nothing felt sure.

"Has my father said anything more to you, Auntie?"

"Be glad you are difficult, and no one wants to wed a headstrong woman." Auntie reached for more seagrass and began a new basket. "Enough gazing out the window. The mountain has not erupted for thousands of years. It is as it has always been. The tide ebbs and flows, but the nature of the water stays the same. Your longing will not determine the outcome."

"I have no control over my life."

"It is good for you to realize that. Family and clan are more important than any individual."

"I do not accept it. I will be in command of my own life."

Auntie laughed, "Agrefena, only Bozhe has control. We humans just think we do. He will help you accept what you cannot change."

Agrefena clenched her jaw and bit the inside of her cheek. She stared at Mt. Edgecomb. Ten thousand years with no eruption—she felt ready to blow. She was encouraged that her father's efforts were not going well. But still frustrated she couldn't find a way to make Mike acceptable to her family. Agrefena wiped her eyes, blew her nose, and bent over the weaving materials.

Her father had never spoken of his visit to the Café but had not forbidden her continuing there. What would she have done if he had? She pushed the thought away but knew eventually, she would have to choose.

"Mr. Evans, Mike, I'd like to thank you for putting me in touch with Mr. Bravebird. I have learned a lot from him. I could stay out to sea forever." Ade Bunderson had filled out these last few months. He would always be slim, but muscles bulged beneath his shirt. His whiskers were no longer sparse and wispy, although still blond. He attacked the plate of food Mike set in front of him.

Mike grinned as he wiped the counters and refilled the salt and pepper shakers. "Quite the fisherman, are you?"

"I'm getting there. I'm learning about tides, currents, shoals, wind, weather, fish species and their life cycles, and the crab and shrimp. It will take years to know everything. Someday, I'll have my own boat. But that's not what I wanted to talk to you about."

"What then?"

"Mr. Bravebird has been telling me about Tlingit history and culture. How important lineage and clans are—" Ade stopped talking, the heat rushed to his face, and he stammered, "—how important marriages are."

Mike stared at the young man, who was not yet old enough to vote. The salt continued to pour out of the canister, overfilling the shaker and spilling onto the counter.

Ade shoveled another forkful of eggs into his mouth, swallowed without chewing, choked, and said, "What I mean is, I'm grateful for all you and Agrefena have done for me, and I want to help you."

"Help me what?" Mike scooped the salt back into the container, refusing to look at Ade.

"Oh, good grief. I'm young, but I can tell you love each other. I think Agrefena would marry you immediately if you proposed."

"And what would that do to her family? Her clan?"

"You know she would choose you over them."

"That choice would break her heart, if not now, when we had children." Mike shook his head, picked up the coffee pot, and refilled Ade's mug. "I won't ask her to marry me."

"There might be a way. I've been talking to Petrov Bravebird about it."

Mike slammed the pot back on the burner. "You what?"

"Don't get upset. I'm helping you."

"I don't need some snot-nosed kid putting his nose into my love life."

Ade stood and threw money on the counter for his half-eaten breakfast. "You don't have a love life, and you're not getting any younger. Look, all I'm saying is there might be a way for Agrefena to marry you with her family's blessing." Ade glared at the indignant Café owner. "It would be difficult. Maybe you're not man enough to try." He stomped out of the Café without seeing Mike's expression turn from exasperation to hope.

Mike and Ade tip-toed around each other for several days. Agrefena couldn't get to the bottom of it, which irritated her. When Ade joined Petrov on a week-long fishing trip, Mike's mood improved, but he wouldn't talk about the young fisherman, just mumbled something about a love life. As far as Agrefena knew, Ade didn't have a love life.

"Fine. Don't talk to me. I'll grill Ade when he returns." Agrefena slapped the dishrag into the sink. Mike stomped out of the kitchen.

Saturday morning Agrefena placed a plate of eggs and hashed brown potatoes in front of Father Alexi and sat at his table.

"You look worried, Agrefena, or perhaps angry?" The priest's lips moved in a silent prayer, and then he picked up his fork.

Agrefena looked toward Mike and then at the priest.

"That's the way of it, then? I have seen you looking at each other in church when you should be paying attention to my sermon."

"I am sorry, Father."

"Not sorry enough to pay attention." The smile almost reached his eyes.

Agrefena lowered her head briefly and then looked into the priest's face. "I have tried to forget him because he is white, and our marriage would hurt my family and clan. But Father, the trying hurts me." She put her face in her hands.

"I know what it is like when you cannot have the one you love."

Agrefena raised startled eyes to the priest. She saw the pain in his eyes. "Father, I..."

"You know the rules. Mike Evans is not Orthodox but has been attending the church. I will marry you with your family's permission if he is baptized. Although he is not Tlingit, not Eagle." The priest sighed and reached for his coffee cup. His eyes were full of pity for the lovesick girl. "I fear he will always be unacceptable."

"I am afraid to ask for their blessing. Marriage is to strengthen the house and the clan, not for love."

"I am sorry, Agrefena. It seems there is nothing to be done, but I will pray. Bozhe has ways of doing the impossible for His children." The priest turned his attention to his breakfast.

"Marriage should be for love," Agrefena whispered as she returned to her work.

Spring came once again to Sitka. The rain fell soft and misty. Thick, dense fog was replaced by thin, lacy wisps. Agrefena's heart remained in hibernation like a bear in deep slumber.

"Auntie, I shall never marry. No matter who my father chooses for me, I will refuse."

"You would shame your father before all?"

Agrefena felt the tears on her face and the constriction in her chest. "Is there no way for me to be happy?"

"You must go to Miss Ruth. She is held in high regard by the ANB."

"How can the Alaska Native Brotherhood help me?"

"The government says we must be civilized to be citizens..."

"I don't care about citizenship," Agrefena snapped and then apologized.

Her Aunt continued, "They strive to help us gain equality. Perhaps this would include marriage between whites and Natives. Miss Ruth might be willing to advocate for Mike Evans."

Agrefena's shoulders slumped, and she fiddled with the silver bracelets on her wrists. The gentle clinking sound gave her little hope. The carvings on the bracelets told tales of Tlingits overcoming incredible odds, almost miracles. A miracle was what she needed. Did Miss Ruth have one?

The white woman in old-fashioned black attire and the Tlingit girl on the edge of womanhood met at the head of Totem Park's coastal trail. The towering spruce and hemlock canopied the path and diffused the light. The marine climate greened the area year-round. Several kinds of moss grew on downed trees and stumps. The forest ended at the rocky beaches of Jamestown Bay. The twitter of forest creatures and the call of shorebirds added to the tranquil scene.

"I have always loved this place," Miss Ruth said as they began their walk, "I like to sit by Indian River where it empties into the bay. Water and islands on one side, trees and mountains on the other."

"Eagles, gulls, crows, and ravens scavenge for their meals along the tidal flats," Agrefena said.

"All kinds of waterfowl and shorebirds live together. If only man could do the same," Miss Ruth shook her handkerchief and swiped debris off a fallen log.

"They live together but do not mate together," Agrefena sighed and bit her lip.

Miss Ruth took the girl's hand, "Ah, these creatures are different species. Man is not."

"Then why do some think so."

"I can't answer that, dear one. I suspect there are many reasons, none good."

"Auntie told you why I wanted to see you?"

"Mike Evans is a good man."

"Have you ever been in love, Miss Ruth?"

Miss Ruth patted the log, and Agrefena sat next to her. The older woman gazed at the horizon and remembered her voyage on the China Doll, a beautiful clipper ship, some thirty years ago. As a twenty-year-old, the excitement and adventure almost overwhelmed her, as did the ship's handsome captain, Harlan Walker. She had come to love this man of the sea almost without realizing it. Her eyes clouded with pain when she thought of the shipwreck off of Kodiak Island just a few years ago and the grief that consumed her when she learned of his death.

Agrefena remained silent. Miss Ruth looked at a whale breaching in the bay, smoothed her skirts, and said, "What do you want of me?"

"My father seeks an alliance with Eagle Moiety. It is tradition."

"And?"

"Will you be my advocate?"

"In place of your family? That would never be allowed."

"An advocate for Mike Evans. Talk to my parents and the ANB. Convince them it will be good for our house and clan if I marry a white man."

"You credit me with too much power."

"Auntie and Father Alexi say nothing is impossible with Bozhe."

"Do you follow after Bozhe and His Great Son?"

"I try."

"It's a start. But Bozhe requires more. He wants you to walk in union with Him so that you are one. Can you give Him all of yourself, even your love for this man?"

"Bozhe would not ask that of me!" Agrefena's eyes filled, and she swiped at them.

"Bozhe's love is great, and if you want to belong to Him, you must surrender everything."

"You sound like Father Alexi, only he seems stern when he says such things; it fills me with dread. Your voice is gentle and gives me hope."

"Bozhe is our hope, and He is always good. If you can put everything into His hands and accept what He returns to you as His perfect will, you will be fine."

"That is asking a lot."

"Everyone comes to this turning point, this struggle to surrender, and it will be difficult, but if you genuinely believe, you will be victorious." Miss Ruth placed her hands on the girl's head and prayed.

"Thank you, Miss Ruth. I have a lot of thinking to do."

"You have a lot of praying to do. Everything in you will fight against surrendering to the God of the universe."

Miss Ruth gave the girl a long hug, and then they finished their walk beneath the silent totems, each woman lost in her own thoughts.

EIGHT

———

The following days and nights blended together as Agrefena struggled to understand who she was and what she believed. Her family had been Russian Orthodox for over a hundred years, but for her, it seemed more cultural than personal.

Miss Ruth talked to Bozhe as if He stood next to her. The older woman knew Him as a friend. How could the Creator be friends with His creatures when He was holy and they were not? How could He be her friend when she was constantly scheming to get her own way and not caring about His? Agrefena wanted the peace Miss Ruth had, but she also wanted Mike Evans. She wanted Bozhe to speak to her as He did to Miss Ruth. Miss Ruth said that only came with surrender.

Agrefena's mind and heart would not let these thoughts go as she wove baskets with Auntie. What if Bozhe required more than she was willing to give? What if Mike Evans was not a part of Bozhe's plans for her? Who did she esteem more, Bozhe or Mike Evans? She did not speak her thoughts.

These questions interfered with her sleep, and she lost her appetite. After a few days, she felt weak but had a plan. Agrefena asked her mother to pack a lunch and promised to return by dark.

"I will make a large lunch since you have not eaten. Where are you going?"

"To the top of Harbor Mountain. I want to see the water and the islands, be near the sky."

"It's a long hike, just a few deer trails. Only the best hunters climb that mountain, and I don't want you going alone."

Agrefena sighed and pushed her still-short hair out of her eyes. "I knew you wouldn't. Petrov Bravebird is taking several of his nephews up the mountain to hunt. I will go and return with them."

Her mother's face settled into a frown. "I don't like it."

"Please, Mother, I am on a spiritual quest."

"You are not seeking a spirit animal, are you? We are Orthodox."

"I am seeking Bozhe. I want to love Him and do what's right like Miss Ruth and Father Alexi advise." She knew in her heart she would ask Bozhe for a way that she and Mike could be together. She was uncertain what she would do if she could not hear His answer or if He said no.

"That is a good thing. Perhaps it will settle you. Be careful."

The trek up Harbor Mountain was hiked in silence. Petrov had coached the boys for many days. Only the most obedient were allowed to accompany him. It was a privilege that had to be earned. Several of them grumbled when they saw Agrefena, but a stern glance from Petrov settled them.

They reached the summit after an exhausting climb. Sometimes Petrov had hacked away brush and branches, but mostly, he had followed the ancient deer paths. His nephews trailed after him like ducklings waddling after their mother. Agrefena was last in line.

The sun broke through the cloud cover and glistened off the waters of Sitka Sound. Petrov Bravebird, wise Tlingit that he was, spread a blanket on the grass. "Do not stray from this area. The boys and I will hunt on the east side of the mountain. If we are successful, we will fetch you. If not, we will continue pursuing the deer until evening."

Agrefena nodded and sat on the blanket. She opened her pack and took a long drink of water. Petrov laid his hand on her arm. "Drink often, but only a little at a time. It will be a long day. I pray your quest will be successful."

"What quest?" one of the boys asked.

"Uncle Petrov told her to sit on the blanket all day, that's all," another said.

"I'm glad I'm not a girl."

"Let's go hunting."

Agrefena waved and then turned her attention to the vista before her. Sun, sea, sky. Seabirds, shorebirds, and the ubiquitous ravens. Eagles and hawks high overhead. The birds knew their place. In the distance, she saw a whale breach. Was she the only one who struggled to figure out life?

Her heritage taught that one lived for the clan. "I am a modern woman. I don't have to bend to the will of the clan. I do not have to protect my father's honor. I do not have to shield my mother from shame." She paced the small clearing, slamming her fist into the palm of her other hand to emphasize each statement. She often paused to look over the shimmering waters of Sitka Sound. Today, they did not bring her solace or comfort.

"What kind of a daughter would I be if I did not respect my parents or heritage? Miss Ruth said Bozhe placed me in my family specifically and at this point in time. She said Bozhe requires that I honor my parents." She argued aloud, sometimes muttering, sometimes groaning—what did it all mean?

The sun continued its journey across the sky. Her stomach rumbled, but she did not eat. Minutes, hours, unaware of time, she saw only Mike Evans's face.

She sank to the blanket and let her tears fall. The birds ceased chatting, and the lone foraging ermine retreated to its den. The sun hovered over Mt. Edgecomb and would soon disappear behind it. Agrefena, emotions spent, had not arrived at a solution. How could she honor her parents, please Bozhe, and marry Mike? It was impossible.

Did she want to love Bozhe more than anything or anyone? That seemed to be the essential question. She lay on her back and stared at the clouds through the overhanging trees; no answers there. She put her arm over her eyes and spoke to Bozhe as she drifted to sleep. "Miss Ruth says you are a God who makes Himself known. Make yourself known to me."

A light brighter than the sun infused her dream. Sweet sounds, never before heard, filled her with longing and awe—music in a language she did not recognize spoke to her soul. She stood and circled herself to see where she was in this dream time. Eternal time, beyond space. A place of light and love, a place not of this earth. This was Bozhe's land, and in the distance, she saw a mighty throng on their knees before a great throne. She could not see the personage on the mist-shrouded throne, but she knew it was Bozhe. She scanned the crowd as she walked toward Him but did not see Mike Evans among the kneeling multitude. So be it.

Shadows covered her, and a chilly breeze blew over her. The sun's slanting rays and the distant cheers of Petrov Bravebird's nephews woke her. A successful hunt. Had she been dreaming for two minutes or two hours?

Agrefena looked to the sky, raised her arms, and said, "Thank you." Seeing how the creation trusted its Creator infused her soul with a resolve to do the same, even as she grieved the death of her dream to marry Mike.

Serenity was something she had never known, but she carried it down the mountain like the boys carried the deer meat. Petrov had taught them how to field-dress the buck. They placed the butchered animal in empty canvas salt sacks and slung the packs over their shoulders.

As they reached the base of the mountain, Petrov's look penetrated deep into Agrefena's soul. "It is good. Carry this peaceful resolve with you; do not let go of the joy that shines from your eyes," he said, handing her a salt sack containing two venison roasts. She could not put the reality of her dream into words, but somehow, the old man could see it in her eyes.

Agrefena stood at the window and pulled back the curtain, her favorite spot during family discussions. Sitka Channel was alive with a family of whales bubble-feeding between Indiantown and Japonski Island. They looked peaceful and free. The young whales bobbed and weaved among the adults. They had no worries for their future. She sighed and turned her attention to the conversation behind her.

It seemed so easy on the top of the mountain. What she had promised Bozhe on the summit must be lived out in the valley. A vow was sacred and must not be broken.

"It is settled," her father said.

"What?" she asked.

"You will marry Bob Tom's son."

"He has no sons, only daughters," Her voice, flat and dull, reflected her feelings.

"He has recently adopted a man from a distant clan who has proven himself worthy. Petrov Bravebird has investigated him. Your husband-to-be is honorable and true."

"Who is he? What house is he from, and what clan? What does he look like? How old is he?" Agrefena willed her voice to remain calm and stilled her emotions. It was decided, and she would honor her vow and her family. *Help me, Bozhe, my heart is shattered. Obedience and duty weigh on me, heavy as a stone. Where is the joy I felt on the mountain?* She blinked her tears away and took a deep breath as she heard her father's words, "He is now Eagle, Hawks Nest House of Wolf Clan, the house and clan of Bob Tom. The other things you asked are unimportant."

Agrefena shrugged, then attempted a smile. "Very well. When will the ceremony take place?" *I trust that joy will come. I trust You.*

"In three days," her mother said.

"There is no time to prepare," Agrefena lowered her eyes lest they see her despair.

"You know the groom's people host the ceremony and provide the honor gifts to us. All has been done properly. Everything is as it should be," her father said.

Except for me, Agrefena thought.

Her mother opened a large cedar chest and held out a dress. "For you. Jazz age."

Agrefena's little brother danced around the white confection in his mother's arms. "I found a movie magazine someone threw away. It had a picture of this dress. I told Mama to make it."

"Look," her mother said.

The gown was tea-length with a scalloped hem, a dropped waist, and the straight, loose-fitting style the flappers of Hollywood loved. The white satin shimmered like the snow on Cross Mountain.

"Look," her mother said again. But Agrefena couldn't look at anything except her mother's face. Why had she sewn such a dress? She did not embrace the modern age or white ways. Was it a bribe to ease the pain of this arranged marriage? Agrefena looked into her mother's eyes and knew it was a gift of love.

Auntie took the dress and held it up to Agrefena, "The bodice and cap sleeves are covered with tiny white beads in the shape of the Sitka rose. Old and new. It is good." Auntie stood beside her and kissed her cheek, "Your mother has also made you a long white cape woven with traditional raven patterns, trimmed with ermine."

There was an unfamiliar pain in Agrefena's chest and a lump in her throat she couldn't get the words around. The dress was perfect, if only her groom could be. Agrefena wanted to thank her mother, but all her feelings had frozen.

Once again, her mother turned to the cedar chest. She pulled out a lacy white cloche with a veil attached. It was adorned with tiny feathers and shells, "This is from Miss Ruth."

Auntie's voice held a hint of caution. "You will be beautiful, but it is best we tie you down before you can escape and shame us all."

Agrefena bowed her head. "I shall honor my family and my clan." All feelings were gone; only duty remained. She wondered how this could be. She had determined to live in the reality she experienced on the mountain. Somehow, she thought Bozhe would solve all her problems and life would be easy. Now, she was pledged to marry a stranger, not the man she loved. *Bozhe, you must show me how to bear it. Please. Restore to me the joy I felt on the mountain.*

As she crossed Lincoln Street, the familiar smells of the Cafe welcomed her. Once she opened the door, her senses were assaulted. Bacon sizzled. Coffee percolated. Silverware scraped against the crockery. And somehow, Ivan Mishkin's voice could be heard above it all. The aromas intensified and were mixed with a cacophony of other sights and sounds.

Tourists complained, especially about the oblivious fishermen who had fish scales clinging to their clothes and knee-high boots. The offensive aroma took their appetites away. As did the disinfectant that adhered to the nurses from the Pioneer's Home. They tried to cover the industrial cleaner's fumes with cheap cologne.

During the all too often rainy weather, the locals hung wet wool scarves, hats, and jackets trimmed with fur on the backs of their chairs. Those odors mingled with the cigar and cigarette smoke that wafted through the crowded room.

Agrefena breathed in the place she loved so much. As offensive as these smells were to the tourists, they were home to her, a heady perfume. She greeted the regulars on the way to the kitchen.

"You've been quiet all morning, Agrefena. What's wrong?" Mike said as they prepared for the noon rush.

"I am to be married in two days. It is the will of my father."

Mike picked up the dishcloth and threw it into the hot water. He attacked the stack of dishes waiting to be washed.

"Did you hear me?" Agrefena stepped closer to him and tugged on his arm. "Don't you have anything to say?" She tried to keep her face expressionless but felt it crumple. She bit her lip.

Mike half turned toward her but kept his hands in the hot water. "I don't know what to say. Your father wants what's best for you."

"What he thinks is best," she spoke in such a low tone he had to bend to hear her. "Oh, Mike, I don't know what to do."

"What did Father Alexi say in his last sermon? All we can ever do is love Bozhe and do what's right. It will be okay, Agrefena."

"It won't."

"It will. Have faith."

"I will do my duty," she whispered. She spent the afternoon wandering through the trails of the Russian Cemetery. The towering trees and shrubs gave the holy place a forest-like feel. She read the gravestones and thought how burdensome life had been for those buried there and now for her.

NINE

The door closed behind the newly married couple. She turned to him and growled, "I am going to kill you. How could you do this to me?"

"Wife, be reasonable." He moved toward her, arms outstretched.

She backed away. "Do you know how I suffered, how my heart was ripped from me?"

"I am your husband—nothing can change that."

"I walked into the church with puffy eyes, my heart frozen. I forced myself to put one foot in front of the other, not knowing what awaited me. And then Father Alexi decided there were too many people and more coming, so we must all march down Lincoln Street to the ANB Hall."

"It was a wonderful parade. Bob Tom and I led all your relatives. Your parents were right behind me. The kids ran back and forth. Your brother led them like a chief."

"And me at the end between Father Alexi and Auntie. She insisted I walk slowly with dignity. I tried craning my neck, jumping, anything to glimpse my betrothed. Auntie glared, and I had to match my pace to hers."

"You are such a short little thing." He laughed and swung her around.

"Put me down." She turned away from him. "I don't remember the ceremony, my vows, the music, nothing." She remembered everything, but he didn't need to know that.

"It was beautiful. Your mother and Auntie cried. Your father looked so proud."

"I have no memory of it, and it's your fault. You could have spared me."

"I gave my word to your parents and my new father, Bob Tom. I was ethically bound not to speak."

"I don't understand their reasoning. Why would they do this to me?"

"I tried to change their minds, but I think your father wanted to know if you would honor him and the old ways."

"The old ways must accommodate the new and the new, the old. We have to find a way to blend, to live together."

"We can do that, you and me."

Agrefena took off her veil and laid it on the table. She did not let him see her smile. He deserved to suffer a little longer. "I was devastated. My life was over." She sniffed and watched him from under her lowered lashes.

"Again, I am sorry. How can I make it up to you?"

"You are now honor bound to share everything with me for the rest of your life. No secrets."

She stood on her toes and lifted her face to his. Even so, he had to bend to reach her lips. His bright blue eyes gazed into her dark ones for a long moment, and then he said, "I love you, Mrs. Mike Evans."

"Perhaps I am Mrs. Mike Tom since you are adopted."

"Maybe you are. The whole ceremony was in Russian and Tlingit. The only English spoken was when I said—I do—and you had to nudge me with your elbow at the right time."

"Tlingits do not adopt lightly, especially outside of the clan."

"You can thank that kid, Ade Bunderson. He told Petrov Brave-bird we loved each other, and I wouldn't propose or declare my feelings because I refused to come between you and your family. Bravebird thought that was honorable, and after further investiga-tion, he and Bob Tom decided I was of good character and worthy."

"I could have told them that."

He grinned and reached for her again. She scooted away. "Don't kiss me. I'm still mad at you. As I entered the ANB Hall, Father Alexi motioned to Ivan Mishkin, who ran past me, mum-bling, 'I fix. No worry.' Bob Tom stood at the altar, and I wondered if I had misunderstood and he was my would-be husband."

"Nope, just me. Father Alexi had left the wedding license and official papers at the church, but when Ivan got there, the door was locked."

"Nobody in Sitka locks doors, and the church is never locked."

Mike nodded and continued as if she had not spoken. "Ivan tried to ease his squat body into a small window. Apparently, he got stuck, half in, half out," Mike laughed.

Agrefena could picture Ivan hanging in the window, although she tried not to chuckle. She crossed her arms and frowned, "Mean-while, back in the hall, the ceremony was delayed, and I didn't know who my groom was."

"It was me." He tried to kiss her again.

She pulled away and said, "What happened with Ivan?"

Mike answered, "This is the story I heard: A dog growled; a voice behind Ivan demanded to know who he was and what he was doing—Ivan said it wasn't anyone's business.

"It's mine since I am the Chief of Police."

"I know Chief. Is not you."

"Two hours ago, your Chief was mauled by a bear and is being transported to Juneau. He would have been killed if Bull hadn't intervened." He scratched his companion behind the ears.

"Is no bull, only dog." The dog growled, and Ivan muttered through a clenched jaw. "Very big dog."

"The name is Stormy Durand, and for better or worse, I am the new Chief."

"Better—worse!" Ivan struggled to push himself through the window.

Stormy motioned to the canine, who gripped the seat of Ivan's pants and pulled. They grappled. The dog growled and pulled. Ivan swore and pushed. Finally, Ivan sprawled on the ground. The dog, which I learned was an English mastiff, stood over him, drooling. Of course, Ivan cursed and howled." Mike laughed.

"In Russian or English?" Agrefena asked.

"Russian, and this stranger didn't understand a word. He signaled the dog, who threw his bulk against the front door. It wasn't locked, just stuck. Ivan dashed in, grabbed the papers, and ran with the dog on his heels."

"I'm surprised the mastiff didn't catch him."

"Ivan heard the man say—"chase, no catch,"— Mike tried to imitate Ivan's accent.

Agrefena smiled and put her wedding flowers in a mason jar of water. "Ivan crashed into the hall, waving those papers above his head, cursing the dog, and yelling the wedding should have been in the church. He nearly knocked me down,"

"It was a wonderful wedding despite Ivan and that huge dog. I think everyone in town was there."

"Too many people thought no man would have me. They wanted proof I was wed," Agrefena said.

"I tried to wave to you from the alcove where Father Alexi stashed me. The dog lay in the opened doorway behind you, panting. Our new police chief leaned against the doorframe and watched."

"I hope they enjoyed our wedding. I didn't." Agrefena's words were stern, but her tone had softened. She remembered Mike with the Eagle clan's headdress made of rabbit fur and ermine skin, trimmed with sea lion whiskers. A carved wolf head rested on his brow. She remembered the tall wooden staff he held with the two eagle feathers attached to the top. She recalled his awkward Eagle Dance down the aisle and the tufts of eagle down he blew over the people, signaling peace.

"I promise you will enjoy our marriage, and it will be a great story to tell our grandchildren."

"I do not know if we are truly married." She tried to sound stern, but there was a smile in her voice and a twinkle in her eye.

Mike leaned against the Café's counter, crossed his arms, and frowned. "Of course we're married."

"We followed some Tlingit traditions, and Father Alexi performed the Russian vows, but I do not recall that you ever said you loved me or proposed—like a white man—on one knee." She pointed to the floor in front of her. Mike dutifully knelt and took her by the hand. "First, you must give me your ring," he said.

Agrefeena held out her right hand with the Triple Rolling Ring of three thin bands. One of yellow gold, one of rose, and one of white. "For Russians, this ring symbolizes the Holy Trinity: Father, Spirit, Son. It also speaks of our past, present, and future," she whispered.

Mike took the entwined ring and said, "After I propose, I will place it on your left hand, which is the white tradition."

Agrefena nodded, "Whenever I see it, I will know how we have blended our cultures."

Mike reviewed their past, expounded on their present, and shared his hopes for their future. The proposal was all Agrefena hoped it would be, and she melted into his arms. "I will tell our grandchildren you made a valiant effort to do the Eagle Dance."

"I was pretty good, wasn't I?"

"You were wonderful." She had glimpsed the man in the eagle regalia at the end of the aisle. She had shivered, but as soon as he began to dance, she knew this was no Native.

At that moment, the dancer looked up and winked. It was Mike! She stared, then tore her eyes away from him and glanced at her father. A man of few words, he nodded and grinned. Her little brother mouthed—I knew it—and her mother and Auntie wept.

Agrefena's trembling had increased, and her breathing deepened. Bob Tom's hand on her arm restrained her from running down the aisle and embracing her groom. Mike's dancing resembled an awkward sea lion rather than a majestic eagle, and most of the wedding guests had great difficulty keeping their decorum.

"I looked handsome in that eagle outfit, and you looked beautiful in that silky white dress."

"Stop talking and kiss me."

TEN

He tugged on his earlobe and placed his notes on Miss Ruth's desk. "This is a rough draft if you want to review them." As Miss Ruth scanned the typed pages, he pulled on his ear and muttered, "I'm not the man for the job."

Miss Ruth adjusted her reading glasses and finished the last few lines. "Perfect. You have captured the essence of Agrefena and the flavor of the time."

"I should have included more historical facts, dates, documentation, references, etc." The Professor wiped his hands on his thighs. Why did he seem to sweat whenever he was in her presence? He forced himself to leave his earlobe alone.

"Nonsense. You are documenting anecdotal history, making these people real to future generations."

Miss Ruth took off her glasses and laid them on his report. "Agrefena refused to be interviewed, didn't she?"

"How did you know?"

"She is an old friend. I knew if you could get her story, the rest would be easy."

"I approached almost everyone in Sitka. Only one was willing to talk. Mike Evans arranged it."

"You know that old adage, *in Alaska, don't ask.* I hope Ade didn't bore you with too many fish stories." Miss Ruth laughed at the surprised look on his face. "Ade Bunderson is a talker," she said.

"Sometimes, while telling me Agrefena's story, Ade started to talk about his own. I had a devil of a time organizing my notes. I'm glad I recorded everything. He called me the Professor, and now everyone does." He squirmed again. "I didn't finish asking my list of questions. I just scribbled."

"And?"

"It didn't feel professional. I was not an interviewer or a researcher. I was an audience."

"Hmmm." Miss Ruth scanned the papers again. "If I know Ade, he's told you everything he knows about Agrefena and Mike. It will be different when he talks about himself. Write out your questions beforehand. Take breaks when he starts down a rabbit trail. You'll do fine. You are going to make a fine professor one day. Just pretend these are your students and lead them. But for now, let's give the citizens of Sitka a little break and take a trip to Kodiak."

"The old priest?"

"He's quite frail, although I don't think he's ill. While you interview him, I'll visit friends. I will phone you when the arrangements are made. I'm hoping we can go in a few weeks. I'd like to be there for Selaviq. "

"Huh? Selaviq?" The Professor scratched his head. Miss Ruth continually confused him. He wrote down the word Selaviq, determined to find out what it was before he saw her again.

Miss Ruth put on her coat, picked up her handbag, and stuffed the Professor's notes into it. "I'm sure there is at least one fish story in this."

The Professor blushed. "I'm not sure what angle, what hook I can use to make Ade Bunderson's story interesting."

"Hook? Sounds fishy," she laughed, "Just tell it like it was told to you, Professor. You don't have to make it fancy."

He blushed again. "You are keeping me busy, Miss Ruth. I need to edit and polish Agrefena's rough draft, listen to Ade's story and write it. And I have an appointment next Thursday with Stormy Durand."

"There are depths to Stormy. Try to plunge into them."

"How can I do that?"

"Lock the door on your way out." Miss Ruth patted his shoulder. "And stop pulling on your ear. It's quite red."

ELEVEN

Ade Bunderson nursed his third cup of coffee in Sitka's newest hotel restaurant. Everything around him was fresh and modern, with bright Formica and chrome tables. He shifted in his chair—uncomfortable; he missed the homey feeling and the history of Mike and Agrefena's place. Even the smells were wrong. He sniffed his shirt—fish, crab, acrid seaweed. So familiar, yet they seemed out of place in the hotel's dining room. He was sure the tourists were turning up their noses. *Let them. They are happy enough to eat the king salmon or crab I caught for this place.*

His unobstructed view through the large windows across the channel to Japonski Island did not ease that discomfort. Ade turned his face away as the locals shuffled across the dock and stepped onto the Dorothy, one of the four shore boats that ferried people between Sitka and Japonski Island. The town's most popular shoreboat pilot, Jake Steiner, started the engine and backed away from the dock. Ade didn't want Jake or any of the passengers to recognize him.

Much to Ade's relief, it was newcomers and tourists who filled this room. The smells from the kitchen made his stomach rumble and his mouth water. The waitress, some college kid in Sitka for the summer, was friendly and recommended the daily special. He gave a brief nod and hoped his luck held. Agrefena must never learn of his culinary disloyalty.

Sitting alone instead of with his cronies at the big round table felt odd. Ade hoped the Professor would ask his questions quickly so he could have a late breakfast or at least coffee and crullers with the guys at the Sitka Café.

A large stack of pancakes and ham was set before him, and the waitress refilled his coffee with a wink and a flourish. After a few forkfuls, he pushed the plate away. Not bad, but it didn't compare with Agrefena's cooking, and he'd take reindeer sausage over ham any day.

His watch indicated the Professor should be here any minute. Ade wondered what his name was, then discarded the thought—Professor would be the young man's moniker from now on.

Ade had some questions of his own. What exactly was the purpose of this project, and whose idea was it? Mike had told him Miss Ruth was involved, and the thing had to be completed before statehood. The middle-aged fisherman didn't get it.

Ade grumbled to himself about federal interference and how statehood might affect the balance in the Territory. The movers and shakers in Alaska had been corrupt and greedy since before the Russians left and the gold-seekers arrived. Bribes offered and accepted. Claims jumped, backs scratched, palms greased, and pockets lined. It was always the Natives and ordinary folk who suffered. Today, the politicians in Washington seemed as mercenary as the gold diggers of yesterday. Even if a few had good intentions, they were too far away to regulate things properly. They were not Alaskans.

The fishing industry had declined in the almost three and a half decades he had lived in Alaska. Something must be done soon, but he didn't know what. All of Alaska's natural resources were under siege. Too much greed. Too many regulations. Too many politicians. Too many outsiders.

Disgusted with the thought of statehood, Ade turned his thoughts to the questions the Professor might ask. Some memories he would share, and some he determined to keep to himself. He poured more syrup on the half-eaten pancakes, took another bite, and pushed the plate away for a second time.

Where had the years gone? It seemed like he had finished grammar school last month. It wasn't easy to realize he was over the half-century mark. That unhappy schoolboy in California had come a long way.

"I won't go. You can't make me," Ade stomped his bare foot on the aged plank floor.

"It's important, especially for a boy," his mother frowned and looked to her husband for support. "Tell him to pay attention."

"Leave him alone, Madge. The law says high school is optional once you graduate eighth grade. He can join me in the grove."

Ade looked from one parent to the other and moved closer to his mother. He tried to keep the whine from his voice, "I already work with him after school and on weekends, Ma. I want to get a different job."

"Everybody knows you can get more pay with a high school diploma," Ade's mother said, then ignored him and directed her comments to her husband. "I want the boy to get a decent job and earn better wages than a mere field hand. He needs a diploma to do that." After glaring at her husband, Madge threw her hands back into the soapy water. "Heaven knows I can't depend on you."

Ade saw his father's shoulders sag. Whenever his mother talked like that, Ade's stomach hurt, and he was embarrassed for his father and ashamed of his mother. "Isn't school important for the girls? They miss a lot when they're not even sick."

His mother whirled around, sending soap suds cascading down her apron. "Don't you worry about your sisters! Auditions are more important than school if they're going to be silent film stars," her voice had risen, and she thrust her hands back into the dishwater, scrubbing an already clean plate.

"You've dragged them around Hollywood since they were toddlers, Madge. Nobody is interested in them." Ade's dad kept his voice soft.

Madge saw how worn-out her tall, slim husband had become—skin wrinkled and tanned as an old saddle. She sighed and thought about how good-looking he was when they married. Life wasn't fair, not to her. She was determined to make it better for her girls.

Tap. Tap. Tap. Their too-small tap shoes clacked on the wooden floor in the living room. "Shh, they'll hear you. What kind of father are you anyway? You have never believed in my dream for them. Never earned enough for them to have the proper clothes or dancing and singing lessons. I've had to squeeze the money out of my household budget, which doesn't pay for the best teachers. And second-hand clothing stores are not where I want to shop for them." She thrust a sizeable greasy pan into the sink, and water sloshed over the rim. "They don't even have decent tap shoes, not ones that fit. It's your fault they haven't made it into the pictures. I've had to do everything myself," she bit her lip and muttered, "has a husband ever been so useless?"

Ade's father hung his head and sighed, as he often did when his mother began her litany of his shortcomings. After every negative assessment of his inability to provide, his father worked longer and harder. Ade never heard the man argue with his mother; it might have been better if he had.

Startled customers looked up as a young man dressed in a rumpled suit and tie stumbled into the restaurant. He zig-zagged through the occupied tables, holding his bulging briefcase and tape recorder aloft, nearly knocking a few heads. Diners ducked and watched with curiosity as he pushed up his glasses with the back of his hand and his briefcase bumped a waitress. She swayed but held onto the plates of pancakes and eggs. Embarrassed, he made his way to the table in front of the windows, and his glasses slid to the end of his nose.

Greetings were exchanged, the tape recorder plugged in, reels set in place, pen and paper pulled out of the worn leather briefcase. The Professor signaled the waitress for coffee and turned to Ade. "Ready, Mr. Bunderson?"

Ade, pulled from his memories, swallowed and said, "My father left home the day I graduated from eighth grade. I did the same."

"When was that?"

Ade scratched his head. "Before the war was over and before the Spanish flu had everyone afraid, so around 1917 or 18, I guess."

"You don't remember the year you graduated eighth grade?"

"The school had no ceremony or celebration, and there was so much contention in my family that I wasn't sure what day it was—much less the year."

Ade pictured his boyhood home, an unpainted clapboard house on the edge of an orange grove outside Los Angeles. His parents had one small bedroom, his sisters shared the other, and he slept on a lumpy couch in the cramped front room. He couldn't remember having a restful night in that house, and it wasn't because of the uncomfortable sofa.

His mother took his two young sisters to Los Angeles every few days to audition for the silent film industry. Ade supposed his sisters were pretty enough. Both looked like their mother, who he considered beautiful when she wasn't frowning and angry. Darla had long dark hair and freckles, while Moria had her hair bobbed in the newest flapper style. They both had the longest eyelashes he had ever seen. Despite their frequent lessons, with the mediocre teachers his mother complained about, neither girl could carry a tune, and their tap dancing was dismal. The moguls in Hollywood must have agreed. The trio always came back rejected and despondent.

Upon returning, Madge paced the living room, ranting about the fools in Hollywood who clearly could not recognize the talent of her girls. Darla and Moria were in tears. Darla's were tears of embarrassment. Moria's, ones of anger.

Ade and his father retreated to the orange groves whenever the threesome was due home.

"Why are things the way they are, Dad? Why is Mom so—so—"

"I don't know, son. She had a difficult childhood. Wants better for the girls."

Ade slumped against a tree trunk, tossing an orange with one hand and catching it with the other. *What about me? Doesn't she want better for me?*

On the next toss, his father reached out and grabbed the fruit. He inhaled its citrus scent but found no solace in it. "Look, son. This orange is a beautiful round ball." He pulled the peelings free, let them fall to the ground, and gave Ade a couple of sections. He stuffed them into his mouth. The bright liquid dripped down his chin.

"The sections are connected, making a whole, but watch." His dad's fingers contracted, and the orange was crushed. The pulpy mess spilled their juice. "The fruit is ruined. It's lost its juice, its flavor."

"Huh?"

"You and I are two crushed sections clinging to each other. Your mother is a damaged segment. I don't know how to put all of us back together. God knows I've tried." He threw the mangled fruit to the ground, where it lay scattered among the peels. California's ubiquitous ants crawled over it. He wiped his sticky hands on his handkerchief. "Sometimes I wonder if your mother has considered your sisters' feelings about this moving picture thing."

"Darla knows she has no talent and dreads each trip to Hollywood." Ade felt sorry for his sister, but there was no way to help her. "Moria is convinced she will be a big star."

Ade's dad picked up the lopper and clippers and inspected the trees for dead branches. His face, leathered by the sun, showed no emotion, although he often sighed as he removed the lifeless limbs.

Beyond the grove, below the cliff's edge, the Pacific Ocean called to the boy, and he stood there whenever he had a spare moment. The water was ever-changing—from serene blue to turbulent green to stormy gray. The infinite distance to where the sea met the sky filled him with unexplainable solace and longing—for what exactly? Escape? Purpose? Hope? Happiness?

The continuous flow of the tide—in, then out, assured him the rhythm of life was ongoing, always certain, but constantly altering. These were more feelings than thoughts to Ade, barely in his teens. The salty sea breezes filled his lungs with an assurance he would be somebody, and the waters soothed his soul in a way he did not understand.

TWELVE

Ade raised sad eyes to the Professor. "It seemed like my parents always fought—fight isn't the right word." Ade rubbed his hand across his eyes. "My dad never raised his voice, never argued. My mother constantly complained and harangued him. She threatened to divorce him almost every week. She finally hired a lawyer; who knows where the money came from? Dad took off before he could be served with legal papers. I followed. He tried to send me home, but I wouldn't go. Don't make my mom sound like a harpy when you write this story. She was, but don't make her sound that way. I think she tried, but Dad constantly disappointed her."

The Professor nodded and erased several sentences from his notes.

"We left Los Angeles to work on a ranch in Nevada. Dad's goal was to make more money—and send most of it to Mom. I guess he thought she wouldn't file those divorce papers if the money kept coming. I convinced him we could send Mom more if I worked alongside him." Ade reached for his now cold coffee and signaled the waitress for a refill.

"As caretaker of the grove, our house had been part of Dad's compensation, and the owner was willing to let Mom and the girls stay—for an unduly high rent." Ade shook his head, reached for his cigarettes, and remembered his wife wanted him to quit. She said she heard rumors smoking wasn't healthy. He unwrapped a stick of Juicy Fruit chewing gum instead.

"The Nevada rancher didn't think you were too young?"

"This was well before Child Labor Laws were passed, and kids younger than me did a man's job. I was a hard worker, skinny but muscular, almost as tall as my dad, and picked up things quickly. I don't think anyone knew my actual age. They wouldn't have cared if they did."

"So, how did you get from a ranch in Nevada to Sitka?"

Ade Bunderson rubbed his hands together, and all thoughts of his cronies and Agrefena's crullers fell away as he realized he had a captive audience. "Well, that is a long story, and I'll need more energy to continue." He looked at his half-eaten breakfast, waved for the waitress, ordered a steak, and hoped it was better than the mediocre pancakes.

"I found mucking out manure was not for me. I disliked the dust, the flies, and the absence of ocean breezes. I griped about the smell quite a bit, so Dad shoveled out the stalls while I groomed the horses—sweaty, smelly beasts." Ade spat the gum into his napkin and longed for a cigarette. Didn't his wife know smoking relaxed a man and kept him calm and healthy? That's what all the radio advertisements said, so it must be true.

"None of that seemed to bother Dad. The pay was good, our expenses low, and I think he would have stayed if I hadn't constant-ly complained. As we approached our second summer, Dad took what money he hadn't sent to Mom and put a down payment on a small farm on the edge of the Mojave Desert." Ade shook his head and rubbed his hand over his chin. "I think he was conned into buying the place, but he never admitted it. It was back-breaking work with little to show for it. I don't know why Dad thought he was a farmer. After a while, the burning sun and lack of water convinced him that nothing would grow, no matter how much we labored. He sold that worthless land to another dreamer and bought holdings in Idaho."

The Professor sharpened his pencil. "Well, that's closer to Alaska anyway."

"It was farther away from my mother. Despite everything, I cared about her and regularly wrote—to my sisters, too. They never answered, and Mom's return letters complained about the producers in Hollywood and begged for more money. She was often behind in the rent. Mom said it was beneath her to take in laundry and ironing to make ends meet. I know she spent all the money we sent for lessons and fancy clothes. She should have paid the bills promptly and bought decent food."

"Did you save any of her letters?"

Ade shook his head. Why would he keep the letters? There was nothing positive in them, no concern for a lonely teenage boy doing a man's work and sending almost every penny home. No questions about his health or well-being. There were no statements of respect or love, nothing saying he was missed. He struggled to answer her complaints and dreaded the arrival of each letter.

Ade let his mind wander to when he and his father took the train to a small town in the Bitterroot Range near the Idaho-Montana border. The locomotive often chugged up impossible inclines and hugged the edge of cliffs as they traveled through the mountains of the West, majestic and powerful.

The teenage California boy had been away from the coast for too long and couldn't remember the ocean's smell or how the sun glistened off the water. He looked out the train windows and tried to picture the Pacific's roaring breakers on a stormy day. He failed to recapture the feelings he had when standing at the water's edge gazing at the horizon. He felt out of place in the rugged Rockies, just as he had on the ranch and in the desert.

They disembarked at their journey's end and showed the stationmaster their map. He marked the route to their cabin. "My son can take you as far as the Old Miller place. My horses won't be happy in this bitter cold, and neither will my boy," the stationmaster laughed as he pulled snowshoes out of a storage room. "Neither will you. I'll rent you these snowshoes for the last four miles. There's no road, and I'm sure the trail hasn't been cleared. It should take about two hours if you keep the lake on your left."

"How will we return the shoes?"

"You can bring them by when you up and quit." He laughed again.

"We're not quitters," Ade mumbled, then realized they had quit the ranch in Nevada and the farm in the Mohave. Hopefully, Idaho would treat them better.

Ade chuckled as he remembered that trek in the Bitterroot Mountains. "Dad and I had never been on snowshoes. In fact, I had never seen snow before. I must have fallen a dozen times before I got the hang of it. It took us a lot longer than two hours." Ade pulled a cigarette from the package and ran it under his nose several times. The smell was enticing, and he wanted to light up.

"Whose bright idea was it to buy a property sight unseen in these mountains," the cold, wet, snow-covered boy asked, "and in winter?"

"I thought it was yours," his father lowered his pack and fished a key out of his pocket.

"Seems silly to lock an isolated cabin near the top of a mountain, miles away from anywhere." Ade leaned his snowshoes against the porch railing.

"Just be glad there is a cabin."

"And a well, don't forget there is a well."

"I'm sure we will find it once the snow's gone. In the meantime, we'll melt snow for our water. Check that shed. Let's hope it is full of dry wood like we were told."

Ade made the mistake of not donning his snowshoes and slogged through knee-deep snow to the woodshed, soaking his pant legs. His father laughed, and Ade glared over his shoulder. He walked into a low-hanging branch, and his father laughed again.

The shed was stacked with aged wood and a few tools, including a snow shovel the previous owners had left. Ade cleared a path from the woodshed back to the cabin. Inside they found some foodstuffs and three books: a Bible, selected works from Charles Dickens, and a copy of The Legend of Sleepy Hollow. There was also a well-worn mountain survival guide.

Ade found heavy jackets, snow pants, and long johns in a storage cupboard. "Look, Dad, these will keep us warmer than anything we've got. Hope they fit."

They unpacked, and when his Dad lit a fire in the fireplace, smoke poured into the room. Ade checked the damper, which was open, but the cabin still filled with smoke. Burning eyes and throats forced them outside.

"I thought you knew how to build a fire," Ade coughed.

"Must be something stuck in the chimney." His father took an axe from the woodshed and selected an eight-foot sapling from a nearby stand of trees, chopping the small outcropping branches until he had a reasonably clean pole. The older man rolled a barrel from the porch to the side of the cabin near the chimney. He told Ade to stand on it, then climbed onto the boy's shoulders.

Ade's legs shook, and the empty barrel wobbled.

"Steady," his father growled and heaved himself onto the roof. He promptly slid off and crashed into Ade. They landed in a heap in the soft snow.

"Get that small leafy branch over there. I'll use it as a broom. The snow on the roof is ice-crusted and slick," Dad said.

Ade brushed the snow from his hat, swore as it melted, and ran down the back of his neck. He turned his collar up and handed the branch to his father.

The older man stood on his son's shoulders again, sweeping the snow from the roof.

"Why can't I stand on your shoulders and sweep. You're much heavier than I, and your big feet dig into my shoulders."

"I'm taller than you, so my reach is longer; besides, I'm your old man. Age has its benefits."

"I always seem to be on the bottom—of everything," Ade grumbled.

"Quit complaining and shove me onto the roof."

Ade stood on tiptoe, wrapped his hands around his father's calves, and shoved. The force knocked him off the barrel, and he lay in the drifted snow again. The older man crawled on his hands and knees toward the chimney, occasionally sliding toward the roof's edge. He swore and kept trying, finally bracing himself against the brick chimney and poking the pole into the opening. The leaves attached to the tiny branches he had left on one end knocked the soot loose, and the pole dislodged a thick bird's nest that had forced the smoke into the cabin.

They cleaned up the mess, stoked the fire, and soon a cheerful warmth permeated the place. They hung their damp clothes near the fire.

Although the cabin was snug and cozy, the long, cold winter in the Bitterroot Mountains of Idaho was brutal—so different from the California coast's temperate climate and the Nevada desert's summer heat. Ade spent much time standing on the cabin's porch, looking at the snow-covered woods, beautiful in their own way, but they didn't pull at his heart like the ocean.

They read and reread the tattered pages of the mountain guide and ran a trap line following the directions, learning more through trial and error. They stretched the animal skins over wooden frames they found in the woodshed. Hopefully, they could sell them in the spring.

In the deep mid-winter, the lake froze. Ade cut a hole in the ice and let a line down, but the fish seemed to have disappeared. Every day, Ade went into the woods with his father's old .22 rifle, gradually improving his aim. The forest provided small game for the stewpot.

As Ade cleaned the gun one night, he said, "I'd do better killing dinner if I had a better rifle than this old thing of yours. We have some money left. I could hike into town and see what's available."

"That money's for your mom. I have to take care of her."

"We need to take care of ourselves, too."

"We'll get by."

"But, Dad—" Ade swallowed his arguments and continued to clean the old rifle. He didn't like it, but he'd have to make do. Mom always came first.

That spring, Ade found a tiny rowboat under the cabin's porch. After replacing two rotten boards and patching a small hole, he christened the boat *The High Seas*. While it wasn't the ocean, the lake's calm waters seeped into his soul. The surrounding trees budded in soothing yellows and greens.

They stoked the fire in the evenings and read Sleepy Hollow and Charles Dickens. Ade picked up the Bible once or twice but didn't understand what he was reading. His Dad told him to keep at it because he was smart enough to figure it out. "Everyone needs a little religion. Maybe if your Mom and I had some, we wouldn't be in this mess."

"Have you read it, Dad?"

His dad turned away and picked up the fireplace poker. "Always meant to, never had the time."

Ade pulled the curtain back. "Raining again. We got nothing but time." Ade put the Bible on the stand beside his father's bunk but never saw him pick it up.

THIRTEEN

The acres around the cabin had been described as a hardwood forest they could log come spring. They surveyed the property thoroughly once the snow had melted and were bitterly disappointed to find remnants of a forest fire several years prior. The regrowth was too young to be logged. Most of the mature trees were scorched and charred. Some were burnt most of the way through, not fit for lumber.

"Well, kid, we can find another fool to buy this place or walk away."

"Plenty of fish and game, even wild berries, and the trees will grow."

"It's too isolated."

"We could build a bigger boat and really do some fishing. It's not like the ocean, but the lake is teeming with fish."

"Without mature trees to log, there is nothing here for us, no way to make money."

Ade circled himself with his arms spread wide. "Don't you want to see what it's like in the summer?"

"We need to send your mother more money." The older man rubbed his hands together. "Besides, the winter cold gets into my bones, and this spring rain makes my joints ache."

"I want to stay."

"Your mother was right. You should be in school."

"I'm not ever going to school again." Ade glared at the older man. His father stared and ignored his remark. "I need to make more money."

"Where will we go? What will we do?"

Ade finished his coffee and pulled out his Camels again. He fondled the package, crumpled and then smoothed it. After a moment, he shook out a slightly smashed cigarette. He struck a match, and soon the aromatic smoke swirled around his head, more satisfying than Juicy Fruit, "Don't write this down, but my dad and I had words. Mean, hateful words about leaving the mountains and my returning to school. I talked to him in a way no son should talk to his father. He didn't get angry; just said he didn't want me to end up a bum like him. Moving from place to place, job to job. Never making enough money."

Ade looked through the hotel's giant wall of windows and saw a pair of whales cruising the channel, bubble-feeding. He wondered what life would have been like if they had stayed in the Bitterroot Mountains or if his father had come to Alaska with him. He stubbed out his cigarette as the waitress brought the food and refilled his coffee. "He was a hard-working man who was loyal to my mother. I should have told him I was proud to be his son."

Ade grabbed the steak knife, sawed the large slab of meat, and told the Professor how they left Idaho in late spring and traveled across Montana, North Dakota, and Minnesota. They hitchhiked from town to town, pausing to find odd jobs here and there as their funds dwindled. It was field work mostly, although they did milk cows in Minnesota for a few weeks and worked a month in a cheese factory in Wisconsin. Eventually, they made their way to his father's people in Michigan. His Dad immediately found a construction job and enrolled Ade in school.

"You're going in the wrong direction, Mr. Bunderson." The Professor chuckled, clicked off his machine, and shrugged into his jacket. "Let's take a break. I need to stretch my legs while you finish eating. I'll be back in a few minutes."

Ade nodded and leaned back in his chair. He closed his eyes and rested his folded hands on his chest. He remembered how difficult it was to be the new kid in school. Although he could read well, he was behind in history and arithmetic, and his spelling was atrocious. The teachers shook their heads and made comments, and the students took their cue from them. Ade had trouble keeping his reactions civil.

Several young hooligans decided he was fair game and waited for him every day after school. He rarely made it home without physical evidence of those encounters. Ade was strong but lacked the skills of a fighter. Four against one was too much for him.

One day, a member of the varsity football team saw the commotion. He was huge, black, with a missing front tooth. He tossed those four boys off the sidewalk and into the street. He shook his fist and growled at their retreating backs. He pulled Ade to his feet and said, "You need to learn to fight. I will teach you. That is, if you, well...."

"Well, what?"

"You're white." The black boy traced a circle in the dirt with his bare toe.

"Yeah—and you're not. Is that a problem?" Ade wiped his bloody nose on his sleeve and wished he hadn't sounded so gruff.

"Name's Sylvester and it's not a problem for me." He grinned, and his white teeth gleamed against his dark face.

Ade rubbed his jaw. "Aren't you afraid those toughs will get their friends and gang up on you?"

"Naw, I've had to fight nearly everyone in this school. I beat them all, so nobody bothers me anymore. Besides, football is a big thing here, and I'm the biggest linebacker on the team, fifty pounds heavier than anyone else. They don't like it but can't win without me, and they know it. Come to my house after school, and I will show you how to fight."

"To box, you mean?"

"I'll teach you to box and to fight."

Ade soon learned boxing and fighting might overlap, but there were definitely some differences. This proved invaluable over the years. He and Sylvester became firm friends, an unusual occurrence for the time.

"You know you will have to fight them before they leave you alone?"

"All of them?"

"You should challenge them singly, although I think you could take them all at once."

"You really think I'm ready?"

"Only one way to find out." Sylvester grinned. "I'll hide and come to your rescue if necessary."

Ade punched him on the arm. "It won't be necessary."

After the inevitable altercations, Ade was left alone. His friendship with Sylvester continued, although both boys spent most of their free time doing household chores or looking for odd jobs.

For months, Spanish Influenza had raged worldwide, and most schools were closed. It seemed as if every family in town had lost someone to the horrible disease. People were uncertain and fearful, and most remained hiding in their homes. Many businesses closed, people quit their jobs, and others were laid off.

Ade's dad dug ditches for the city's water department and filled potholes with a road crew. The foreman was hospitalized with influenza, and most of the crew quit. Ade's dad brought him and Sylvester to fill the vacancies. At least they were outdoors breathing fresh air, although fear about the epidemic hovered in their minds.

With his first paycheck, Sylvester bought a pair of shoes and gave his mother the rest of the money. Ade looked at his worn and too-small shoes and longed for new ones. But both of his sisters needed new tap shoes. He gave his wages to his father.

A few months later, Ade 's grandparents sent a telegram to his father. They had received a letter from the owner of the orange grove, who found their address among his mother's papers. Darla, Moira, and their mother had succumbed to the dreaded disease. Their belongings were boxed and stored in one of the grove's outbuildings.

"We should have never left California," Ade hiccupped and hoped his father didn't notice the wetness on his cheeks or the pain in his voice.

His father's tear-stained face told Ade his father felt the same, "It was your mother who wanted the divorce, not me."

With her death, his mother's constant harping faded away, and the boy remembered her cooking and how pretty she was. "You could have done more."

"Her dream was to get your sisters into the silent pictures. My dream was to make her happy—give her what she wanted." He stuffed his hands into his pants pockets and turned away. "We both failed."

Ade's young mind couldn't comprehend the complexities of adult relationships, but the hurt in his father's voice caused him to regret his accusing words and tone.

"I tried to fix the place up how she wanted and give her money for the girls. It was never enough. You know I sent her more money than we could afford. What else could I have done?" The grieving man pulled a clean, white handkerchief from his back pocket and blew his nose.

Ade watched his father leave the room, shoulders slumped, head bowed, the same way he did when his wife harangued him. The boy vowed to be more careful of his father's feelings.

A few days later, his dad told him about a job opportunity in the South. "We are going to a large farm in Mississippi, forty-five hundred acres of prime cotton land. We'll get paid by the cubic yard of dirt we move. We're both strong and quick."

"I don't want to leave Sylvester; he's my only friend."

"We'll earn enough money to buy a marble marker for your mom's grave by the time our contract ends."

"Can't we stay? We have jobs here."

"We'll make more money in the South and get that marker."

"Dad! I don't want to leave." Ade wondered if his dad would ever put him first. All the man thought about was making his wife happy, even when she was dead. He sniffed, wiped his nose with his sleeve, stuffed his guilty feelings, and said, "She'd like that." He turned his thoughts away from his parent's relationship and his own feelings of isolation and loneliness. "I don't get it. Where are we moving the dirt to, and why?"

"Farm's near a swamp. I think they are going to drain it or divert it. We'll be shoveling mud and laying drainage pipes. Owner's going to turn that swamp into viable farmland."

"You should come with us. It's good money."

"My Pa would shoot me before he let me go back to the South." Sylvester stared at his new shoes.

"It can't be as bad as you say."

"It's worse." Sylvester looked at Ade with eyes full of pain. "You'll see. The way they treat us coloreds is different from how they'll treat you. Although some hate Yankees as much as they hate us. Don't let on you got a colored friend."

"You are the only real friend I've ever had." Ade patted his vest pocket where he had put the scrap of paper with Sylvester's address. "I won't forget you."

"I wish you weren't going." Sylvester dug the toe of his shoe into the dirt, then spit on his hand and polished the dust from the shoe leather. He couldn't raise his eyes to Ade's. "Yeah, I won't forget you either."

FOURTEEN

"Don't we have enough money for bus tickets?"

"Nothing wrong with walking or hitching."

"But we could ride the bus? We have the money?" Ade stopped and fished a pebble from his shoe. Several weeks ago, he had cut the front uppers from his shoes, exposing his toes. How he longed for a pair that fit.

"Listen, son. We'll save every penny and buy your mother the biggest gravestone the monument company has."

Ade mumbled unkind words under his breath, took both shoes off, and tied them to his belt loops. He stumbled after his father, barefoot, feet burning on the dusty unpaved road. Finally, he walked on the dead grass at the road's edge. Like his father, he held his thumb out and hoped it wouldn't be long before someone stopped. The day was hot and humid, the road dusty, and his canteen empty.

Fortunately, enough kind people gave them a ride in the back of their trucks or wagons, and once they rode the rails. They reached Mississippi in just over a week. They had run out of food and were hungry and dirty when they arrived at the large farm and were given a baloney sandwich and two apples. The cost would be taken from their pay. After eating, they were immediately put to work.

Ade could hardly wait for the day to end. Standing knee-deep in swampy water and shoveling mud in that humid heat proved unbearable. The mosquitoes, biting flies, and other monster insects were attracted to the sweat on his face and body. They feasted, and he itched and scratched at their painful bites.

He wiped his face with the back of his hand, leaving streaks of mud. He saw the nearby colored crew had covered themselves with the thick Mississippi mud. Odd.

"I wish we hadn't come here," he mumbled. "There's not a cloud in the sky, and I'm covered in bug bites."

The foreman overheard and laughed. "You could cover yourself in mud like them darkies. They think it protects them. 'Course, then we'd have to put you on their crew." He laughed again and slapped his rawhide whip against his thigh. Ade hoped the whip was just for show.

All thoughts the weather would change died. Perhaps laying the drainage pipes would be easier than shoveling the thick Mississippi mud. He wondered if he and his dad could get on that crew tomorrow.

"Watch out for snakes and other critters," the foreman yelled in Ade's direction.

"Hey, Yank, 'gators been known to bite your leg off." The man working next to Ade spat tobacco juice and taunted the boy.

Ade blanched and slapped his shovel on the surface of dirty brown water as he had been advised, causing the others to laugh and jeer.

"Aww, leave him alone. He's just a dumb Yankee."

"That's why I warned him. Them Yankees don't know nothin.'"

While working alongside his father in Michigan, Ade learned to keep his mouth shut and ears open. He was intensely focused on this first day in Mississippi. He wanted to prove Sylvester wrong, but this particular crew of men seemed to be the kind his friend had warned him about.

"I don't like this place," Ade grumbled as they dragged their exhausted bodies into the bunkhouse after rinsing as much mud from their bodies as they could.

"Room and board are provided. Pay's pretty good."

They made up their beds, a thin sheet that was no longer white and a scratchy surplus army blanket that was much too hot for these humid Southern nights. Ade glanced around and kept his voice low. "I mean, I don't like these people."

"Not so loud, son. We don't want any trouble."

The bunkhouse members played poker or cribbage, smoked, and told tall tales. Some sipped boot-legged whiskey from Mason jars they hid under their bunks.

Ade moved closer to his father and whispered, "Sylvester's right. The bosses don't treat the colored crew the same as us."

The white men worked together, and the coloreds formed another crew. The whites got a morning and an afternoon break, and the boss supplied fresh water. The coloreds worked longer hours for less pay and were assigned the dirtiest parts of the job. They even had to bring their own water and were housed in ratty army tents, surplus from the Great War or perhaps the Civil War.

No one on the colored crew had met Ade's eyes or returned his greetings all day. They refused to look into any white man's face. Ade jerked the pillowcase over the lumpy pillow and thought about his friendship with Sylvester. He wished the large football player were here, then changed his mind. Sylvester wouldn't do well facing all the injustice. He stuffed the wool blanket under his bunk, stripped down to his underwear, threw himself on his bunk, and focused on his dad's words.

"...and so, it's an explosive situation. There are about eleven colored people in Mississippi for every white person. Most are still treated like slaves. Those who work for this farmer or any other are not paid enough to live on. They are always in debt to the company store, and I heard it's an unwritten law that you can't move without the owner's permission if you have any outstanding debts. They're stuck, and they resent it."

"I don't blame them."

"It's nothing to do with us. Just keep your head down."

"It's not fair."

"We need to get along. Keep your thoughts to yourself."

Ade had never paid much attention in history class and couldn't recall the circumstances during the aftermath of the Civil War, but it seemed that little had changed in the last sixty years. His anxiety increased the following day.

The owner appeared on a white horse as the crews picked up their tools and headed toward the swamp. "I'm paying you top dollar and expect you to give me your best. You'll get used to the bugs. Ignore the heat and humidity." He stared at Ade and his father, the only ones not acclimated to the weather in Mississippi. "I'll be getting daily reports on everyone, especially you Yanks. You'll be paid when your contract ends. If you make it that long. Alright, men, get to work, and remember, if you quit before your contract ends, you get nothing." He jerked on the reins and rode off.

The white men marched toward the muddy water, and the coloreds shuffled behind them. The foreman badgered, insulted, and threatened the colored crew on the short walk to the work site.

It appalled Ade that a threat of being beaten, or worse, hung over any black who crossed a line. Ade didn't know where that line was, but he was sure they did. He thought about Sylvester's family, who had experienced several horrifying incidents in Detroit when they first moved North. Ade was glad his friend's family had moved to the small town where football reigned, and Sylvester was tolerated, if not respected. If the truth be told, Ade had only half-believed the stories Sylvester shared. Now, he was convinced they were entirely accurate.

In the bunkhouse, Ade heard rumors of whippings and thrashings administered on this farm and those in the surrounding area. And even several murders. He had great difficulty pushing this evil from his mind. It reinforced his father's advice to keep his head down and his thoughts to himself.

The days and weeks dragged on. Work. Eat. Sleep. Ade tried to stifle all feelings, especially his desire to be near the ocean. Several months later, rumors flew that a colored man in the next county had killed his boss. The men worked themselves into a frenzy.

"I heard the boss had the man's wife."

"Still ain't right for no black man to kill a white."

"They'll put him down like the animal he is."

"I'd like to get my hands on him. Uppity…"

All day, the agitated men talked about what they would do if they got hold of that darky. The talk continued through supper and into the evening. The men in the bunkhouse could not settle. Ade and his father kept silent.

The foreman burst through the door, pulled the cigar from his mouth, and growled. "Bonus pay for everyone who joins the search. We are going to get that monster."

Mason jars were drained, knives and guns were strapped on,

and a few hateful stares were aimed at Ade and his father as if daring them to say anything.

"I ain't been on a good 'coon hunt in a long time."

"We'll git him."

The foreman threw his cigar on the floor and stomped it with his boot. "C'mon, boys. It's huntin' season."

Ade's skin crawled, and he almost threw up when he heard the word hunt. His heart pounded, and his palms grew damp. Ade and his father stared at each other as the bunkhouse emptied.

"Let's get out of here, Dad. I don't like this state."

"We don't get paid until the end of our contract."

"How much longer?"

"About three weeks. Then we will go."

"As far away as we can."

"Wherever you want."

Ade picked up a worn copy of National Geographic and flipped it open to a picture of snow-covered mountains. "What about Alaska?" Ade asked. "That's about as far away from Mississippi as you can get."

His father laughed, "First, California and your mother's marker, then we'll go north."

Ade did not sleep that night. Near dawn, the crew returned. Before entering the bunkhouse, they visited the army tents and took out their rage on the sleeping colored men. The foreman intervened before anyone was killed. "Them darkies got to work tomorrow. Be gentle, boys." He laughed and left them to it.

Ade shivered under the covers, kept his eyes closed, and hoped the others would assume he was asleep. Slowly, he pulled the covers over his face. He knew it was childish, but he felt safer even though he heard the men recount how they had cornered the black man and rushed him, not knowing he had a Winchester pump gun and a thirty-eight revolver. He shot and killed nine whites, including two from this bunkhouse. He was then gunned down.

Although he knew nothing about that far-off land, Ade dreamt of Alaska.

The following day, the crew glared and muttered curses toward the colored men as they marched to the work site. The black men kept their heads down and did not respond as they limped along.

Ade sidled close to his father. "I don't know if we can make it another three weeks."

"We're not leaving without our pay."

"I'm scared, Dad." The boy whispered.

"Buck up, boy. Your mother is going to have that marble headstone."

Ade bit his lip. "Sure, Dad. Sure."

FIFTEEN

The Professor spoke as he changed the reels in his tape machine. "That's quite a story, hard to believe."

"Imagine my shock when I arrived in Sitka and saw signs in the store windows saying NO INDIANS OR DOGS ALLOWED."

"What?" The Professor's eyes widened.

"Learn your history. Sitka was segregated. Oh, there weren't any Jim Crow laws. It was more subtle, but I didn't like it. It's a story for another day." Ade reached for his coffee.

The Professor was quick to follow his lead. He'd do some research on Alaska and racial discrimination later. "I assume you and your father traveled by train to Seattle and then a ship?"

"Not exactly."

"I meant after you bought the gravestone."

"Not exactly," Ade said again.

"I'm beginning to wonder if you ever made it to Alaska," the Professor joked.

Ade laughed along with him. "We stopped in California to get those headstones for Mom and my sisters. Once we stood by their graves, Dad fell to his knees, broken. Overcome with grief. It was as if they had died that day instead of months before. Finally, I pulled him to his feet and away from the cemetery."

"My condolences."

Ade nodded. "Dad got his job back as caretaker of the orange grove. We moved into our old house, more of a shack, really, but I couldn't get the idea of Alaska out of my head." Ade gulped and almost swallowed his wad of gum. It was much easier to take a drag from a cigarette than try to drink coffee around his gum. He rolled the gum between his fingers, stuck it under the table, gulped his coffee, and longed for a cigarette. "Dad started fixing the place the way Mom had always wanted. He unboxed her few belongings. I could understand putting the dishes and pans in the kitchen, but he hung her clothes in the closet." Ade shivered and said, "It scared me then, and I don't understand it now. It's like he thought she would return."

"What did you do?" the Professor sounded genuinely concerned.

"I didn't know what to do. I tried to talk to him, yelled, begged, and pleaded. He said he left my mother once and wouldn't do it again."

"I don't get it either; it makes no sense." The Professor scratched his head and doodled on his notepaper, avoiding Ade's eyes.

Ade finished his coffee and signaled for more. "Remember that old Bible we found in the cabin in Idaho? I took it when we left, always intended to read it." Ade shrugged his shoulders. "I gave it to Dad, thought it might help him. But he never opened it."

The Professor tapped his pencil on his clipboard and then realized his tape recorder would pick up his nervous noise-making.

"Dad insisted I return to school, but it was too late."

"What do you mean?"

"The kids in school seemed so young and carefree. I had nothing in common with them. I grieved for my mother and sisters, and I was used to working all day, not studying, so I stopped going."

"What did your dad think about that?"

Ade shook his head and looked away. After a moment, he said, "He went to the groves every day and then visited Mom's gravesite, weeping about what might have been, what he should have done." Ade took a large handkerchief from his back pocket and blew his nose. "He didn't say anything when I finally told him I quit."

Ade picked up his coffee with shaking fingers, then set it back in the saucer without drinking. "On my sixteenth birthday, Dad gave me his blessing, six dollars, and told me to live in Alaska or anywhere else. Added to the little I saved over the years, those dollars came to a third of what I needed for Alaska."

"So, you left home. Notice I'm not assuming you made it to Alaska this time."

Ade almost smiled. "I felt myself dragged into his grief, and that scared me. I even went to see the boss, but he said there was nothing to be done as long as Dad did his job and wasn't physically sick. I felt guilty about leaving, but Dad insisted. Looking back, I think he realized I was imprisoned by his depression and grief. He did a good thing by forcing me to go."

"Hey, you! Wharf rat."

Ade turned in the direction of the voice.

"Looking for a job?"

"Yes, sir." Ade trotted to the sandy-haired longshoreman and saw he was at least ten or twelve years older but carried himself with a quiet assurance and confidence that Ade had never experienced.

"Got your dockworker's card?"

"I don't know what that is."

"That building over there is the Union shack. Ask for Mac. Tell him Bill Wall sent you."

"Thanks, Mr. Wall, but I can't see giving part of my pay to some union when I do the work; I intend to keep all my wages."

"You will join the union, or you won't work on these docks or any dock in Los Angeles. You may get beat up or worse if you try. With your dockworker's card, you can be hired for casual labor. It takes years to become a longshoreman. You can't do either without the union."

Ade felt his stomach sink but forced himself to stand straight and thrust his chest forward. "I can take care of myself."

Well-muscled but thin, Bill set his work aside and stood a little too close for Ade's comfort. "There was a strike about a dozen years back. Owners brought in scabs—non-union workers. My dad was killed in the violent confrontations with the scabs. He wasn't the only one."

"That's tough, sorry."

"This is a union dock, boy. A complex world." Bill looked around and lowered his voice, "A dirty world. Lots of waterfront scum. I'm outta here as soon as I have enough to buy passage North."

Ade grinned and stuck out his hand, "I'm going to Alaska. Where are you headed?"

"Same. Uncle's foreman at a logging camp in Baranof, Alaska."

"Maybe we can go together? I have some money saved, and I'll earn more."

Bill ignored the outstretched hand. "Keep your voice down, and don't let any of these wharf rats know you have money, or you won't have it long."

Ade fingered the leather pouch around his neck. "Thanks for the advice, Mr. Wall. Alaska, here we come."

Ade's voice faded, and he gazed into his coffee cup. After a few minutes, the Professor realized Ade had finished his story. He turned off his tape recorder and gathered his notes. "Thank you, Mr. Bunderson."

Ade jerked his thoughts from the past and laughed, "Don't leave me on the docks in Los Angeles amid those thieving scoundrels."

The young man sat down, ordered more coffee for the both of them, and said, "Tell me, but don't try to slip in any fish tales."

"I'm not making any promises, Professor." Ade spat out a piece of tasteless Juicy Fruit. "I had been sleeping in doorways, behind buildings, anywhere I could find a corner. One morning, Bill Wall found me shivering and cold. He took me back to his place that night. Wasn't much, just a cheap boarding house. He made me sneak in the window, and I slept on the floor, but it was warm and out of the weather. More importantly, I was safe from the unsavory elements on the waterfront. I thought I knew my way around but was a naïve kid." Ade made and held the Professor's gaze. "I realized my father had always looked out for me, then Sylvester. Now, Bill was doing the same. I was grateful." Ade pointed his finger at the Professor and said, "Never be too proud to accept help, my boy."

"Did you work on the same pier as Bill?"

"Like Bill said, it would take years to work my way up to long-shoreman, but with my dockworker's card, I could do casual labor, which didn't pay much. Between rent and food, saving even a small amount took forever." Ade unwrapped another piece of Juicy Fruit, then traded it for a cigarette. "I loved the waterfront. The smell of the sea, the ships coming and going. Hearing the seamen brag about their adventures. I didn't mind the pungent odor of fish, even when they were past their prime. It turned Bill's stomach, and he suffered when the fishing fleet offloaded their catch. He preferred cargo ships."

"But you eventually bought tickets to Sitka?"

Ade shook his head, drained his coffee cup, and frowned at the memories flooding his mind. "One night, we were mugged on our way to the boardinghouse. Bill carried all his cash in a money belt fastened around his waist. I had a small leather pouch I hung around my neck. The thieves got them both. Bill was beaten pretty bad and missed a few weeks of work."

Ade felt the stubble on his chin and rubbed his hand over his graying hair. "Thanks to Sylvester's training, I only had a few cuts and bruises and recovered quickly. I borrowed Bill's longshoreman card and took over his job."

"Didn't you get caught?"

Ade slammed his coffee cup, and the dark liquid sloshed over the rim. He cursed and wiped it up with the white linen napkin. "Yes. And it cost me plenty to bribe the foreman to let me continue. I was glad Bill never found out, or it would have been worse for me. On the docks, I kept my mouth shut and my ears open. Listening to those captains and their fish tales finally paid off." Ade eyed the Professor, hoping he would see the importance of listening to fish stories.

"How's that?"

"With our money gone and Bill out of work, it didn't look like we were going North any time soon, at least not the conventional way. But I talked an Old Salt into taking us on as deckhands to pay for our passage."

"You had never been on an ocean-going ship, right?"

"He didn't ask, and I didn't volunteer that information. He was only going as far as Seattle, and his rusty old scow didn't look like it would make it. The captain was as aged as the steamship he piloted," Ade chuckled.

"I assume you reached Seattle and then worked your way to Sitka on another ship."

Ade continued as if the Professor had not spoken. The memories were coming fast and furious. "Bill wasn't completely recovered from his beating and couldn't find his sea legs. When he did, he stumbled to the rail and gave his breakfast to the sea. The other deckhands were merciless in their ribbing. He spent most of the trip moaning in his bunk. It was worse for him when we encountered severe storms along the Oregon Coast and a fierce one in the Strait of Juan de Fuca."

"What did the captain do when Bill couldn't work?"

Ade grinned, and his eyes sparkled. "I was young, strong, and not too bright. I told the captain I would work Bill's shifts and my own. It nearly killed me."

"How did you manage?"

"Lots of coffee, little sleep, and sheer doggedness. Captain Jensen was actually a kind old fellow and saw to it that I learned how to read charts, tie knots, and stay safe when working on deck in gale-force winds. It was thrilling!"

"But not for Bill?"

"Every pitch and roll of the ship was agony for him. He didn't eat, just a few crackers, but still tried to throw up. The retching and dry heaving caused him to ache all over. I was in the cabin with him whenever I wasn't working, although the smell nearly gagged me. Between the body odor, sweat, and—well, let's just say he never made it to the bathroom on his own. I cleaned him up as best I could, half-carried him into the tiny shower, puking, moaning, and swearing he'd never get on a ship again. Once I got him back into bed, he fell into a disturbed sleep, rolling from side to side and talking. It was like listening to one of those popular drama programs on the radio."

Ade leaned back in his chair and remembered how Bill thrashed on the small cabin's lower bunk. He grabbed Ade by the shoulders as the teenage boy tried to hold him still. "Don't let that man you married send me away, Ma."

"Bill, wake up! You're talking crazy." Ade wiped Bill's sweat-soaked face with a damp cloth.

"Don't let him send me away," Bill kept begging.

"I'm not your Ma."

Bill continued as if he had not heard Ade. "He's not a good man. I wish you hadn't married him after Pa died."

"You're on a ship, Bill. Seasick." Ade grabbed Bill's shoulders and shook. Bill twisted out of his grasp and continued tossing and talking while Ade stood by with the damp rag and the vomit bucket.

"Please, Ma."

"Your father thinks it's for the best."

"He's not my father. He never will be."

"And that's why you have to leave." Bill's stepfather barged into the room and whacked the rolled-up newspaper against Bill's shoulder. "You've never accepted me. Never allowed me to be a father to you."

"My Dad was a good man, always treated my mother kindly. I can't say the same for you."

The angry man tossed the newspaper aside, his fists clenched, and he stepped closer to Bill. "On Friday night, you graduate from high school. On Saturday morning, pack your bag and leave."

"Please, dear, give him some time to find a job and a place to live." The distraught woman wrung her hands and knelt before the man she had so foolishly married. Bill turned away from the sight, his stomach churning.

"I made my way in the world when I was much younger than him." The man he would never call father picked up the newspaper he had thrown aside and fell into the shabby, overstuffed chair. He held the paper in front of his face— a signal he was finished with the conversation.

Mother and son sat at the kitchen table and tried to think.

"Come with me, Mom. We don't need him."

His mother placed her hands over her still-flat belly. "I can't. I'm expecting."

"A baby?" Bill glanced toward the front room. "I hate him."

"We need to make a plan, son. I have a little money saved that he doesn't know about."

"You might need it, Mom."

"Write to me in care of my friend, Elsie." She scribbled an address on the back of an envelope. "Her husband works on the docks in Los Angeles and can probably get you a job. It's not what I would have chosen for you. The waterfront can be a vile place. Promise me that you will go to my brother in Alaska as soon as you can. You can build a good life there."

"Uncle Joe's letters are exciting, but I want to be close in case you need me."

"I'll be okay and feel better knowing you're with Joe."

SIXTEEN

Ade stubbed out his cigarette, vowed it was the last one he would ever smoke, and unwrapped another piece of gum. "I admit I was curious about Bill's life, and I kept him talking. Shouldn't have done that. From his ramblings, I learned Bill skipped his graduation and left home that night. He got his dockworker's card and later a longshoreman's card, although it took him several years. His mother's friend had married a man like poor Bill's stepfather." Ade shook his head and spat his gum into the ashtray. "Bill found his own place as soon as he could. His Uncle Joe offered to buy him a ticket north, but he refused. He vowed never to be beholden to anyone after having to depend on his stepfather."

The Professor said, "Poor Bill."

"Captain Jensen told me that a person can hallucinate in extreme cases of seasickness. Bill thought he was in his past. He was still weak when we docked in Seattle, so I half-carried him ashore. He said he'd find a way to get to his uncle's logging camp by land." Ade laughed and reached for more gum. "He didn't appreciate it when I reminded him Baranof was an island."

"How long were you in Seattle?"

"Too long for me, not long enough for Bill. He was a Class A longshoreman and got a job almost immediately. Even though I had my dockworker's card, I didn't want to work as casual labor; the hours were long, and the pay was lousy. I finally found work in a fish cannery further along the waterfront. Again, we stayed in a cheap boardinghouse. The room was drafty and cold, but I didn't have to sleep on the floor. The food was good, and I ate a lot."

Ade excused himself to go to the bathroom. All that coffee needed to be released. The Professor took the opportunity to read over his notes. He wondered if he was getting the information Miss Ruth wanted. He could understand her putting Agrefena on the list. After all, she was a Native Alaskan, and how she had to adapt and learn to live in a white world was intriguing. While this simple fisherman was interesting, he didn't seem remarkable, and his friend, Bill Wall, wasn't even on the list. Many young Scandinavians, just like the now middle-aged Ade Bunderson, had come to Alaska for the fish. He shook his head and shuffled the papers as Ade returned to his seat.

"Where was I?"

"On the docks in Seattle."

"Bill wanted to travel on a large sailing ship like the Star of Alaska. He thought there would be less pitching and rolling. The tickets were more expensive, and we didn't have enough money to eat in the ship's dining room. So, we brought a sack of apples and Pilot bread to last the nearly week-long voyage."

"Pilot bread?"

Ade shook his finger at the Professor, "How can you live in Alaska and not know what Pilot bread is—something between a cracker and hardtack. Good stuff. Sticks to your ribs."

The Professor ignored Ade's remark. "I'm surprised you didn't offer to work in the galley in exchange for meals."

Ade laughed, "The cook chased me out of his domain with a meat cleaver in one hand and a rolling pin in the other."

The waitress hovered over them with her ever-present coffee pot. Both men waved her away. She fluttered her eyelashes at the not-bad-looking grad student and left. With all the winking and batting, Ade assumed she was a flirt, although the intense young man sitting across from him didn't seem to notice. He shrugged and returned to the business at hand.

"The National Weather Service predicted storms along the Inside Passage for the next several days, but I lied and told Bill the forecast was for calm seas and fair weather. He never did forgive me."

"How did you like working at the logging camp?"

"Young man, did I say I worked at the logging camp?" Ade tapped his fingers on the table and scattered the half-dozen gum wrappers. "As soon as we docked in Sitka, Bill headed for his uncle's. I didn't see him for a month."

"Let me put a new reel in the machine," the Professor said.

Ade watched the other man fiddle with his recording machine, then scratched the stubble on his chin and said, "I think I had seawater in my veins all my life but didn't know it. I decided to learn everything there was to know about these Alaskan waters and vowed that someday I would have my own boat. I would teach myself to fish if I had to."

"Mike Evans told me how the white skippers saw you as a competitor when you arrived in Sitka, even though you were just a teenager."

"I offered to apprentice, work for food only, and they still wouldn't take me on. I was pretty discouraged, but Mike contacted the Tlingit—Petrov Bravebird. I owe a lot to both men. In fact, Petrov introduced me to my wife, Olly."

"Was she Native?"

"A Yupik from a little village called Ninilchik on the Kenai."

"I heard most Native cultures embrace family and clan and are matriarchal; I'm surprised you didn't settle near her family."

Ade leaned against the chair back and crossed his legs. "Her village was originally a Russian retirement settlement. The wives were from separate tribes and clans in different areas of Alaska. There were no clan houses or tribal structures. The culture was mostly Russian. Olly's only family was a sister here in Sitka. In fact, my buddy Bill was married to her—for a few years anyway."

"Was?"

"Long story. Tragic."

"Wait. Olly? Ollyanna?" The Professor pulled a packet of papers from his vest pocket. "Bill Wall's not on my list, nor are there any other Bundersons, but there is an Ollyanna Oskolkoff."

"That's her. She didn't like the name, Bunderson—couldn't wrap her tongue around it. Would only use it for official paperwork and stuff. Women." Ade twisted in his chair, saying, "I can tell you whatever you want to know about her."

"Thanks, Mr. Bunderson, but it's in my notes that I am to interview everyone directly, if possible. Miss Ruth's orders." He removed his glasses, squinted, and held the list close to his eyes. "There is a hand-written note here in tiny letters, 'Ollyanna's faith.' What does that mean?"

Ade groaned, "Ask her. I mean, I believe in God and everything. You can't live in Alaska without knowing somebody had to create all this. I've been in impossible situations when fishing alone, and I know Ollyanna's prayers saved me. She talks to God like she knows Him personally and listens as if He talks to her." Ade reached for his coffee cup and dumped in a lot of sugar, which he only did when he felt nervous.

"Yeah, I think Miss Ruth is the same. She sees the invisible and hears the inaudible."

Ade shivered. "Spooky. I'd say they were religious fanatics, but they are the kindest and most honest people you will ever meet. Fearless."

The Professor fiddled with the knobs on his recording machine. "I'd say formidable. At least, Miss Ruth is."

Ade laughed, "So is my wife, but in a good way. Until she gets too preachy, that is." Ade cleared his throat and tapped his spoon against his coffee cup. "I do sometimes envy the faith she has."

"Yeah, well…"

The two men looked everywhere in the restaurant except at each other. Throats were cleared. Coffee cups rattled against their saucers. Napkins scrunched. Water glasses lifted.

Finally, Ade swallowed the too-sweet coffee and said, "Bill's an interesting guy. He's in a tuberculosis sanitarium, not doing well, but he wouldn't talk to you anyway."

"Why not?" Relieved about the new topic of conversation, the Professor asked for the name of the sanitarium.

Ade closed his eyes, and his face screwed up as if he were trying to think. "Bill never talked about his past, and I never asked. Everything I know, I heard when he was seasick. When he turned twenty, Bill figured he could take on his stepdad if it came to a fight. He wanted to rescue his mom, but strangers lived in the house. He contacted his mother's friend, Elsie, who said they left one night, and she didn't know where they went. His mom, stepdad, and the baby. It was a girl. Poor Bill, he had no one."

"He had you."

"Guess I never thought of it that way. Yeah, we were like brothers. I miss him."

"Even if he's not on Miss Ruth's list, I'd like to know more about him." The Professor's curiosity was in high gear, and he reminded himself to pay attention to the task at hand.

"I heard you were a curious fellow. It surprises me you don't want to hear about my fishing adventures. Over two decades on these waters, I could make your skin crawl, have you laughing out loud, or bring tears to your eyes."

Heat pulsed in the Professor's face; he chuckled, turned off his tape recorder, and leaned back in his chair. He tugged on his earlobe, then laced his fingers together behind his head. "Alright, Mr. Bunderson, against my better judgment, I'll listen to one of your fish stories, but only one."

"You won't be satisfied with one."

"One."

"I was fishing off Little Biorka Island and saw a violent downburst in the distance. The damaging winds intensified, and I saw this was no ordinary storm."

"Wow! I had never heard of a snow squall! There is a professor at the University who could help you write your stories and maybe get them published."

Ade's heart leaped. Published! What a thought. Before he could respond, the Professor asked, "So why Sitka? There are fishing villages throughout the Southeast."

"I've spent time in Wrangel, Ketchikan, and Petersburg, good places, but all on the Inside Passage. Sitka faces the ocean and feels right to me."

The Professor sharpened his pencil, scooped up the shavings, and let them fall into his empty coffee mug. "Mr. Bunderson, you don't strike me as a man who does things because of a feeling."

"Let's call it a gut instinct, then." Ade chewed on the inside of his cheek. "I understand you're from up around Fairbanks. Born there?"

"My grandfather was a gold-seeker. Never found any, but opened a bakery in the newly incorporated town of Fairbanks. My family has been there ever since. What's that got to do with anything?"

Ade Bunderson, now in his fifties, took a deep breath. "You're an Alaskan through and through, born and bred. Alaska is home. I suppose you never had to think about it, never wondered what Alaska meant to you or your people." Ade scratched the stubble on his chin and tried to find the right words to express the feelings that were deep inside. "I never fit in the orange groves in California or bumming around the Midwest with my Dad, and I don't even want to think about Mississippi." Ade drummed his hands on the table. "I sometimes wonder how life would have turned out if Dad and I had stayed in the Bitterroots." He shook his head. "No, the mountains of Idaho weren't enough."

"Enough?"

Ade picked up the pencil and sketched on a napkin. "I know each shoal, outcropping, current, hidden cove, and every small island in these waters, even the unnamed ones. I know all the best fishing spots and spawning grounds, but I keep those to myself. I guess what I am trying to say is I'm comfortable here. I fit. I know and am known." He pushed the napkin across the table. He had sketched a perfect picture of Sitka Sound and the surrounding islands.

The Professor rubbed his eyebrow and looked puzzled. Ade sighed and wondered if he could explain this feeling, even to himself. "Mike and Agrefena took me in and steered me in the right direction. Petrov Bravebird showed me how to be a man. Ollyanna gave me a family and showed me what it meant."

"But Sitka?"

Ade reached for the napkin and wiped his eyes; he stared through the window, letting the water calm him. "These waters—this town—they grew me up—matured me." After a moment, he continued speaking with tears in his eyes. "I stand on the bow of my trawler or skiff and picture that California teenager at the edge of the orange grove. The boy who gazed into the ocean and longed to belong." Ade stared out the window, then down at his hands. He sniffed, looked at the Professor, and whispered,   "Ollyanna says Alaska and especially Sitka draws the people who are meant to be here; of course, she meant by Bozhe." He shrugged. "All I know is Sitka made a place for me."

The Professor nodded as if he understood and wrote down everything Ade Bunderson told him.

SEVENTEEN

Interviewer's note: I met with Mr. Durand over several days. He was uncomfortable and reluctant to be interviewed, although he did open up to me on two separate occasions. He seemed to be a literary man, although he never attended college. I imagine he was self-educated, although he tried to hide it.

I am confident his actions in the Great War—World War One, marked him and caused him to try to lose himself in Alaska. Although he now appears whole and mentally healthy, I saw remnants of pain and sensed a deep sadness within him.

I believe there is more to his story. I have been unsuccessful in my attempts to interview him further.

The dog's breath fell heavy and hot on his face. The warmth felt good to his half-frozen body, although the smell was terrible. He thought the dog's last meal must have been rotten fish. The large animal licked his face, whined, and lay next to him, offering its warmth. The broken man nestled next to the canine.

Moonrise lit the night. No overcast clouds obstructed Orion or the Great Bear. No one in the North called it a Dipper. Big Bear and Polaris stood proud in the bright navy sky. He squinted into the distance and knew the sun would soon crawl over the mountains.

He stretched and yawned, then flinched when his side reminded him of his injuries. He wiggled his toes and fingers, then felt his arms and legs. No broken bones, except perhaps, for his nose. He tried to sit, but the pain caused him to slump next to the sleeping beast. He pressed his hand to his side, feeling the congealed blood on his shirt. Wincing, he pulled an extra pair of long johns from his knapsack and tied them around his midsection. His ribs, bruised and possibly cracked, sent shooting arrows of agony through his body. He didn't think they were broken. And since he was still alive, he assumed the knife had missed his vital organs. Pain. The dog moaned and sat up, causing him to keel over.

"Did you see anything, big fella?" the man moaned, "like who attacked me and why?" The images of the assault refused to come into focus, and he didn't know if his memory would return. Where was he, and where had this protective canine come from?

"Sun's coming over the mountains, boy." The animal licked the man's face and stood.

"You're as big as a bull! Is that your name, big fella?" The dark-haired mastiff barked, grabbed the man's arm, and attempted to pull him toward the docks.

"Not so fast, boy. I've lost a lot of blood." He stumbled to his feet, pressed his side, and winced. The dog pulled on his arm with a stronger tug. "Good idea, Bull. I need to get out of this town. But slowly, I don't want to start bleeding again."

The dog whimpered, and his chocolate eyes implored the scruffy, beaten man.

"Okay. **We both** need to get out of here." After checking his pockets, he swore and said, "They've taken my stake and pouch of nuggets." He scratched the mastiff behind the ears. "There's still gold in those mountains if you know where to look."

The dog looked up the street and growled deep in his throat. The man glanced over his shoulder. "That looks like an angry mob gathering at the end of town, and I don't want any company."

Again, the dog whined. The man laughed. "Okay. **We** don't want any company." He scratched the dog's ears. "You must be lost, or maybe you've run away from your previous owner. I'm sure you had your reasons."

The man's battered body did not allow him to move quickly. The dog matched his pace to the man's, although he whined and nudged him continually as they took the back alleys to the docks, avoiding everyone. When they reached the wharf, the man took off his shoes and socks and retrieved several bills. "My pappy always told me to keep an emergency stash where others wouldn't look. We'll go as far south as this money will take us."

"I can take you as far as Sitka if you think you can travel. You look like heck." The short, squat skipper of the small steamer chomped on an unlit cigar. "Not in any kind of trouble, are you?"

"I was hoping for Seattle."

"Leave the dog with me. He'd bring a fair price, enough to cover your passage to Seattle."

He felt the dog move closer to his knees. "We'll go to Sitka."

The skipper shrugged, took the money, and said, "I need your names for the ship's passenger list."

"Stormy Durand and my partner is Bull." He laid his hand on the dog's massive head.

The skipper laughed, "Biggest dog I've seen in Skagway or anywhere. But you both look hungry. The ticket price doesn't include any grub."

"Well, Bull, I guess we'll tighten our belts."

The skipper reached into his pocket for some change. "There is a chowder shack on the other side of the cannery. I'll give two blasts of the whistle when it's time to leave."

"Thanks, Skipper."

Later, Stormy Durand and his newly acquired mastiff joined a dozen or so would-be passengers back at the pier, but the steamer was nowhere to be seen. Curses, murmurs, and empty threats could be heard. Some scowled and shook their fists at the open water.

A young couple with a child in their arms looked at Stormy's battered face, blood-soaked clothes, and Bull's fierce expression; they moved away.

The man put his arm around his wife. "We have our tickets and returned within the hour like the Skipper said. I don't know what to do." The woman gnawed on her lower lip, hugged the baby tighter, and cried.

Stormy slung his knapsack over his shoulder, winced, and looked away with a heavy heart. He had no money or resources to help them.

An old sourdough cursed and swore, "This is Skagway, the most corrupt town in Alaska—has been ever since Soapy Smith took control of the place during the Klondike Rush. Ole Soapy must have inspired that low-down skipper."

"He sure found a way to make money from us unsuspecting, honest folk," a well-dressed man slapped his derby against his thigh and walked away. "I paid good money for my ticket. Someone is going to hear about this."

"I should have known better." The old sourdough cursed again and spat tobacco juice out of the side of his mouth. It landed near

Bull's front paw, and the mastiff growled. The sourdough squinted, stepped back, and spoke in a low tone, "Ain't you the fella wanted for robbing the bank?"

Bull bared his teeth and leaped forward. Stormy grabbed him by the ruff of his neck. "Easy, Bull."

"Makes no-never-mind to me. I don't trust them cheatin' bankers, just as money-grubbing as Soapy." He pulled his hat over his eyes and shuffled toward town. "Anybody asks, I never seen you."

"The skipper gave us money to get some lunch before we sailed." The woman cuddled her baby and looked at the others. "He seemed so nice."

"He obviously sold more tickets than he had space for."

"I bought a ticket to Wrangel, and all I got was a bowl of chowder."

"Me too. Ketchikan."

"I guess it was first come, first served, and when the ship was full, he left."

"Heck of a way to run a business, but I guess it's profitable."

Stormy and Bull faded toward town as the small crowd grumbled and milled about. "Best we stay out of sight, boy. My memory's coming back, and those thugs that beat me will be upset to learn I'm still alive." He stumbled and grabbed his side. "One of those ruffians was good with his knife; my wound's bleeding again."

The chocolate-colored mastiff led Stormy to an alley behind the fish cannery. He stood guard as the weary man collapsed beside a pile of packing crates. Stormy spent most of the day and night in and out of consciousness. Near dawn, he sank into a deep sleep and dreamed of the only woman he had ever cared about. He supposed every wounded doughboy in France was half in love with Nurse Kate.

While in the hospital, he and Kate discussed great literature, poetry, history, and philosophy. Whenever she came into the ward, he followed her with his eyes. He did not join her other patients when they whistled, teased, and made outrageous comments to her. He wanted to knock heads together and protect her. He thought she knew because she would look at him with a smile and a wink.

Those weeks in the hospital healed more than his body. Kate's attention and care began mending his soul. All too soon, he was sent back to the trenches with wounds barely healed.

Kate gave him her London address, and he promised to find her after the war. Her last words to him were—till we meet again.

The Great War ended on November 11, 1918, and the guns on the Western Front ceased their firing. Stormy Durand finagled a pass to London. War-torn London was a tangled mess. Streets and buildings had been bombed, first by zeppelins, then by aeroplanes. It took two days to find the address Kate had given him.

He was shocked to learn the ship carrying her back to Britain had been attacked and sunk while crossing the English Channel. He spent an uncomfortable afternoon with her parents drinking cup after cup of tea. They were thirsty for stories of Kate, and he forced himself to remember every conversation, every look, every thought he had.

How could she have died so many weeks ago without him knowing? He had assumed her letters were lost in the unreliable mail service to the front.

He left her parents' flat in a daze, not remembering how he returned to his unit in France. He finished his discharge paperwork and the mustering out process in a fog. He didn't remember much about the transport ship back to America, so deep was his grief.

Dawn broke, sending shafts of chilly sunlight onto Stormy's face. He didn't want to wake up, but the pain was intense. "You are a good nurse, Bull, but I wish Kate was here." He pushed her image away, although he would never forget her English rose complexion and honey-colored hair. Her gray eyes still haunted him. Life was easier when he didn't think about her.

"You still here, Bull? Good boy, best you go find yourself some food and water. I'll be okay." The dog licked his face and ran out of the alley. Stormy lay back and gripped his side. The blood in his wound no longer flowed, but he was afraid to move. He moaned, closed his eyes, and dozed.

"What are you trying to show me, boy? Where are you taking me?"

A woman's voice, solid yet curious, penetrated his pain. He struggled to open his eyes but could not. He felt gentle yet firm hands examine him and a sharp intake of her breath.

"Stay, boy. I am going to get help."

He didn't know how long, but when the woman returned, he felt himself raised to a semi-sitting position. "Hold him still, Shorty. I want to clean and bandage this gash in his side before we move him." She untied the longjohns and cast them aside. The metallic odor of dried blood filled the air.

"You collect stray dogs and children like they was Easter eggs, but this is a man, beat good. I don't like it. We don't know if he's a honest one." Shorty turned away and spat tobacco juice on an empty packing crate.

"Good or not, honest or not, we are going to help him."

"Don't forget your boat sails in thirty minutes." Short Shorty shook his head and handed her the bandages. "We don't know what he's done or who knifed him. Maybe the other fella is dead. Killed."

"Hush now."

"Miss Ruth, this fella could be someone we wouldn't want to meet in a dark alley, and this is a dark alley."

"Yes, it is. Step to the side. You're blocking my light."

Stormy tried to express his thanks but could only utter a groan. His eyelashes fluttered, and he passed out as his wound was probed.

"We'll take him to your house, where I'll finish cleaning him up, and you can fetch a doctor."

"Are you sure, Miss Ruth? He looks evil to me."

"He looks like someone I've seen before. I can't place him, but the dog is loyal to him, and that's good enough for me."

Stormy Durand was unaware as the duo loaded him in a wheelbarrow and pushed him through Skagways back alleys. He heard their voices as if he were in a long tunnel and tried to answer. "Stor—Dur—Sitka."

"After I get the doctor, I'm going to find out about this fellow," Shorty said. He figured folks in Skagway's several speakeasies would know all the latest gossip. The ship's whistle blasted. "You've missed your ship, Miss Ruth, on account of this ne'er-do-well."

"There will be other ships and, as you know, I love visiting with you."

As they neared the crowded street, Miss Ruth said, "Stop a minute." Short Shorty stretched his shoulders as the middle-aged Miss Ruth pulled the shawl from her shoulders and the hat from Shorty's head and set them loosely over Stormy's face.

"What did you do that for?"

"We want people to assume we're carrying a dead body. Fewer

questions that way."

Shorty Shorty scowled and spat tobacco juice in the street. Bull growled and trotted beside Miss Ruth. No one in Skagway gave them a second look.

EIGHTEEN

Short Shorty pulled the man into the parlor and onto the leather settee. He grabbed his hat and promised Miss Ruth he'd send the doctor over and then learn all he could about this stranger.

Miss Ruth was grateful the doctor appeared to have a significant lack of curiosity about his patient. Even though the chaos and lawlessness of the gold rush were in the past, remnants remained, and in Alaska, it was prudent to mind your own business. Curiosity and corruption were not good bedfellows, not in a Skagway that was still unprincipled, unscrupulous, and notorious.

The doctor complimented Miss Ruth on her medical skills and stitched his patient's side and a gash on his shoulder. The doctor was careful to never look at the man's face as he made small talk about the weather. Miss Ruth paid him and promised to call if the man's wounds did not heal properly. Bull never took his eyes off of the doctor.

Miss Ruth made tea and waited for Shorty to return. An hour later, he burst through the door, "I told you he was no good! The Canadian Imperial Bank was robbed, and the law is looking for a man of his description."

The barely conscious wounded man shook his head and tried to sit but fell back against the sofa pillows. Miss Ruth, calm and serene, poured Shorty a cup of tea. "The real thieves met him about a half block from the bank. They assumed he saw the robbery, so they attacked him and dragged him to the back of the bank, leaving him for dead. They gave his description to everyone, pretending they had witnessed the whole thing."

"You believe him?"

"Here's your tea. He was on his way to Sitka. We must get him there with no one the wiser." She looked toward her patient and saw that he had fallen asleep again. It was the best thing for him. "I am going to shave his beard. No one will be looking for a clean-shaven man. Maybe then I will recognize him."

"Best shave his head too." Shorty rubbed his hand over his own thinning hair.

Once she had shaved him, Miss Ruth gasped. "Shorty, this is the fellow from beyond Dyea, the one I found freezing to death in the abandoned cabin."

"Last winter was a bad one, for sure. He still looks like an evil ruffian." Shorty paced the room, throwing several glances at the newly shaved man asleep on the sofa.

"What was his name?" she asked herself.

"Something about the weather, I think you said," Shorty muttered.

"That's right. Stormy—Stormy Durand." Miss Ruth pulled the blanket up and tucked it under Stormy's chin. She patted his cheek.

"Just because you know his name doesn't mean he's a good man. Beard or not, they're looking for a fellow who's been stabbed and has a broken nose. Besides, the doctor seen him."

"We'll hide him until he's well enough to travel," Miss Ruth said.

"What will we tell the doctor?"

Miss Ruth scratched her ear and tilted her head, lost in thought. "I don't think the doc will ask any questions. He didn't ask for Stormy's name and said he doesn't keep any records of his patients."

"Are you sure this here, Stormy Durand, ain't the robber?"

The dog growled, and Shorty shrank back in his chair. "Okay, big boy, I guess we'll trust your judgment."

Miss Ruth smiled, "I have found dogs are usually better judges of character than most people."

Bull wagged his tail.

NINETEEN

The tape recorder clicked off. "Looks like I need to change the reel. It will just be a moment," the Professor said.

"Not much left to tell. Short Shorty hid me in his attic for several weeks. Once my wounds had healed, Miss Ruth shaved my beard again and clipped my hair, although she didn't think the law was actively searching for me any longer. They smuggled me down to the docks and into their friend's fishing boat. I've been in Sitka ever since."

"I assume you weren't born in Alaska."

Stormy Durand's lips turned down, and his eyes glazed. He seemed to shrink into himself. The Professor quickly said, "Perhaps you can tell me about the day you arrived in Sitka instead. I heard something about an old man stuck in a window, a wedding, and the long arm of the law."

Stormy laughed, "Something like that, Professor. Miss Ruth had given me enough funds to survive for a few days, but I needed to find a job and a place cheaper than the hotel. Besides, Bull seemed to intimidate the hotel's guests."

The interviewer glanced at a framed photograph of the beloved dog. Stormy reached down to the young animal resting at his feet. "This is Bull's great-grandson. His father and grandfather were also named Bull."

"Nice, doggie."

The dog made a noise that sounded like a human snort, licked Stormy's hand, and rested his head in his master's lap. Stormy continued his story as he absently scratched Bull's ears.

"The dog and I were on our way to a small place in the woods just off Sawmill Creek Road near Indian River. The hotel clerk said it was for rent. We heard scuffling and screaming and a rifle shot as we neared it. Bull took off toward the sound snarling and barking as loud as I'd ever heard him. I ran after him and saw a man knocked aside by a bear's gigantic paw. It would have been fatal if Bull hadn't leaped and fastened on the bear's leg, deflecting the blow."

"Everybody knows bears are easily spooked by dogs, especially a huge one like your mastiff."

"At the time, I didn't know that." Stormy ran his hand over his unshaven face. "I was shaking and thought I had lost Bull for sure. The bear shook Bull off and turned toward me. I grabbed the man's rifle and fired three times in rapid succession. The bear, head weaving back and forth, took several steps toward us. Bull growled, and I yelled at him to get behind me. Instead, he grabbed the unconscious man by the leg and pulled. The bear stumbled and finally fell. Bull had minor wounds, but the man wasn't so lucky. I carried the poor fellow back to town. Bull licked his cuts and gashes, then caught up with us." Stormy swallowed the last of his coffee and scratched Bull's great-grandson behind the ears once more.

"Then what happened?"

"Others had come running when they heard the gunshots. Two went to check on the bear, and the others helped me get the man to the doctor, who patched him as best he could and arranged to send him to the hospital in Juneau. Turns out the man was the Police

Chief. Since I saved the Chief's life, the Doc said I should have his job. Whenever I refused, Bull growled and pushed me toward the men. We were toe to toe when one of them said, "That dog wants you to be the Chief so he can be your deputy."

Bull sat up and wagged his tail as Stormy continued, "I told him Bull could be the Chief, and I'd be his deputy. They laughed and pinned a badge on me. This is where I keep it." Stormy twisted Bull's collar so the Professor could see the shiny badge attached. "A couple of the men hurried away, saying they had to attend a wedding. The others wandered off as well. As we approached the middle of town, Bull discovered a bandy-legged little man trying to break into the Russian Church."

"Who are you, and what are you doing?" I hollered.

"Not your business," he answered.

"As Chief of Police, I'm making it my business."

The little man pulled his head out of the window and glared at me. He chewed on his mustache and said, "I know Chief. Is not you."

He continued to try to stuff himself into the window.

"Your Chief was mauled by a bear and is going to the hospital in Juneau. I'm the new Chief."

"Who say?"

Stormy looked at the younger man and chuckled, "I wasn't sure who hired me, so I told him it was a group of townsmen on their way to a wedding. That startled him, and he tried to shove himself through the window again. I motioned to Bull, and he and this would-be thief had a little tug-of-war. Bull won."

"No wedding without papers. Must get." He waved his arms and fell off the wooden barrel he had been standing on. "The Father. He send—door locked."

"Turns out the double doors were stuck. Bull pushed against it. The little fellow ran in, grabbed some papers off the altar, and ran. Bull chased him all the way to the ANB Hall."

The Professor laughed out loud and wiped his eyes with his sleeve, "I only heard part of the story. This is great. Bull's first official act as Sitka's chief law enforcement officer was to grab a citizen of Sitka by the seat of the pants and crash a wedding."

"And we've been the law here ever since." Stormy Durand rubbed his eyebrows and laughed, "But like I said, Bull was more the law than me. I just tagged along, especially when we went hunting."

"What do you mean?"

"You have to understand we still lived a pretty subsistent life back in the day. If I had men in prison for any length of time, their families would go hungry. That didn't sit well with me, so I took them into the woods or out on the water. After their families were provided for, I hauled them back to jail to finish their sentences."

The Professor shook his head and laughed, "You gave them guns?"

"And gaff hooks, clubs, and knives," Stormy chuckled.

"I'd like to see you try that today or down in the States."

"My prisoners had breakfast at the Sitka Café and were ordered to return to the jail after dinner. If there was a dance on a Saturday night or a double-header baseball game, I let them attend if they promised to return by midnight."

"Like Cinderella, huh?"

"Believe me, they were the ugly stepsisters, and no glass slippers were in sight. If they were really bad, the town bought them a one-way ticket to Seattle."

The Professor checked his notes. "Thank you, Mr. Durand, er, Chief. That's how you and Bull settled in Sitka, but what brought you to Alaska in the first place?"

The taciturn lawman leaned back in the chair and closed his eyes, reluctant to answer. Old Bull's great-grandson whined and put his head on Stormy's knee. Absently, he rubbed the dog's nose.

"After the war—the Great War," Stormy opened his eyes and looked at the Professor who fiddled with his tape recorder, "While in France, I received a letter that my parents had died of Spanish Influenza. I didn't know my sister had succumbed a few weeks later. The neighbors said they wrote, but I never received their letter."

"Sorry, sir."

Stormy pulled a handkerchief from his pocket and blew his nose. "Those of us who fought in the Great War were changed. Those who didn't lose their lives or their minds lost their futures."

"What do you mean?"

There was a faraway look in Stormy's eye and tension in his face. Bull whimpered and nudged closer to the wooden rocker as if to comfort his master. "My father was a scholarly man, a college professor. I planned to follow in his footsteps. My mother was a gentle soul who loved poetry. All I knew about a man's capacity for carnage and horror I read in books. The reality of the trenches, mud, blood, and bodies—destroyed all the goodness in me. I returned to the United States empty, unfeeling—as empty as the house I grew up in. I packed a bag, gave the key to the neighbors, and visited the cemetery on my way out of town."

"And you never returned?" The questioner scribbled as fast as possible and quietly turned the recorder back on.

"I saw things and did things in the War that killed the poet in me. It was all I could do to breathe."

"You wanted to be a poet?"

"I wanted a thoughtful, peaceful life." Stormy Durand tried to smile, "I might have been a good teacher. I was never a good poet but enjoyed playing with words and looking for meaning." Stormy fiddled with his watch and wished he hadn't spoken about such things. No one in town knew this side of him, and he'd like to keep it that way.

"And what made you decide on Alaska?"

"I wandered aimlessly and couldn't settle. I had no motivation, no dream to pursue, and no cause to believe in. Followed the crops for a while, working in the fields. Eventually, I ended up in the woods of the Pacific Northwest. The beauty of the forests and woodlands soothed me for a time, but logging was dangerous, and accidents occurred nearly every day. I saw too many men die. It reminded me of the war. Met a few lost veterans like myself. One of them knew the captain of a fishing vessel bound for Alaska, so we all signed on. We fished for a couple of seasons, and then the ship went down in the Yaiya Inlet at the north end of the Lynn Canal. The rescue cutter brought us to Skagway."

"Did everyone survive?"

"Yes, most returned to the States—said Alaska was too wild and lawless, as dangerous as the trenches in Europe. I wandered around the gold fields and tried running a trap line in the interior."

"Why did you stay when the others left?"

Stormy shrugged, looked at the ceiling, and closed his eyes.

"Mr. Durand? Chief? Stormy?"

Stormy fidgeted and fought against answering but heard himself say, "I suppose it was the poetry."

"What?"

"The harsh, wild poetry of this land, the sea, and the sky. It's difficult to explain."

"Can you try?"

Stormy felt his cheeks warm. He pulled Bull closer and rubbed his chin on the dog's head. The dog gave a soft bark, turned, and licked the man's cheek. "Thanks, boy. You always know what to say."

Stormy remembered the autumn he spent in the interior near the mountain the Natives called Denali and the Americans called Mt. McKinley. He had traveled north with a Native guide who promised to teach him to run a trap line. They found an abandoned cabin, chopped a wood supply, and set out their lines. All was well for a few weeks. The Native was a good teacher, and Stormy an apt pupil, but the game was scarce.

They worked their way south as the weather deteriorated and winter neared. They found another abandoned cabin near Finnegan's Point. After the first snowstorm, his guide wanted them to travel to a Native village north of Dyea and remain there for the winter. Stormy refused.

Being surrounded by people was not to the ex-doughboy's liking. He needed the remoteness and isolation of this cabin. The Native looked at the sky and told Stormy it would be a bad winter, and they needed the safety and security of a tribe. Stormy grunted and said they had a supply of vittles and wood. The Native shrugged, but in the morning, Stormy was alone. No matter. He was better off.

After a series of wild weather, days of brilliant sun returned, and calm skies soothed his soul. The snow lay over the landscape like a shroud; perhaps a newly starched sheet would be a better description. Fresh. Crisp. Bleached. He hoped this sunny weather would last.

Less than a week later, a severe storm roared out of the North. The arctic wind forced him to abandon his trap lines and hibernate in the cabin. The firewood was unseasoned and did not supply adequate heat when the temperature dropped to minus thirty. Stormy put on all the clothes he found in the cabin's loft.

He pulled several good-sized rocks from behind the wood stove and heated them in the oven for several hours. When placed in his bed, they kept him from freezing.

The cabin held very little in the way of entertainment. There was a deck of cards, a cribbage board, and a Bible. After playing endless games of solitaire with cold, stiff fingers, Stormy gave up. He picked up the Bible and thumbed through it. He'd read a page, stoke the fire, climb back in bed, and pull the covers up to his neck, trying to conserve his body heat. The blizzard lasted two weeks.

The coffee was gone, and so was the bacon. Plenty of beans were left, but the wood was in short supply. It wouldn't last, and Stormy knew he would freeze to death. He grabbed the ax and demolished the table and benches. They burned hot, and the cabin was warm, but only for a short time, then the cold set in again. Outside, the wind howled, and so did the wolves. The temperature plummeted. His Native guide had told him it was not unusual for the temperature to reach forty or fifty below.

He shoved the last of the wood into the stove, crawled into the bed, and waited. Even though this was the end, he was glad he had come to this land. The isolation and beauty of this pristine, untamed wilderness unmarred by man's evil had healed him or, at least, covered his scars. He closed his eyes and drifted into a deep, almost fatal sleep.

TWENTY

When he opened them, he found himself strapped into a dogsled, traveling at high speed. There were two sleds; the one in front was driven by his Native friend. He craned his neck, and although it was hard to tell beneath the furs, he thought the musher was female. The wind rose. He ducked his head and closed his eyes.

The dogs barked and yipped as they raced along the trail. Stormy, too weary to think about where he was going, thought about the female musher instead. Who was she, and how had she learned to drive a team? The rocking of the sled lulled him to sleep.

Miss Ruth had spent some time at the Native village and learned about this white man who did not trust the experienced advice of the Native guide.

They traveled through a land few people had ever seen. Forests, meadows, rugged mountains, and hidden valleys were all covered with thick snow. Each day was colder and darker than the last. Stormy's heart broke with the beauty of it. He felt a thaw in his soul.

As they camped at night, Miss Ruth questioned him, and the usually reserved man who did not share his past tried to explain how he felt about Alaska. She told him it was not Alaska that gave him peace but the Creator of this magnificent land. How could he put all of this into words for the Professor?

"Mr. Durand?"

"I spent some time with my rescuer, Miss Ruth."

"Our Miss Ruth?" The Professor gasped.

Stormy nodded. "One day after we had made it to Skagway, I saw her sitting on a log at the edge of Lynn Canal, and a poem came to me. The only one I've written since the war."

"Can you recite it for me?"

"It's not a good poem." The words he had written so many years ago revealed a deep yearning. Stormy cleared his throat, "I can't remember it."

Bull whined and put his paws on Stormy's thigh. The Professor looked at the mastiff and then at the Chief. "Bull thinks you can remember, and I think it would benefit your story. I'd like to include it. Please."

Stormy glared at the Professor who kept his face impassive. "It's been a while. Let's see, how did it go?" Despite his fear, Stormy reached into his memory and reluctantly whispered the words:

Creation's trinity
Confronts
The woman walking near the
Shore.
Sand! Sea! Sky!

Her personal trinity
Longs for
Communion with the Eternal.
Body! Spirit! Soul!

Beyond the horizon
The Holy Trinity
Invites.
Father! Spirit! Son!

Waves of joy yearned for
Tsunamis of peace hoped for.
Glory!

She glimpsed His beauty.
She sensed His presence.
Contentment!

"Yeah, ah, really cool." The Professor twirled the pencil like a baton and looked everywhere except at Stormy. "I mean, I don't know a lot about poetry. Can you explain what it means?"

This so-called professor apparently had no thought for the poem's meaning and nuances. Stormy shifted in his chair and pursed his lips. Despite his inclination to keep such thoughts to himself, the teacher in him said, "Alaska is called the Last Frontier, but to me, it was more like a pristine Eden, especially on a clear day in winter. The sun intensified the blue sky and reflected off the white snow. Its low angle bathed everything in amber light. Mountains on the edge of the horizon, their craggy peaks stable and strong, overwhelmed me with their majesty. A silent milk-white expanse. A large cerulean cloche covering it."

"Cerulean?"

"Blue."

"Cloche?"

"It's a sizeable dome used to protect plants or food.

"Huh?"

"It's a lid, son." Stormy put his hand over his mouth and coughed to hide his amusement. What do they teach in college nowadays?

The graduate student couldn't hold back his nervous laugh or his embarrassment. "I guess you do like words."

"I can't find the words to express how Alaska awes me, and Sitka calls to me. Anyway, the whiteouts speak of the Creator's power; the fierce howling winds and glacial temperatures tell of His strength. The soul snow goes deep into a man."

"Soul snow?"

"Once amid Alaska's fierce and wild weather, there was a calm like the eye of a hurricane. I stood as large, gentle flakes fell like feathers shaken from a pillow. They filled the atmosphere. I mean, the space between the flakes seemed to have substance."

The Professor scratched his head with the point of his pencil. Before he could form a question, Stormy continued.

"That ethereal moment was steeped with serenity. The sounds of stillness carried awe and tranquility. I looked up, and the aurora glittered like a silk curtain and lit up the heavens. It filled my soul with eternal wonder. The beauty of that crystalline snow and the intricacy of individual flakes...." Stormy shook his head and frowned. "I have no words."

"I don't get it. Sounds mystical."

"If you want the science behind it, freshly falling snow traps the sound in the gaps between the flakes. That's why it gets tranquil and quiet." Stormy considered the Professor and wondered if he had any imagination at all.

"Okay. I get it. I am surprised you don't live farther north."

Stormy put his fingertips together and chose his words carefully. "Sitka's forests are primeval. Some of those old-growth trees seem to reach heaven. The various greens of flora and fauna are bursting with life, as is the sea. Those Southeast Alaskan waters affect me the same way the Northern climes do. All of Alaska infuses my soul."

"The poem, your descriptions, they all seem kinda religious. Are you devout, like Miss Ruth?"

Stormy crossed and uncrossed his legs and side-stepped the question. "If you spend a lot of time with her, you will find that she isn't overly religious but has an other-worldly aspect about her. Peaceable. I think she sees and hears things the rest of us are unaware of—like maybe a sixth sense, a spiritual sense."

"It must be the poet in you. I've met her several times, and she just seemed like a forceful old lady." He made some notes and then scratched them out.

"That she is my boy, that she is." Stormy laughed, and his reflective mood seemed to dissipate. "If there's nothing more...."

"It seems Alaska has been good to you, Mr. Durand. I'd like a follow-up interview. Perhaps you can share some of your law enforcement exploits." A low growl came from the young dun-colored mastiff. "Or Bull's. I bet all your dogs have had many adventures."

Stormy Durand stood and held out his hand. "I'm sure you have more interesting people to interview than me. Come, Bull, time to patrol Sitka's neighborhoods. If we're lucky, and we usually are, everything will be quiet and calm."

TWENTY-ONE

With a sad smile, Miss Ruth removed her spectacles and thought about what she had just read. The Great War had destroyed so many lives. It was supposed to be the war to end all wars, but just over twenty years later, the world erupted again. She rubbed her temples and brought her thoughts back to Stormy.

He kept the peace in Sitka with a smile, a calm demeanor, and perhaps, some fierce growls from Bull. But how effective and influential would his life have been if he had spent it teaching or writing.

She thought about the twists and turns of her own life. Internal choices and outside forces had changed the direction of her life many times. *I suppose no one's life is what they thought it would be, Lord. I'm so glad you are in control.*

She perched her spectacles on the end of her nose and smiled at the Professor. "I've arranged for you to visit Ollyanna after our jaunt to Kodiak."

"When are we leaving?"

"Meet me tomorrow morning at the float plane dock. We'll take off whenever Robbie arrives from Angoon. I must tell you, it took some work to convince Ade he should go fishing when you meet with Ollie. He insists he could tell her story much better." Miss Ruth winked at the Professor. "She is reserved and shy, but you'll be fine once you get her talking."

The Professor rubbed his chin. "I'm still unsure I'm handling these people and their stories correctly."

"That you are concerned tells me much about your character." Miss Ruth reached across the table at the Sitka Café and patted his hand. "From the feedback I've received and the drafts you've shared, I think you are doing just fine."

The Professor pulled on his earlobe. He was used to being graded daily. Was 'just fine' a C- or a B+? Was it 75% or 90%? He pulled on the lobe again and decided not to ask.

KODIAK ISLAND

Haven Ray Turner pulled off her gloves, tucked the errant strand of gray hair back into its bun under her knitted hat, and opened the envelope with the spidery Spencerian script. The beautiful and precise swirls written with an old-fashioned fountain pen let her know instantly who the letter was from.

She waved it over her head as she hurried away from the post office, unmindful of her boots crunching on the salted sidewalk. "She's coming. Miss Ruth is coming and in time for Selaviq!" Passers-by turned and wondered who this middle-aged woman was talking to. She smiled back and danced down the sidewalk. A small slide and near fall slowed her speed, but not her enthusiasm.

It didn't matter that she had no one to share this news with, not even a cat. She had read somewhere that old maids and widows should have felines for comfort. "I don't have time for cats, not with working double shifts and all the visits from veterans and former patients. "You never had a cat, did you, Miss Ruth?" she asked the letter.

A widowed nurse on Kodiak Island was giddy that a spinster teacher was flying across the Gulf of Alaska to visit. Haven Ray didn't imagine the residents of Kodiak were impressed.

She turned the corner and approached her little cottage. It was a small log cabin she purchased when WWII ended, and she decided to stay in Kodiak. It reminded her of the one she and her mother lived in for several years when they left Afognak. Over the years, she had slowly renovated and decorated it in the English country style, somewhat out of place in Alaska, especially in the dark winter months, but she loved the flower-splashed chintz slipcovers. They reminded her that spring always comes.

As she unlocked the door and entered the cold living room, she wondered if her mother would have fared better during Alaska's sunless winters had she been surrounded by images of bright flowers.

When Haven Ray was a young girl, her father's job took the family from sunny California to Afognak Island, north of Kodiak. Ray Rutledge was a surveyor and map-maker for the Territory of Alaska. The other surveyors had families in Seattle and San Francisco whom they visited every six months.

Papa told Mama Alaska wasn't for everyone and wanted her to stay in California. His contract was for two years; then, he could transfer to a warmer climate, and they could accompany him.

Mama insisted they come north. He suggested she stay in Anchorage while he was on Afognak, but again, Mama had her way. She thought Papa could come home every few days or weekends. It didn't happen. She was shocked to learn Afognak was a Native village. The only whites were the saloon owner, the storekeeper, and several Swedes at a nearby fish cannery. None of these people were the kind Mama felt comfortable around. Haven Ray thought it exciting and adventurous. When Papa was absent for weeks, Mama took to her bed.

Haven Ray shook off her memories and reread the letter. Her memories of Miss Ruth warmed her soul just as the fireplace warmed the living room. She loved Miss Ruth for the lessons she taught and the stories she told of old Alaska. She imagined herself in every tale. She felt as if she had lived Miss Ruth's life along with her. From her first Selaviq on Afognak until today, Haven Ray felt a special kinship with her former teacher. She had corresponded regularly with her for nearly fifty years. Miss Ruth's visits had been infrequent, but now she was coming! More than a teacher—Miss Ruth was a friend and mentor.

As she fixed a simple meal, Haven Ray made mental lists of groceries, household chores, and things she needed to do before Miss Ruth arrived. She must find a Selaviq they could enjoy together. Those who remembered and celebrated the old ways had decreased as the years passed. Surely, some small villages near Kodiak kept the old ways. She transcribed those mental lists to her notepad, then put the last log into the old stone fireplace and gazed into the crimson flames.

The wood box was now empty. Although her house was heated by an oil furnace, Haven Ray pulled on her snow boots and winter coat. She slogged to the woodshed. It was just a few steps outside her back door, but the minus twelve degrees ripped through her. She quickly filled her arms with the dry wood but paused to gaze at the Milky Way that cut a swath through the pinpoints of lights shimmering in the night sky.

Although shivering, Haven Ray continued to wonder at the brilliantly lit sky. There was no sign of Lady Aurora. She felt her cheeks burn and her lips crack. She should have wrapped a scarf around her throat and face. The arctic air burned her lungs, but she stared at the sky for another minute.

The hinges squeaked with an icy chuckle that echoed her own when she struggled to open the back door. Once inside, she kicked it closed and remembered the first time she had seen the Northern Lights. She was a little girl, trembling and holding Miss Ruth's hand. Perhaps she would again see the lights of Lady Aurora with her old friend.

Miss Ruth and a young man she called the Professor should arrive late next week. They were working on an official project. Haven Ray hoped she and Miss Ruth would have time for a heart-to-heart without this Professor.

She settled before the fire again and creamed her cold, chapped hands. She grabbed a large handkerchief and coughed into it. She rubbed her chest and took several slow, deep breaths.

Chopping the kindling and cleaning the ashes had become a problem, perhaps from aging or fatigue, but she could not abandon the solace of staring into a cheery fire. The warmth that emanated from the fireplace hugged her like a soft blanket. The flames crackled and danced before her, and in their depths, she saw a little girl on Afognak Island just after the turn of the century.

"You're a big girl, Haven Ray Rutledge. You can get your own breakfast." Mama wiped her eyes with the edge of the sheet and pulled the blankets up to her nose.

Nine-year-old Haven Ray had prepared her breakfast hours ago. It was now mid-afternoon. She felt her chin quiver, bit her lip, and said, "I'll have bread and cheese. Do you want some?"

"I only want to sleep." Mama sighed and closed her eyes. "I

wish your father hadn't brought us to this dismal island—so full of darkness."

Haven Ray looked out the window at the dusky twilight. "I thought you wanted to be close to Papa?"

"I didn't know he would be gone so often."

"I like it here, even when Papa is away." Haven Ray spoke the words softly so Mama wouldn't hear. This little Native village on an island north of Kodiak Island was different, and Haven Ray loved it.

When Papa was home, he took her sledding, and they made snowmen. Mama got out of bed and didn't talk about the darkness or the cold. She baked cookies and watched them from the window. Papa didn't know how sad Mama was when he wasn't there.

Little Haven Ray fed the woodstove, ate the bread and cheese, and drank a cup of weak tea. She took a tray to the bedroom, but Mama was asleep.

She left the food beside the bed and bundled herself into the heavy woolen coat Papa had given her for Christmas. A hat, mittens, two pairs of socks, boots, and a scarf wrapped around her neck gave her a roly-poly appearance. She thought Mama would sleep for several hours and felt free to leave the little unpainted house at the end of the road.

Haven Ray waddled through the village on her way to the schoolhouse. She turned her head away from the saloon. Bad things happened there, or at least she thought so. The general store owner leaned on his snow shovel and greeted her, "Going to the Starring, Haven Ray?"

"Huh?"

"Never mind. You better scoot; school is almost over."

She waved and hurried along. Mama said the school was only for Native children, but Miss Ruth smiled whenever Haven Ray appeared.

Mama was supposed to teach her from the lessons sent from the correspondence school in the United States, but most days, the gray, dingy darkness soaked into Mama's soul. That's what she said. Anyway, it made her tired. Haven Ray didn't mind; she liked it better at Miss Ruth's.

The sun came up after breakfast and went to bed before supper. It didn't even travel across the sky, just hovered near the horizon. It wasn't yellow like the sun back home, which reminded Haven Ray of buttercups, but rather a pale golden white. "What color are you?" she asked. The snow caught the sunlight and held it. Snowflakes melted on Haven Ray's eyelashes, then froze, and the wind chafed her face. She crunched along and wondered why there was never any snow where they used to live. Haven Ray stuffed her mittened hands into her pockets, shivered, and wished Papa would come home soon so Mama would be cheerful.

The door squeaked, and heads swung at the sound. Faces smiled, a few hands waved in greeting, then turned their attention back to the front of the room. Haven Ray listened as she peeled off her winter wear and slipped into the seat in the back Miss Ruth had said was just for her.

"...as you know, children, today is Christmas Eve, and the Selaviq will begin as soon as school is out." Miss Ruth saw Haven Ray's confusion and declared, "Where I come from, there is no Selaviq." A groan arose from the classroom as the students looked at one another. No Selaviq! How was that possible? There was no Christmas without it.

"And we celebrate Christmas on December twenty-fifth, not January seventh." Again, heads swiveled in every direction as the children looked at each other with great confusion. How odd these white people were. They didn't even know what day baby Jesus was born.

"This will be my first Selaviq, and I am excited. Can you explain it to me?"

Many hands were raised, and Miss Ruth called on her students one after the other. Most couldn't wait, and comments burst from the children like snowballs during their recess games. Haven Ray tried to pay attention, but it was all so new.

"The Father has a huge wooden star, and it spins."

"He makes it go round and round," Miss Ruth's youngest student said.

"Why does it spin?" Haven Ray asked.

"Nobody knows, but the Father says the star has to keep moving."

"He will lead us from house to house to look for the baby."

"He's lost, you know." The girls nodded to each other and wondered what kind of mama could lose her baby.

"We will sing and get treats."

"And the people from the first house will go with the Father to the next and so on."

"Whoever finds the baby will be wise." A chubby-faced boy said.

"I'm smart enough." The tallest boy slouched in his too-small chair.

"He's always at the church. Why don't we go there first?" A smug little boy demanded.

The boy behind him flicked him on the back of the head, "Because then we wouldn't get all the cookies, cakes, and special treats."

Before a ruckus could erupt, Miss Ruth glared at the flicker, smiled at the flicked, and clapped her hands. "Thank you, children. We will follow the star and find the baby. It's already starting to get dark. Now rush home and get ready."

The children scampered out amid cries of 'Merry Christmas' and 'Hooray for the Selaviq.' Haven Ray made her way to the front of the room.

"Miss Ruth, is the Selaviq for me too? Can I look for the baby?"

"It's for everyone, dear. I'm sure you and your mother will enjoy it."

The little girl's face fell. "What if I came without Mama?" Her voice quivered, and she couldn't meet Miss Ruth's eyes.

"Hmmm." Afognak's only school teacher knelt before the sad little girl. "Has your Mama given permission for you to attend school? I confess I've been so busy I haven't visited."

Haven Ray shook her head. "Mama mostly stays in bed. It always looks like nighttime to her. Please don't tell her I come here."

Miss Ruth hugged the child. "Everything will be okay."

"Mama is afraid of the dark. At least she won't go out in it." Haven Ray hiccupped and tugged on Miss Ruth's sleeve. "I have to find the baby, Miss Ruth. I have to."

"I promise He will find you." Miss Ruth buttoned the little girl's coat and wrapped the scarf tightly around her neck. "Everything will be okay," she repeated the words more forcefully this time.

Haven Ray remembered when Mama used to button her up and ensure she looked tidy. Tears froze on her cheeks as she trudged home. She knew everything would not be okay. Mama would be mad, and what if nobody found the baby?

❧

"Mama, can I go to the Selaviq?"

Mama had pulled herself out of bed and shuffled around the kitchen, fixing a simple dinner. She dished out the soup, and they sat together. "What are you talking about?"

"It's Christmas, and the Selaviq is tonight."

"Christmas was two weeks ago."

"I mean the real Christmas. The Russian one."

"Have you been going to the village again? You know you are supposed to stay in the house when I'm not feeling well."

"You said I'm a big girl, and it's not far to the school, and the other kids like me, and Miss Ruth doesn't mind." Haven Ray's words tumbled out in a rush, and she saw Mama's lips tighten.

"I don't like you wandering around in the dark by yourself. It's not safe."

"It's not dark, Mama, and they will have torches and lanterns for the Selaviq. Can we go?"

"What's a Selaviq?" Mama sighed and pushed her hair away from her face.

"They find a lost baby and eat cookies."

"Who lost their baby?" Mama's voice rose. "Did they send out a search party?"

"I think that's what the Selaviq is. Singing and looking in everybody's house for the baby, but he's never there. The Father spins a star, and everybody keeps their coats on, even when it gets too hot because it's Christmas."

"Silliest thing I ever heard. Whoever is in charge needs to find that baby now. It's so dark."

"The baby's lost at the church, Mama."

Mama frowned and dipped her spoon into her soup. "If only

we could have gone to the United States for Christmas. Home."
She brushed a tear away and let the spoon clatter into the bowl. She
clasped her hands tight in her lap. "We've had our Christmas. You
got new underwear, a picture book, and that nice coat from your
Papa. Your stocking had nuts, candy, and an orange."

"Yes, Mama." Haven Ray bowed her head and took several slurps
of her soup. Somehow, she knew the holiday was more than new underwear and a handful of mixed nuts that had to be cracked open
with a hammer. "But this is the real Christmas, and I want to go."

"We don't know these villagers. I haven't met Miss Ruth. Your
father's not here. It's too dark to wander about with spinning stars
looking for lost babies."

The little girl bit the inside of her cheek. *It's better if I don't say
anything. It would make Mama sad if she knew what I was thinking.*

Haven Ray cleared the table and sat by the woodstove with a
book while Mama did the dishes.

"Would you like me to read to you, dear?" Mama asked as she
put the last dish away.

Haven Ray shook her head as she silently stumbled over some
words. Not because she didn't know them but because tears blurred
her vision. She closed her book and thought about the baby. Who
was he, and how did he get lost? Was he really at the church, like
the one boy said? She glanced toward the window and wondered
when the Selaviq would start. Haven Ray chewed on the inside of
her cheek and worried.

Mama lit every candle and lamp in the tiny house, stealing
glances at the little girl pretending to read. Mama then sat in the
wooden rocker with a blanket over her shoulders and a book on
her lap.

"You look tired, Mama. Don't you want to go to bed?" Haven Ray tried to sound concerned.

"I need to keep an eye on you, especially tonight." Mama leaned back in the rocker and closed her eyes. "I'm sorry, dear. I promise to take better care of you. This gloomy darkness drains me, wears me out."

Haven Ray held back her tears and put more wood into the stove. Did she hear muffled singing from the villagers? The voices got louder, and soon there was a powerful pounding on the door. Haven Ray flung it open and stared.

Before Mama could say anything, the Father, with a fur parka over his long black robes, entered carrying a large four-foot-tall wooden star attached to a three-foot wide reindeer hide frame. It barely fit through the door. He gave the star a spin every few seconds so it continually rotated. People crowded into the small room, singing in a language neither Haven Ray nor her mother understood.

Haven Ray jumped up and down with excitement. Her mother stood and gripped the back of the chair, eyebrows raised as she looked right and left, and frowned at the villagers causing the noise and confusion. Miss Ruth pushed and prodded her way to the bewildered woman and extended her hand. She leaned close to Mrs. Rutledge's ear and spoke loudly, "I'm Miss Ruth, the teacher. I apologize for not visiting you sooner and welcoming you to the village. This invasion is Selaviq, the Starring. It is traditional to offer a treat to the singers. I've brought tea cakes since you did not know the tradition or had any expectation we were coming."

"You're white!" Mrs. Rutledge fanned her face as sweat broke out on her upper lip. "So many strangers in my house; it's too crowded, too noisy."

"Haven Ray knows everyone." Miss Ruth gave the basket of small cakes to the little girl, who passed them out with a big smile. When she returned the basket to Miss Ruth, the schoolteacher winked at her and said, "Hurry into your coat Haven Ray; we are about to depart."

"Oh, no, we couldn't possibly," Mrs. Rutledge said.

Miss Ruth directed the woman's gaze to Haven Ray, who was already buttoning her coat and pulling on her mittens. "She's so happy; please don't disappoint her."

Mrs. Rutledge shook her head, "It's the darkness, you see. I simply cannot face it."

"I understand. I was once farther North when the sun neither rose nor set for several weeks."

Mrs. Rutledge squeezed her eyes tight and shivered. "How did you endure it?"

Miss Ruth put her arm around the woman's shoulder. "I admit it was a struggle. I forced myself to picture the light when I couldn't see it. I imagined its warmth when I couldn't feel it."

"I'm afraid I don't have that kind of willpower," Mrs. Rutledge shivered.

"My dear, this cannot be accomplished by one's own determination. I had to call on the One who calls Himself the Light." Miss Ruth kept her voice calm and expression soft. "I'm from Texas, where the sunlight is sharp and hot. Alaska took some getting used to."

"The light here is cold and feeble. The sun is so pale. Oh, I can't explain it." Mrs. Rutledge wrung her hands and whined, "I need to escape this darkness."

The Father and the Spinning Star departed, followed by the villagers, who were now hot and sweaty in their heavy coats but still singing exuberantly.

"The Alaskan winters affect many people that way, but please come. I will stay by your side, and you will find the light."

"Where's Haven Ray? Where's my daughter?" Mrs. Rutledge turned her head from side to side. "I can't see her."

"She tucked a doll's blanket into her pocket and left with the other children." Miss Ruth lifted a coat and scarf off its hook by the door. "It's the Selaviq. She will come to no harm."

Mrs. Rutledge allowed Miss Ruth to bundle her into her heavy winter coat. She clung to the schoolteacher's arm as they followed the procession through the village. She saw Haven Ray run ahead of the priest, circle back, then run ahead again, singing all the while.

The little white girl sang the Christmas carols that were familiar to her while the Natives sang in Old Slavonic, Yupik, or Alutiiq.

"Look, Mama, even the snow twinkles from the starlight." She dashed off again.

House after house welcomed them, each more crowded than the last as families joined the trek to the next place. Hot drinks and fancy treats were provided at each stop. No one noticed how overheated they became indoors or how cold they were when tramping through the snow. It was Selaviq, and that's all that mattered.

Mrs. Rutledge trudged along, head bowed, chin tucked into her chest. As they neared the church, Miss Ruth said, "Look up. The Creator has made millions of stars and named them all. Let that light into your soul, Mrs. Rutledge."

Mrs. Rutledge pulled her collar closer and sighed, "I admit the stars are brilliant."

Haven Ray shrieked, "What is happening to the sky? It's all green and swirly!"

Mrs. Rutledge's voice cracked as she gasped, "What is it?" She stumbled and grabbed Miss Ruth's arm but kept her gaze on the sky.

The Father raised the spinning star higher, and the villagers sang louder as they lifted their faces to the sky, grinning and laughing.

"It's the Aurora," Miss Ruth said, "I could give you the scientific reason why this happens, but I prefer to think it's the Lord's way of promising spring will come, and everything will turn green again."

For a brief moment, Mrs. Rutledge sounded hopeful, "What a lovely thought."

Everyone thrust their torches into the snow outside the small church and snuffed them out. Light from numerous candles streamed out of the church's open door and many windows.

"The first thing God said, according to the Bible, was *LET THERE BE LIGHT*," Miss Ruth said.

Mrs. Rutledge kept her gaze on the church's open door. "There is certainly a lot coming from the church."

Haven Ray wrapped her arms around her mother's waist. "A baby changes everything, Mama. That's what the Father said." She waved the doll's blanket, "I'm going to keep him warm."

Mrs. Rutledge squeezed her daughter's hand and then spoke to Miss Ruth. "So, they found the lost baby?"

Miss Ruth's eyebrows rose as she considered the question, then she chuckled. "The baby wasn't lost; we were."

"I don't understand."

"It's the Starring. We are wise men following the star."

Mrs. Rutledge nodded. "I've heard the Christmas story, of course, but I'm not religious."

"Do you know what the Bible says about those who believe the Christmas story?"

"I told you I'm not religious." Mrs. Rutledge stiffened.

Miss Ruth ignored the other woman's sharp tone. "People living in darkness have seen a Great Light—darkness engulfed the world and shattered our souls. But if you follow the star, it will lead you to the Light."

Haven Ray tugged on her mother's coat sleeve. "We followed the star to the church, Mama. The baby is in there. I want to see him." She danced around her mother and Miss Ruth, then ran to the front of the church. She tucked the blanket around the baby Jesus and spoke sternly to the priest, "Don't you ever let him get lost again."

"Child, if you keep Him in your heart, you will never lose him."

She ran and told her mother the baby lived in her heart. Miss Ruth hugged the girl and laid her hand on Haven Ray's head. "We must follow that baby all the way to the cross."

"I'm still confused," Mrs. Rutledge said, "and getting colder the longer we stand out here."

"The Father will explain everything. First in Russian, then in the two Native languages. I will translate as best I can." Miss Ruth raised her head to the stars. "Above the radiant stars, the God who made them sits on a Throne of Light."

Mrs. Rutledge swallowed and whispered to herself, "If only I could believe."

"There are several kinds of darkness, dear Mrs. Rutledge, but only one Light. You can meet Him tonight."

"Anything to rid myself of this oppressing darkness."

Arm in arm, the two women and the little girl entered the church.

TWENTY-TWO

"How was your flight?" Haven Ray said as she hugged Miss Ruth who introduced her to the Professor.

"A little bumpy, lots of thermals, but young Robbie here is almost as good a pilot as his father was," Miss Ruth answered matter-of-factly.

The ashen-faced Professor climbed out of the small plane and faced the middle-aged woman. "We were attacked by solid winds with blowing snow. Heavy wet snow that I thought would press us into the Gulf."

"We were in no danger," the red-faced pilot brushed past the Professor and extended his hand, "Name's Robert Nelles. Here's my card if you ever need a pilot."

Haven Ray pocketed the card and smiled at Robbie, as Miss Ruth called him. He pulled the luggage out of the plane and set it on the tarmac of Kodiak's small municipal airport.

"The waters across the Gulf were treacherous, and sometimes the snow was impenetrable. I couldn't distinguish the sea from the sky. We should have delayed our flight."

Robert gave his disgruntled passenger a look, but the Professor continued grumbling to himself and didn't notice. The pilot tipped his cap to the two women, accepted a hug from Miss Ruth, and strolled toward the small hanger to make his report and order more fuel.

"Thank you, Robbie." Haven Ray grinned at Miss Ruth as she called after the bush pilot. She turned her attention to the young man picking up the luggage. "You must be the Professor. Just put the bags in the Jeep."

"Yes, Mrs. Turner." The Professor eyed the battered Jeep, flung the suitcases into the back seat, and scrambled in after them. No one seemed concerned about the flight except him. "I don't know how we made it here alive."

"I see you haven't joined the modern world yet with a decent vehicle," Miss Ruth said as she patted the dented fender.

"Is everyone going to ignore my concerns about our flight?" The Professor muttered.

"It's just weather, my dear." Miss Ruth threw the words over her shoulder.

"I'm used to adverse weather, but I stay on the ground where I belong, where it's safe."

Miss Ruth handed him a lemon drop and winked. He stuffed the unwanted candy into his coat pocket.

Haven Ray patted the dashboard. "This old girl and I have been through many battles. I admit we're both aging. She is rusting, and I'm going gray. She has scratches and dents. I have wrinkles and aches."

"Is this a surplus World War II Jeep? I don't see any markings, but it looks right," the Professor asked.

"Clever of you, Professor. It's a Navy Jeep; they were not marked like Army vehicles. This old girl proudly served her country during the war."

"Are you talking about yourself or the Jeep?" Miss Ruth laughed.

Haven Ray put the key in the ignition. "It was a wedding gift from the base Commander."

"Can they do that?" The Professor leaned over the seat and stared at Haven Ray.

'It wasn't my wedding, and I never did find out the details. Wrap yourself in those blankets. It's only three degrees, but it will feel colder on the drive."

"I'm from Fairbanks," the Professor said, putting on his hat and wrapping his scarf around his neck. It had stopped snowing but was still overcast, and there was a bite to the wind. "This is positively balmy." He wanted to know whose wedding it was and how it was gifted. Was that even legal?

The two women were deep in their own conversation. He could only catch a few words here and there and wondered about this middle-aged nurse and the battered Jeep. What was her relationship with the bride that she now possessed this vehicle?

It was a short drive into Kodiak, a town of around seventeen hundred residents, a large city by Alaska standards. The population primarily consisted of Native and Norwegian fisherfolk.

The Jeep stopped at a small hotel at the edge of town; the Professor grabbed his suitcase and said his goodbyes, then turned back and asked Miss Ruth if he might speak to her privately. He stepped to her side of the vehicle at her nod and whispered several questions about Miss Haven Ray and the Navy Jeep.

"Every life is a story, dear boy, and heaven's library holds them. Only in eternity will we have time enough to read them all."

"What did she mean that she and the Jeep had been through many battles?"

"Not what you think, I suspect."

"At least tell me about the commander and the wedding. There is a mystery here, and I don't like mysteries."

Miss Ruth patted his hand. "Nonsense, my boy. You love a good mystery."

"I like solving them, but you aren't giving me any clues."

Miss Ruth whispered, "Haven Ray's story is not for you, not now. It would be best if you focused on Father Alexi."

The Professor's eyebrows crunched together, and he stuffed his curiosity in his back pocket but knew it wouldn't stay there. When this project was over and his duty to Miss Ruth complete, he was determined to find out how a commander in the United States Navy dared to give a Jeep to a civilian.

He rubbed his eyebrow and scowled; maybe she was a Navy nurse and saved his life. Perhaps they were in love, and the commander had a hunch he would go down with his ship. The Professor, his temple now pounding, tried and failed to stop thinking such thoughts. He cursed his curiosity and bit his cheek.

"We will meet you tomorrow at noon in the hotel's restaurant. Be sure to bring Father Alexi. I want Haven Ray to meet him," Miss Ruth instructed him.

"And we must invite him to the Selaviq," Haven Ray said.

Although curious about what a Selaviq was, the Professor rubbed his temple and forced himself to think about what he intended to ask the aging cleric. He glanced again at the woman sitting behind the wheel of that battered military Jeep and wondered about her life.

The Professor, who was actually just a graduate student, set up his equipment quietly in the shabby one-room apartment. Father

Alexi stroked his beard and wondered why he had permitted this stranger to come, then remembered Miss Ruth had made the arrangements. Infernal woman.

As he turned the spigot, the samovar hissed and steamed, and he filled a glass mug two-thirds full of hot water. He lifted the tetera—teapot—from the top of the samovar and poured the concentrated, choice Chinese tea into the hot water. Father Alexi felt the young man taking mental notes about the antique Russian samovar and old-fashioned dishes. The priest handed him the tea and pushed the bowl of sugar cubes across the table. The priest hid his irritation toward Miss Ruth, who sent this person to him, "You want to know why I settled in Sitka?"

"My job is to collect accounts from our eldest citizens. It's important, Father. You are living history."

Father Alexi snorted and watched this interloper's eyes dart around the room. They focused on the Beautiful Corner with the old Russian Bible and chalice, which the priest used for his personal communion, then on the painting of the Tsar and shelves of old books, all in Russian.

"No one is interested in a retired old priest who's no use to anyone anymore."

The Professor sighed and spoke without conviction. "I'm sure many will be interested. Miss Ruth is convinced, anyway."

"Hmmm." The aged cleric refused to think about the many closed and locked doors in his soul—places he had not entered in decades. Rooms abandoned and boarded, almost forgotten.

"Please." The Professor clicked his pen, opened his notebook, and turned on his tape recorder. The reels on the recorder turned, and Father Alexi envisioned strangers hearing his pain. He poured a cup of tea for himself and looked into the amber liquid. He opened his mouth and then clamped his lips together.

"Are you ready?"

"I don't know where to start." Could the reluctance in his voice be heard, the fear in his tone?

"Tell me a little about your family history."

Father Alexi sat silently for several minutes. His breath came in short bursts, and he slumped in his chair. The sweat from his brow dripped into his unfocused eyes.

"Father! Are you okay? Is there anyone I can call?"

"Pills! Medicine cabinet!" The priest sensed rather than heard hurried footsteps.

Between the attack and the pills taking effect, Father Alexi relived his escape from the Bolsheviks and the winter spent hiding in the Ural Mountains. He remembered his despair when his eldest son, Ilya, left to join the White Army. His heart broke again when he pictured his daughter's grave in China and how he had lost the will to live after the shipwreck in icy Alaskan waters.

The Father heard the rustle of papers shoved into a briefcase and the recording equipment packed. Through slitted eyes, he saw worried glances cast his way. Awkward words of sympathy were given by the young man.

Father Alexi rubbed his chest and, against his will, said, "Miss Ruth says you're a fine fellow, Professor. We can continue."

"I think you need to rest. Let me help you to bed, and I'll return this evening."

❧

Father Alexi lay in bed all day. The memories came, and his heart raced once more. He had barely survived living his life; how could he endure revisiting it? *This was Miss Ruth's fault; interfering old woman!*

With his eyes closed, he tried to picture his loved ones. Shameful tears inched down his cheeks and onto his beard. There were no family photographs to hold or cherish. He couldn't see Kira or the children with his heart or soul.

He pushed the covers aside, sat on the edge of the bed, then tried to stand. His breath came in shallow bursts, and he fell back against the pillows and reached for his pills. The memories pushed against the bolted doors of his past. He looked at the bottle in his hand and imagined it was a key. As he swallowed the medicine, he envisioned that key turning the lock. It clicked, the hinges squeaked, and he saw—

TWENTY-THREE

Ilya Dimitri Alexi, the grandfather he was named for, had come to Kodiak Island as an employee of the Russian Fur Trading Company. He married a Yupik Eskimo woman, and their children were Creoles.

Father Alexi's brow wrinkled. As a child, he was told Creole combined Russian words for man and woman. Later, he learned the term had a Spanish origin and was brought north by French sailors from Louisiana. It meant mixed offspring. Focusing on a word's meaning and origin was a temporary respite that kept his emotions in check, an old trick. It didn't work this time.

He ran his hand through his hair, tugged at his beard, and tried to put those jumbled memories in order.

The Russian American Company attempted to create a race of Creoles who would tame this northern wilderness. They were a legal class with high status in Russian America. It did not remain so when the Americans came; Creoles were neither one thing nor the other. They were the—*so what*—people, half-breeds. They were discriminated against and classified with various indigenous peoples. A people the Americans called Indians.

The old priest rubbed his eyebrows, twisted in the bed, and hoped his physical and emotional discomfort drained away before the Professor returned. His thoughts continued as he scrambled some eggs and made toast.

His father had chosen to remain in Alaska when the United States purchased Russian America. Seven years later, Ilya was born. And following tradition, little Ilya Alexi was sent to Russia to be educated. He was nine years old when his parents put him on the ship with other children and an escort.

Several months after arriving at the boarding school in Kaluga, Russia, the boy received a letter with the news his mother had died. Something inside of Ilya broke. He longed to return to Alaska and sit beside her grave.

His primary and secondary education years passed without further incidents, although his father's letters kept his yearning for home alive. After college, he entered the Russian Orthodox Seminary in St. Petersburg. Ilya planned to return to Alaska after he graduated. Even though the land no longer belonged to Russia, the church was active among Natives, and priests were needed. Marriage and children prevented him from returning home.

A knock on his door pulled his thoughts away from his past. He watched the Professor set up his equipment and wondered how to explain to this young man all that had happened in the previous half-century.

"I hope you are well, Father. I'm anxious to hear about your life, but I don't want to cause you any discomfort."

Father Alexi folded his hands in his lap. "I will tell you the end, but it is painful."

The Professor tapped his pencil on the table. Miss Ruth had not advised him about handling other people's emotions. Father Alexi reminded him of his grandfather and how the old man stuffed his hurts. He muttered to himself that he must proceed cautiously. "You don't have to reveal anything that makes you sad, Father. Just give me a brief overview. It would be helpful if you could start at the beginning."

"I have been restless all day, young man, feeling sad, angry, disappointed, even despairing. I have never shared my history. Perhaps it's time." He rubbed his chest, and at the startled look on the Professor's face, he said, "Do not worry. I am not going to have another attack."

"Where are your pills?"

"Here, behind the samovar. I think it will ease my heart to talk. As I said, I will begin at the end."

The Professor scratched his head and wondered how efficient that would be. "If I have questions—"

"Save them."

Slowly, Father Alexi went through the ritual of preparing the tea. He handed the Professor a cup and said, "The diamond saved us."

"Diamond?" The Professor clamped his lips together.

"My birth certificate from Alaska proved I was an American. My ordination papers declared I was a priest. The American official knew how much danger my family faced in Russia, so he filled out the asylum forms for us. Then we had to wait. The myriad of documents from the British Consulate allowing us to remain in Hong Kong was more complex and challenging to achieve than our asylum papers."

"Hong Kong?" The Professor's pencil hovered over the paper. At Father Alexi's look, he bent over his notebook and left the rest of his questions unspoken.

"The British Mission to China had a relief program for Russian refugees. Many were fleeing the Bolsheviks through China rather than Europe. The mission supported us until we got our work per-

162

mits. I am afraid I was not always a gracious recipient." Father Alexi closed his eyes. The Professor silently turned off his tape recorder and let the older man rest. "I'm not sleeping, Professor. I'm fixing events in my mind."

Memories of the humid heat of Hong Kong caused sweat on Father Alexi's upper lip, or perhaps it was steam from his tea.

Even though it would take longer to save for their journey, Father Alexi said, "We no longer need to take money from the British mission now that the boys are working."

Kira, bless her heart, said, "I think Bozhe wants us to be cheerful givers when we can and cheerful receivers when we must. Do not let your pride shame you when you receive."

Father Alexi, constantly uncomfortable when his wife pointed out a truth he did not embrace, turned to a different topic. "The boys' work at the import/export trading company unloading supplies has given them bulging muscles, and I swear they have grown several inches. I'm proud of them."

"It must be all the Chinese noodles they eat." Kira smiled as she set the table. "They are making friends, picking up the Chinese language, and adding to the English you've taught them. Such smart boys,"

"You work hard at the mission's laundry." Father Alexi took the soup tureen from her and placed it in the center of the table.

"I could make more elsewhere, but I like it there."

"We should be able to save more now that I have been hired by the Vessel Boarding Agent at the American pier. My English and

Russian are helpful to them, and my little bit of French and Spanish is useful."

"In the past, I resented all the hours you spent studying words and languages. Bozhe knew we would need them." She patted his cheek again.

"I've talked to everyone at the Seaman's Center about Alaska."

"I would like to go there sometime, the Center, I mean."

"It's a mission for seaman and sailors; the men are rough and crude. I do not want you or the boys anywhere near the docks. When we have saved enough money, I will book our passage."

Kira set her bowl of noodles aside and reached for his hand. "The boys and I like it here. There is a nice community of Russians. I'm comfortable with them. The weather is good, and besides—" She went to the window and pulled back the curtain. Steep hills and high mountains blocked her view, but she carried the image of her daughter's resting place in her heart.

"What?"

"I thought we could visit her grave when things settled down in China."

"I'm afraid things will never settle down, the government is weak, and the many gangs of bandits are too strong."

She covered her eyes with her hands and wept. Father Alexi put his arms around her. "We keep our daughter in our hearts."

"And our firstborn?"

"I'm afraid we will never see Ilya again. We do not even know if he is alive." Father Alexi bit the inside of his cheek and wished he had not spoken of the son that carried his name.

"Bozhe knows," Kira whispered, and her tears continued to fall.

A few days later, Pastor Walt, the cleric at the Seaman's Center, said, "Do not give any more money to these seamen for sailing information. You cannot know if greed is their motivation or what they say is true."

"I have no more money to give," Father Alexi sighed, feeling foolish.

"I know an honest Captain due in port next week. I will send word when his ship, the Aloha, arrives."

Father Alexi thanked him, but even if the ship's destination was Alaska, they did not have enough funds to purchase their tickets. Head bowed, he trudged back home, disheartened. There was no possible way to continue the journey. Most of the money they earned was spent on rent and food.

As always, Kira attempted to soothe her husband with her calm and serene ways. "We are not supposed to question or understand Bozhe's ways. He parted the Red Sea."

"The Pacific Ocean is much larger."

"Think of Job. We are to trust and obey."

The longer he lived with this gentle woman he dearly loved, the less he understood her. She seemed to accept even the difficult things from the hand of Bozhe and believed that, somehow, things would be as they were meant to be.

Father Alexi's faith was not as all-encompassing. He wanted to understand what Bozhe was doing and why. If Bozhe worked all things together for good, why couldn't He do it sooner rather than later, and why didn't He make it obvious?

"There is a ship arriving next week. Its outward-bound destination may be Alaska, but we don't have enough money for the passage."

"Are you sure we can't stay here?"

"Alaska has always been my home."

"You were so young when you left, and your family is gone. We can make a life here in Hong Kong."

Father Alexi looked at his wife. He struggled for a moment, then took her hand, "We always planned to return to Alaska. You shared my vision to bring the Word to the Creoles of Alaska."

"That was before we had children."

"The Patriarch of the Holy Synod has declared I should do this. The only higher authority is Bozhe."

"I have a feeling." Kira couldn't find the words to continue.

"The word has come from Bozhe to the Patriarch to the Metropolitan to me."

"It does seem like the right thing to do, but my heart tells me differently."

Father Alexi put his arms around his wife and said, "We will be safer in America. Much as I love you and long to make you happy, Alaska is my home. My mother and father are buried there."

"And our daughter is buried in China," Kira spoke softly, "But if you think this is Bozhe's will for us." She kissed his cheek and left the thought unfinished.

It irritated him, and he turned away. "What difference does all of this make? We have no money."

"Bring me my sewing kit."

"Now is not the time to mend my shirt. We have no money."

"Bring me the kit."

She broke open a hollowed-out spool of thread. Out tumbled several rubies and a diamond. "The Metropolitan said we would need these for passage."

"Why didn't you tell me?" Father Alexi fumed.

"He said you might be tempted to spend them earlier, but it must be for our tickets." Kira's soft tone took the sting from the words.

Father Alexi sighed; he knew there were many times and situations he would have relied on those jewels rather than Bozhe. The Metropolitan—the head cleric of St. Petersburg—knew him too well. Father Alexi, glad for the gems but ashamed that the Metropolitan had seen his weak faith, took the jewels.

Captain Harlan Walker of the steamship, Aloha, asked no questions, and the Father offered no information. The Captain accepted the diamond as payment and returned the rubies.

"The ship departs in three days. We'll make port in Shanghai, Manila, Honolulu, then to several cities on the Pacific Coast of the United States, and finally north to Alaska."

After dinner that night, Father Alexi explained his plans to the family.

"Hooray. I want to be a sea captain," Vladi said.

"I like Hong Kong. Can't we stay?" Andrei asked.

As Kira cleared the table, she said, "We have a good life here. The boys will be accepted at the International School next term. We have wonderful friends at the mission. We all have work. Life is good, and I am weary of traveling. But if you are sure..."

"It's settled," Father Alexi huffed.

Her eyes clouded, and she lay her hand on his arm. "We have traveled for so long, but we're settled now. Living on board a steamship for weeks, if not months, troubles me. The ocean is so big. I fear we will never see Alaska. Please pray about it once more. I will accept this from Bozhe's hand if you are certain."

"I have, and I will." Father Alexi pulled on his beard, angry with himself for his irritated tone. He turned away, convinced she was just afraid of the sea. Young Vladi was eager for adventure on the high seas, but Andrei's face fell.

"Andrei, you must tell me why you want to stay in Hong Kong. It will help me make my decision."

"I thought you already decided," the boy sucked on his lower lip.

"Perhaps I will change my mind." The look on his face told Father Alexi the boy did not believe him. "Please, talk to me, son."

He shrugged. "I like it here."

Father Alexi continued questioning him, and finally, the boy said, "You will think I am young and foolish, but I know my heart. There is a girl at the church."

"A girl?"

"Yes, the pastor's daughter. She feels the same as I do."

"It is just young love. Once in Alaska, you will forget all about her."

Andrei stared at his father and then left the house, closing the door softly.

"Should I go after him?" he asked his wife.

"Let him breathe." Kira rubbed her husband's back. "He will return before dark."

"What if he rebels like Ilya?"

"Alexi has a different temperament. He will return before nightfall and not speak of this again."

Kira's words proved accurate, and Father Alexi was comforted. The following day Kira asked if he had received word from Bohze about the voyage.

"The Aloha is sailing in three days, and we will be on it."

Kira stood before him and looked into his eyes, refusing to let him look away. "If you are sure, then Bozhe goes before us."

"Of course, I'm sure!" Only then did he realize he had not prayed about it. No matter. Father Alexi vowed he would renew his faith in the land of his birth.

"There is packing to be done and goodbyes to be said. Three days is not much time, but we will be ready."

Captain Walker's ship was primarily outfitted for cargo. There were less than thirty passengers on board. Different nationalities, most kept to themselves.

Vladi followed the crew, asking questions and generally making a nuisance of himself, and Andrei soon joined him. One evening at dinner, Father Alexi apologized to the Captain, who laughed and called First Mate Jensen. "See that Father Alexi's sons are trained in seamanship. Give them a ship's tour, but keep them away from the engine room. Pay them half a dollar a day."

"You are most kind, Captain."

"I was a cabin boy on my grandfather's clipper ship when I was their age. I remember how much energy I had and how seamanship fascinated me."

"It is not necessary to give them a wage."

"They'll earn it."

Calm seas and fair winds followed them to the ports in China and the Philippines. The vast ocean, stories from the crew, seeing dolphins and whales, and learning the rigorous strength needed to be a deckhand kept Andrei and Vladi busy from sunup to sundown. At night First Mate Jensen regaled them with his sea-faring adventures and showed them how to tie many nautical knots. Soon, life at sea crowded out Andrei's longing for the girl in Hong Kong.

"Come to my cabin," Captain Walker hailed the boys, "I have a large globe; you can see how far you have come. You, too, Father and Mrs. Alexi."

"Look how far we are from St. Petersburg," Vladi said.

"Captain, what is our next port?" Andrei asked.

Captain Walker pointed to the Hawaiian Islands. "We will be there for ten days. Then north to Los Angeles, San Francisco, Seattle, and journey's end in Kodiak."

"Is that where you live, Captain?" Vladi, always curious, gazed at Captain Walker.

"I've spent most of my life on The China Doll, a beautiful clipper ship, then this old tub. This is my last voyage. I have a buyer for the Aloha in Kodiak."

"But what will you do?" Vladi said, "A Captain with no ship."

"I shall live in Sitka, and perhaps I will build boats instead of sailing them."

"Why, Sitka, if I may ask?" Father Alexi said.

"It's a beautiful little town, and I have close friends there." He stared over the boys' heads at a silver-framed photograph next to the globe. "Very close."

Vladi followed his gaze, "Is that your daughter, sir. She looks way too young to be your wife."

Captain Walker ruffled the boy's hair. "Is that your way of saying I'm old?"

"Who is she, Captain?" Andrei asked, "She's very pretty."

Captain Walker picked up the frame. "The photograph was taken years ago, but she is still very, very pretty."

"Does she live in Sitka? Is she the close friend?" Vladi leaned against the Captain's elbow and stared at the photo. "I would like to meet her."

"Enough questions, boys," Father Alexi said.

Captain Walker laughed and replaced the photo on his desk. "She would tell stories of climbing the ratlines on the China Doll, yelling 'Land ho!' from the Crow's Nest, and stealing my breeches."

The boys put their heads together and whispered in Russian. "What are these breeches?" Vladi asked.

"I don't know, but they must be valuable if she stole them," Andrei glanced over his shoulder to the Captain.

"Did he ever get them back?"

"I don't think so, or he wouldn't still be bothered about it."

Kira admonished her boys, "English only, be polite."

The boys laughed, and Vladi said, "I wish there was a Crow's Nest on this ship."

Captain Walker saw a gleam in the boy's eyes that reminded him of Miss Ruth. "Come to the pilothouse tomorrow, and you can steer the ship. Andrei also."

Kira spun the globe and then placed her finger on the middle of China, "So very far away," she whispered.

"It's a big world," Captain Walker saw the torment in her eyes and wondered what caused it, a painful loss, no doubt, "and sometimes we leave our hearts behind as we sail the high seas."

Father Alexi's heart hurt for his wife and himself as well. He put his arm around her shoulder. "Thank you, Captain. Come, boys."

❦

The following day, Captain Walker gave most of his duties to the ship's pilot and the first mate in order to spend time with Alexi and Vladi. They were eager to learn and peppered him with questions, especially about his life on his clipper ship, the China Doll. Whenever they wandered into the galley, the cook fixed them what the seaman liked to eat. At the boys' insistence, he taught them several simple dishes.

Andrei served the Captain the breakfast he and Vladi had prepared this morning. Captain Walker ate with enthusiasm, then said, "This reminds me of the time Miss Ruth—"

"All your stories seem to include that lady. Why is that, Captain?" Vladi asked.

Why indeed, Captain Walker wondered, although he knew the answer. He had never lost his love for her. He was now sixty-five, which made Miss Ruth a mere fifty. The gap in their ages no longer seemed so vast. He wondered if she was ready to settle down—with him. So many years ago, she had chosen to live for the Lord and the children of Alaska. Would she now be willing to live for him—as man and wife? If not, he would stay close and remain her dear friend.

He looked at these precious Russian boys and envied Father

Alexi. The Captain had never felt the joy of parenthood, but he thought he would have been a good father. He pictured all the young seamen he had invested in. Some of those relationships had remained through the years, but none were as close as father and son. Captain Walker shook away his thoughts and poured another cup of coffee. "I will take you into the ship's bowels. It's dangerous, and you must follow my instructions exactly."

"Where are we going, Captain?"

"Some of the seamen say it's the pit of hell."

The boys looked at each other with fearful faces. Vladi tugged on the Captain's arm. "I don't want to go to hell," he stuttered.

"I'm sorry, boys. I shouldn't have phrased it like that. We are going to the engine room. Men shovel coal into the firebox, which boils the water and creates the steam that powers the ship."

"But you said it was hell," Andrei said.

"It's a hot and humid metal room, suffocating, hard to breathe. The men are soon covered in coal dust. It gets in the pores of their skin, nose, and lungs. Horrible. It's noisy, so keep your eye on me. Be careful of the pipes; they are extremely hot and will sear your skin, perhaps burn through it."

The boys were subdued after they toured that cramped room. It fueled their imaginations with pictures of a fiery hell.

"I'm never going to work in a place like that," Vladi cried.

"I hope you never have to, son," Captain Walker said.

"Why do you make them do it?" Andrei asked, "I feel sorry for them."

"I kept my clipper ship as long as possible, but eventually, I had to switch to a steamship to make a living. I do employ twice as many stokers and boiler room workers. That way, they can trade off, have shorter shifts, and work on deck part of the time."

"It's sad, isn't it, Captain, that the Clippers went away. I wish I could have seen one."

Captain Walker slapped his knee and exclaimed, "You will, Vladi. The China Doll is in Hawaii and is mainly used for tourist tours, but I know her captain. Would you like to take a short cruise and be a deckhand on a real clipper ship?"

"Yes, sir!" Vladi and Andrei saluted.

"I'm going to climb the ratlines like Miss Ruth did," Vladi vowed.

Captain Walker watched the excited boys run to tell their parents. He smiled a sad smile. If life had been different, he might have had sons like that.

The waters of the southern Pacific around the Hawaiian Islands were the bluest the Russian family had ever seen, as azure as the sky. The sand was soft and golden, and the weather—beautiful.

Honolulu Harbor, that large bustling port, appeared early the following day. Captain Walker left the wheelhouse in the capable hands of his pilot and stood in the bow. He leaned against the rail and marveled at how the harbor had grown over the years. It was the chief port of call for the trans-Pacific trade. Sandalwood, furs, tea, and spices came through this calm harbor. Presently, sugar was king.

The Russian boys flanked him. Vladi, although not tall enough, crossed his arms and tried to lean on the rail like the Captain. Andrei, now a teenager, disdained his brother's attempt at imitation and pulled him from the railing.

"It's a pretty place, Captain, and the air smells like flowers or something."

"Flowers. And spices from over there," Captain Walker pointed to a crane that had dropped a load of cinnamon. The dockworkers scrambled to retrieve as many spice sticks as possible as the sweet smell mingled with the salty flowery air.

Several children on the pier, accompanied by a tall bronze Hawaiian, waved and hollered. Captain Walker returned their greetings. They ran to the end of the wharf as the ship's pilot steered the Aloha into its assigned berth. The crew expertly handled the massive ropes used to secure the Aloha to the pier and lowered the gangplank.

"Can we go ashore, Captain? Who are those people? Can we play with the kids?"

"Wait for your parents, boys." Captain Walker threw the words over his shoulder as he scrambled down the gangplank and hugged the middle-aged Hawaiian. The children, all five of them, vied for his attention.

"They look fun. I hope we can play with them," Vladi said.

Andrei snorted, "I'm too old to play. I'm not a child any longer."

"Just because you turned thirteen doesn't mean you're grown up."

Andrei ignored his younger brother and turned his attention to the oldest child talking to the Captain. She was tall, slim, and a tan color that reminded him of the hazelnuts Mama used in baking. He punched his brother on the arm. "Go, find Mama. I'll wait here."

Vladi looked from Andrei to the girl on the dock and back to his brother. He shook his head and hoped he never turned thirteen.

Two tiny rubies were exchanged for cash, and the family booked into a hotel on the beach. The boys played on the sand and surf, although neither could swim. Andrei had an eye for every pretty girl that strolled by.

Kira and Father Alexi watched them from their suite's balcony. But always, her gaze turned toward the East. He knew she was thinking of the children they had lost.

"Kira, please don't think about them."

She looked shocked and hurt, and he wished he had not spoken.

"It makes me feel close to them and brings me comfort. Why do you seldom speak of your eldest son or baby girl?"

"I can't."

"I know Bozhe watches Ilya, but my heart yearns for him. I know He holds the baby, but my arms are empty. I am unsettled."

"You will settle when we get to Alaska."

"This voyage has drained me."

She slipped to her knees as he walked away, and he knew she prayed for him. She was a good woman and more than he deserved.

As she did after every voyage, Iolana had the Captain's cottage ready for him. He sat on the lanai, drank the fresh pineapple juice, and ate too many of the macadamia nut muffins she had left on the table. "Kamalei, I want to take the Russian family for a short sail on the China Doll. Can you arrange it?"

"My father will be delighted if Mrs. Alexi shares some Russian recipes. You know how he wants a recipe from everyone he meets. How long a sail?"

"That depends. I think Mrs. Alexi is tired of traveling. Perhaps only the boys will go. The youngest, Vladi, wants to climb the ratlines like a certain girl did long ago."

Both men chuckled, then avoided eye contact as they thought of Old Skookum, that ancient mariner who would no longer be waiting in the Crow's Nest.

"The hardest letter I ever wrote to Miss Ruth—" Kamalei choked.

"He died in his sleep aboard the China Doll. A beautiful, peaceful way to die. We should all be so blessed."

"Happier news—as usual, there will be a luau in your honor at the village. Will you bring the Russian family? You seem to have developed an affection for them. Although I do not like how the older of the two boys looked at my Makana."

"That girl is a beauty even now." Captain Walker slapped his friend on the back. "How will you keep the boys away when she's older?"

Kamalei snorted. "I have to keep them away now. I could send her to a deserted island, marry her off early, or make her wear a veil." Kamalei ran his hand through his hair. "My other daughters are equally pretty but don't have Makana's spirit. There is going to be trouble with her. I know it."

"You keep an eye on her, and I will watch Andrei."

"I have a better idea." Kamalei reached for another of his mother's muffins. "It will be more intimidating if I keep an eye on Andrei. Makana loves her Uncle Harlan and will want to please you. It's only six more days, and the village is several miles from Honolulu."

Captain Walker chuckled at the canny Hawaiian, "Excellent."

"I will not mention the trip on the China Doll, although Makana loves that old boat."

"Ship, my dear boy, ship" Captain Walker had known Kamalei since he was a baby and thought of him as a young boy, not the middle-aged man he was.

"By the way, my children feel like they know Miss Ruth because of my stories and have begged me to take them to Alaska."

"I wish I had a room on the Aloha, for you, your wife, and eight children. I'm overbooked as it is."

"Maybe next trip."

Captain Walker flung his arm across Kamalei's shoulder, "This is my last trip. I'm selling the Aloha and moving to Sitka."

"Tell me you have a plan." Kamalei laughed, "If I remember correctly, Miss Ruth is half a dozen years older than me. It's time for her to retire and maybe settle down, perhaps with a much older sea captain?" He saw Captain Walker wince at the term, 'much older,' Kamalei said, "I meant much more mature."

"That's not a better word," Captain Walker sighed, his shoulders slumped. "I've always thought I was too old for her."

"The older we get, the more the years between us shrink. I'm happy for you, Captain." Kamalei's face crinkled as he grinned and thought about his dear friends and their future together.

Father Alexi's family happily accepted the invitation to the luau, a feast unlike anything they had known in Russia.

The one hundred-pound pig had been heavily salted; its cavity filled with hot rocks. Lowered into the pit, covered with banana leaves and soil, it had been cooking all day.

The tables were covered with brightly colored tablecloths and set with bowls of chopped taro leaves boiled in coconut milk. Squid, chicken, fish, poi, breadfruit, sweet potatoes, and every kind of fresh fruit the Islands had to offer crowded the tables.

Iolana escorted the Russian family around the laden tables and explained how each unfamiliar food was prepared.

Vladi exclaimed, "They cooked a pig in a hole in the ground! I'm going to eat until I throw up!"

Kira gasped and dragged Vladi away by the ear, scolding him in Russian. Iolana laughed and said to the embarrassed Father Alexi, "From young boys, that is a compliment."

Andrei scoured the crowd, saw Makana next to Captain Walker, and hurried over. Vladi joined them as soon as he escaped from his mother. On the way, he grabbed a fruit Iolana called a banana. "Captain Walker, have you ever eaten until you threw up?"

After dinner, Vladi lay on the grass and breathed slowly. He groaned, "I'll never eat again."

"You are such a little pig," his older brother snorted.

"I ate too much pig. Don't tell Mama."

"I won't as long as you say I was with you all evening. I'm going for a walk with Makana," Andrei bargained for his brother's silence.

"I don't care what you do—owww, my stomach." He rolled from side to side, clutching his belly.

Six-foot torches were stuck into the ground, surrounding the area around the luau. Kamalei's oldest girls lit them at dusk, and several villagers brought ukeleles and drums and began to play and sing. Everyone gathered, and some began to dance.

Kira held Iolana's baby granddaughter. Father Alexi noticed the tears gather in his wife's eyes, even as she tried to smile. He sighed and turned away. Captain Walker sat on a log at the edge of the luau, and Father Alexi joined him. "My wife is sad yet happy holding that baby, and my sons are having a wonderful time."

"What about you?" Captain Walker made room on the log for the priest.

"May I speak with you, Captain? I am heavy of heart."

At Captain Walker's nod, Father Alexi said, "In Russia, Bozhe spoke to the Patriarch, the Metropolitan, and the Bishops, but I rarely heard His voice. I trusted my superiors and did as they directed."

"Yes?"

"I served my people, counseled them, but there was no one I could talk to. I could not reveal my concerns to my superiors or those below me."

"What about Kira? She seems deep, spiritual."

Father Alexi raised sad eyes to the Captain. "I cannot tell her of my doubts, not the ones about this trip. Perhaps I could tell you: a man of the sea, a man of the world, a kind and wise man." Father Alexi struggled to get the words out.

"I'm sure I'm not all those things, but go on."

Father Alexi spoke of his decision to leave Russia during the Revolution, the endless weeks of hiding, traveling, and losing his eldest son and only daughter. Kira's reluctance to leave the Urals, then Hong Kong. His sense that she would be happy to stay in Honolulu. Her dread of a further voyage.

Captain Walker listened without speaking until Father Alexi fell silent. "What is it you want me to tell you, Father?"

"Kira and I have always been in agreement. She took care of the house and the children. I took care of the church and the parishioners. But now—"

"Now?"

"She submits to my decisions but is not enthused. It confuses me, and I doubt myself. Kira and the boys would be happy here.

They were happy in Hong Kong. I am a man of the North, a man of the cold. I'm not fond of this warm weather, but it's no reason to leave. There are Orthodox in Alaska who need a priest. I believe we should continue our journey."

Captain Walker rubbed his chin. "My friend Miss Ruth used to say, do not dig up in doubt what you plant in faith."

"So, you agree we should continue?"

"She also used to say, when in doubt, don't."

Father Alexi sighed, "That's not very helpful."

"Have you asked Kira directly what you should do?"

"She has misgivings but no logical basis for them."

"Hmmm. I've never been married, but Miss Ruth and I have had long conversations in person and through letters over the years. She often had a feeling, an intuitive sense of something, difficult to articulate, but it often came to fruition."

"That inability to explain what she's thinking baffles me." Father Alexi rubbed his eyebrows.

"She's not thinking; she's feeling."

"That makes it even more confusing." Father Alexi shook his head.

"I learned to appreciate Miss Ruth's perspective, even when I did not understand it."

"Without understanding, there is only confusion and chaos."

Captain Walker stared at the sea, deep in thought. "Father Alexi, all I can say is listen to your mind and heart and carefully consider your wife's words. Listen to her silence as well."

"Thank you, Captain." After shaking the Captain's hand, Father Alexi wandered through the luau with a muddled mind and a heavy heart.

The days in port passed swiftly; the Aloha's cargo holds were loaded, and the crew was ready to cast off. Kamalei and his entire family came to wish them well. A tearful Makana handed Andrei a fruit basket but said to her father, "We are going to Alaska soon, right, Father?"

The heartbreak of first love on his daughter's face softened Kamalei. He shook Andrei's hand. "The world is in turmoil with the Great War in Europe and the battles in New Guinea and Samoa. I do think the war will not come any closer, and perhaps, we will make our way north soon." He handed the boy a card with their address on it. "You have impressed me, Andrei, and though you are still a boy, I give you permission to write to my daughter."

The young girl and boy touched hands and gazed into each other's eyes. Then Andrei walked up the gangplank, turning several times to wave.

Ports of call in California and Seattle were uneventful. But the farther north they sailed, the darker the waters. The seas became choppy and rough once they reached the Gulf of Alaska. Angry, cold waves followed the steamship. Clouds hung low, like grave clothes covering the sky. The sun refused to penetrate; there was only a sliver of diffused light around the clouds' edges. The ship plowed through dark gray waters. A thick sea fog reduced visibility to nothing, and still, the ship plunged forward into the waves. Father Alexi vowed to remain on land forever once they reached port.

The ship's pitching affected Kira, and she spent all her time in the tiny cabin. Seasickness had ravaged her body and weakened her. Besides his forays into the ship's dining room, Father Alexi spent all his time with her. He bathed her with a wet cloth and held a basin for her retching.

"Please, Kira, just a few sips of water."

"I can't. It comes right back up."

"But you must."

She moaned and turned her face away. "Will this ship never stop heaving?"

"Just a few more days, my dear, and we will end our journey."

"All in Bozhe's time. He is good," she whispered weakly. "How are my boys?"

"They are good sailors. Vladi spends most of his time in the wheelhouse, asking too many questions. He's decided he wants to captain a ship."

"And Andrei? I worry about him."

Father Alexi rinsed the cloth he used to wipe his wife's face. "He asks the Captain a boatload of questions, usually about the Hawaiian girl. I suppose an Alaskan girl will capture his attention when we arrive in Kodiak."

Kira smiled weakly, then moaned again as the ship rolled in another direction.

The following morning the sky darkened even more, and the wind screamed out of the Arctic, bringing its freezing chill. Once it hit the Gulf, it swirled in every direction as if it couldn't decide where it wanted to go. The rain contained stinging ice crystals and slammed out of the sky in great sheets.

Andrei and Vladi had their sea legs and thought the coming

storm a grand adventure. They wore lifejackets under their slick-
ers and were tethered to a lifeline when on deck. Father Alexi told
himself they were as safe as they could possibly be.

The ship's pitch and roll attacked Kira again with a vengeance.
"Make it stop. Please, make it stop."

"Oh, Bozhe, give me this terrible seasickness. Spare my Kira."
Father Alexi groaned.

A member of the ship's crew burst through the door with two
life jackets. It wasn't easy to hear him over the wind. "Your boys are
safe on the bridge with the Captain. Put these on." He was gone as
quickly as he came.

They felt the engines shudder as the ship heaved upward and
slammed into the trough. Poor Kira, nauseous and dizzy, moaned
about the pain in her head—excruciating. Father Alexi lashed her
to the bunk and tied himself next to her.

The winds increased as the day wore on, and the ship rolled
from port to starboard and back again but never leveled itself.

He held Kira through the night and feared morning would
never come. Near dawn, there was a slight lessening of the dark,
enough to see the heavy rain and icy sleet through the porthole.
Another day passed with no relief. This was no mere storm but a
merciless tempest—a gale.

"Abandon ship!" Did he hear those words or scream them in
his mind? It took time to untie himself from the bed and see that
Kira was alive. She lay pale and still. He did not know if she was
unconscious or sleeping in utter exhaustion.

The contents of the cabin had tumbled about. He pushed
smaller items out of the way and crawled over the larger ones as
he made his way to the door. The ship was listing by nearly forty

degrees. Once in the hallway, he saw a deckhand banging on the cabin doors. "Abandon ship! To the lifeboats!"

Kira did not open her eyes but moaned as he struggled to get her out of the bunk and into her winter coat. He gave up trying to get her shoes on, settling for two pairs of his heavy socks instead. The ship's tilt and Kira's inability to keep her balance seemed to be obstacles he could not overcome. He wrapped one arm around her waist, grasping whatever handholds he could with the other. They did not progress because of her stumbling. If he carried her, he could not pull them along. Finally, he stooped over and put her on his back, her hands hanging over his chest. He grasped both her wrists in one hand and pulled them along with the other. She opened her eyes, moaned, retched, and closed them again.

"Bozhe, give me strength to reach the lifeboats. Keep my boys safe," she whispered.

The ship vibrated beneath his feet. The lights went out, and Father Alexi felt his way the last few feet up the staircase to the deck. The ship heaved, and he fell. Kira rolled toward the rail. He screamed, and the wind carried his voice to Captain Walker and one of the few remaining deckhands.

They raced to her, and the deckhand carried Kira to the last lifeboat while the Captain returned to help the priest.

The deckhand held the ropes steady. "Hurry, Captain! We need to lower the lifeboat before the ship capsizes."

"Where are my boys?" Kira opened her eyes as Father Alexi held her in the bow.

"I saw First Mate Jensen put them in the second lifeboat," the deckhand bellowed above the wind.

She nodded, and her eyes closed once more. Captain Walker handed the priest a blanket, but an icy blast of wind ripped it from his hands. Father Alexi removed his jacket and wrapped his wife in it, then stared in horror at the mountainous waves forming around the ship. The water was nearly as black as the sky.

The deckhand manned the pulleys that lowered the boat into the churning water. It took several tries to keep the boat level and ease it into the sea as the waves batted it from several directions. Success came with the third attempt. The deckhand shimmied down the rope, and they cast away. He grabbed a pair of oars.

"Row with all your might," the Captain yelled, "We must be a certain distance when the Aloha goes down, or we will be sucked into the vortex."

A half-dozen passengers huddled in the lifeboat, grabbed the remaining oars, and pulled. The fear on their faces added to Father Alexi's own.

"I sent several Maydays, but I don't think there is much hope of rescue in this tumult. I've never encountered a gale like this."

"We'll make it, won't we, Captain?" the deckhand asked.

"If God wills."

Father Alexi rubbed his forehead and sighed. He set his teacup on the table and said, "I knew nothing more until I regained consciousness in the saloon on Kodiak. It also functioned as the doctor's clinic. I'm not sure he was a real doctor, not even sure he was sober. He told me I almost drowned or died from hypothermia."

The Professor swallowed and searched for words of comfort.

He had none. He laid his pencil on the paper and wrapped his hands around the mug of tea. As the warmth seeped into his fingers, he was almost afraid to whisper, "Your boys? Kira?"

"Three fishing boats looked for survivors and wreckage when the weather eased. That's when the fishermen found me—lying across an overturned lifeboat. They thought I was dead. Several bodies, strangers, washed ashore in the next few days."

"Did they ever find—"

"I railed against Bozhe. Why did He let me live when my family was gone? He did not answer." The older man's hand shook as he uncapped the bottle of pills and held them against his chest. He took several deep breaths and let them out slowly. "Saved alone."

The Professor turned off the tape recorder and said, "I think that's enough for today, Father. Perhaps I should call Miss Ruth." He looked everywhere except at the priest.

"You look wretched, Professor. It's almost as if you have taken my grief and despair. Incredibly, the tears I see floating in your eyes have dried my own. Your discomfort is easing mine." Father Alexi put the cap on his pill bottle and set it on the table.

The Professor, ashen-faced, continued gathering his materials. "I can't do this anymore."

"I'd rather continue," Father Alexi said as he turned toward the samovar. "And there is always tea."

The Professor, emotionally spent, sank into his chair, flipped the switch on his machine, swallowed the lump in his throat, and said, "Whenever you are ready, Father."

"Actually, all that tea has necessitated a visit to the—" He jerked his head toward the bathroom.

The Professor reread his notes and wondered how he would write the priest's story. What words could he use to convey how much this man had lost and what a toll it had taken? His respect for Father Alexi increased, and his heart ached for him.

Father Alexi returned but did not sit. He pulled back the curtain and stared at the boats in the harbor. "It was some time before I regained my strength. I didn't know what to do with myself. Eventually, I went to the Russian Church, although I was still angry with Bozhe. The priest there was old and unable to perform many of his duties. I stepped in to keep myself distracted. I had no sense of devotion to the people, the church, or Bozhe." Father Alexi looked into the Professor's sad face. "In the year Tsar Nicholas II died, I arrived in Alaska. Nearly dead. All alone."

"The last Tsar? 1918?" he asked, "That was nearly forty years ago."

"You know your history." The priest closed his eyes.

"I'm sorry, Father. Your story is a sad one, so much loss."

"If only it were just a story."

"Yes, well, I mean...." The Professor fiddled with the knobs on his recording machine and avoided eye contact.

"I know what you mean, and I want to thank you."

"Me? For what?"

"For making me remember. I've never shared my whole story."

"You still haven't." The Professor chuckled, but his words had an edge.

"Giving you my memories has released something in me."

The Professor looked as puzzled as the priest felt. "What?"

"I'm not sure. I feel lighter, better—"

"I still don't know how you ended up in Sitka, about your early years in Russia, or how long you spent in China. Are you willing to share those memories?" The Professor asked and then doubted his own willingness to hear them. He admitted feeling a little guilty for putting the old man through this emotional journey.

"Come back tomorrow."

TWENTY-FOUR

Father Alexi settled himself in the narrow bed at his usual time. Sleep seemed irrelevant. The Professor was correct; there was much loss, and those losses became the focus of his life. He remembered Kira's last words. "Love Bozhe and do what's right."

"Oh, Bozhe," he cried aloud, "I rejected your love even as I worked in your church and among your people. I am undone. I am an old man, and my life is over. It's too late."

He wept for his son Ilya, whose fate was still unknown, his baby girl buried in China, and his wife and boys lost at sea; his sorrow for the years he had refused Bozhe's comfort overwhelmed him; his grief burst out of the locked rooms of his soul and nearly consumed him. He paced the floor through the dark hours of the night until exhaustion stilled his sobs. He crawled into his bed, totally surrendering. And with that surrender, there was an awakening in his spirit. Something he hoped would grow and flourish.

The sun inched over the mountains. Dawn light filtered through the curtains, even as the darkness lifted from his soul. "Forgive my lack of love, Bozhe, both the receiving and the giving. I have missed so much."

And I will restore to you the years the locust hath eaten..., and ye shall eat in plenty, and be satisfied, and praise the name of the Lord your God, that hath dealt wondrously with you.

"What a beautiful promise from the book of Joel. Thank you, Bozhe," Father Alexi spoke aloud as he changed out of his rumpled nightshirt and prepared to meet the Professor. "I must tell him how I settled in Sitka, but more importantly, I must explain how Bozhe is beginning to settle my soul."

The Professor arrived with a sack of pastries and a thermos of coffee. Tea was alright, but he felt the need for something more substantial. He set up his equipment quickly and set the donuts and eclairs on one of the Father's china plates. He hoped to steer the conversation to logistical rather than emotional questions. "I have so many questions. What was your schooling like in Russia? How did you meet your wife? How did you escape the Red Army? How long did it take you to cross Russia, also China? Why didn't you go south to the Black Sea?"

"I must tell my life in my own way."

The Professor stifled his frustration. "Coffee, Father?"

Father Alexi laughed and held up his hand, "I told you no questions." He turned to the samovar. "Are you ready to spend the winter with me in the Ural Mountains?"

"It couldn't be any colder than Fairbanks."

"It wasn't the cold that concerned me."

The Metropolitan of St. Petersburg looked over his shoulder and whispered, "Enemies of the state are pressuring the Tsar to abdicate."

"The Revolution is only a month old; surely, the army will come to the Tsar's aid."

"Most of the army is far from St. Petersburg, fighting the war, and I do not believe the Tsar has enough troops nearby to withstand these Bolsheviks. This apostate, Lenin, is becoming more powerful."

"What can we do?"

"The Bolsheviks have spies everywhere. Those speaking the truth are watched, followed, and many have disappeared. They have lists."

"Surely, we are not on those lists." The look on the Metropolitan's face said they were.

Father Viktor Popov, an elderly priest, was present at this meeting. He said, "I shall return to my small village south of the Urals. It's isolated, and I believe I will be out of the way, unnoticed. I know many clerics in central Russia have remained faithful. They will help you."

"Help me what?" Father Alexi pulled on his beard.

The Metropolitan took him by the shoulders and said, "You must take your family and go."

"My wife's parents are old and infirm; she will not leave them."

"Do not stop at Father Popov's. Go to the Siberian Coast and take a ship to your beloved Alaska. You will be safe there."

"Perhaps we can stay with Father Popov. My wife's parents can accompany us if the trip is not too strenuous. Kira will not leave her parents."

"In America, you are free to preach whatever you like."

Father Alexi closed his eyes. He had always planned to return to Alaska after his many years of schooling, but he married and had children. To leave Russia in fear, running and hiding from the Red Army seemed impossible and cowardly.

"What will you do, Metropolitan?"

"I am old. I have no family. I will help as many to flee as I can."

"I should stay and help you."

"You must save your loved ones. You were born in America; it should be an advantage."

Father Alexi turned to his fellow priest. "Are we taking the train?"

"This side of the Ural Mountains, the Reds have too much control, even over the railroads. They will check our papers against their lists. You must cross the Urals before you take the train."

His wife wept in her mother's arms, "I cannot bear to leave you. There must be some other way."

Kira's father embraced her and said, "Your brother has joined the Bolsheviks, the Reds. He will betray you as he is sucked deeper into their evil."

His aged mother-in-law wailed and gathered her grandsons in a fierce hug. Finally, she stood on her toes to kiss their cheeks, then crumpled a handkerchief to her face. She gazed at the baby girl and wept again.

Father Alexi stood to the side, not knowing what to say. This Revolution was tearing families apart politically, geographically, and spiritually.

Their goodbyes nearly broke him. His wife's father pressed all the rubles he could spare into his hand and said, "Keep my loved ones safe, even at the cost of your own life."

A heavy burden, but one he already carried.

Father Alexi watched the incoming storm through the lace-curtained window. Violent wind and fierce weather were the norm this time of year, but he loved Kodiak Island. The water in the samovar steamed as he waited for the Professor to speak. He pulled at his beard and vowed not to let his memories attack him like they had the last time.

"Can you tell me something about your journey across Russia? Take a moment to collect your thoughts," the Professor asked.

There was no need to tell him about leaving the city in a farmer's cart under smelly horse blankets and bags of heavy animal feed. The endless weeks of walking, hiding in the hedgerows when strangers approached, sleeping in roadside ditches, huddled and cold.

Father Alexi's sons, Andrei—almost a teenager, and Vladi—three years younger, had adventurous spirits that carried them through the weeks of walking. His oldest, Ilya, sixteen, was sullen, even surly.

"We should stay and fight," he muttered.

"Don't be so foolish."

"I am not afraid."

"You should be."

They left the main roadways and traveled across the countryside. For several weeks they slept under shrubs and bushes or near haystacks. Father Popov developed a cough, and so did the baby.

Kira was determined to board the Trans-Siberian Railroad, even though the Metropolitan had advised against it. "We have our internal travel documents. We're allowed to ride the trains." She shook her head and whispered, "Where is your faith?"

"We have faith," Father Popov said, "the Communists have lists."

The family of travelers continued to walk and glean from fields and orchards. They picked wild berries and mushrooms in the woods between the farms. As the weeks passed, they became thin and weak, and the leaves began to turn. They often stopped for Father Popov to rest. His cough and the baby's came from deep in their chests.

Areas patrolled by the roving bands of Red militias had to be avoided. The White Guard, a counter-revolutionary army that believed in everything the Reds rejected, controlled some areas to the south. How could anyone prove their loyalty to either group? There was no trust left in Mother Russia. No safety.

Autumn was nearly over by the time they saw the Ural Mountains. Gleaning became impossible. For the sake of his family, Father Alexi relieved some chickens of their eggs and once took several loaves of bread cooling on an open windowsill. Although satisfied and full, his stomach soon churned with guilt. For his family's survival, he became a thief.

TWENTY-FIVE

Father Popov insisted, "Bozhe, our great God, goes before us and prepares the way." His cheerful demeanor encouraged Kira and the boys but irritated Father Alexi.

He could not find much faith when he looked into his sons' frightened eyes and gaunt faces. He became angry when he saw his wife's dress hang on her thin frame, her skin sallow, her hair lank, or when he heard the baby cough and cry.

What kind of husband and father was he? Didn't Bozhe see? Didn't He care? Why didn't He do something?

His wife patted his face when he voiced such thoughts and said, "Remember the early believers and the wicked Romans who killed them."

"Remember Jonah, who was eaten by a whale?" Vladi asked.

"You are so stupid," Andrei socked his brother on the arm. "I say remember Pharaoh's army drowning in the Red Sea. I hope Bozhe does that to all the Reds."

Ilya turned away, muttering, "There is no use remembering. Bozhe—if there is a Bozhe—has forgotten us."

Father Popov quietly put his arm around Ilya. "Sometimes the enemy is near, and the battle is fierce. Sometimes, not so close, but life always has its difficulties. I do not speak of the Bolsheviks. I speak of the enemy of our souls."

"Don't forget, dear husband, Bozhe is always good."

"He is our hope," Father Popov insisted.

Father Alexi bristled. They didn't need to lecture him. He believed all that; of course he did, but it did not comfort him when he roused his sons from a night of too little sleep to face a day of too little food.

They continued their journey toward the Ural Mountains on tired, swollen feet. Meandering between two armies, avoiding towns and villages whenever possible. Hiding from friend and foe since they could not distinguish between the two.

"We will part ways in the morning," Father Popov said as he hunched over and coughed violently. The old priest handed Father Alexi a hand-drawn map of the steppes, that vast grassland east of the Urals. He had marked the towns and villages where hopefully, the priests could be trusted. "Learn these names and then burn the paper."

Father Alexi and his sons leaned over the map and studied it carefully.

"The Bolsheviks aim to destroy every person of faith in Russia." Father Popov shook his head, and his eyes filled. "There is a great evil coming. Indeed, it has already arrived." He enfolded Father Alexi in a firm hug and said, "Always love Bozhe and do what's right."

Ilya, Andrei, and Vladi hefted their school bags and bedrolls to their shoulders. Kira tied the baby to her chest with a large shawl, and they faced the Urals after a tearful goodbye to Father Popov.

"We have to cross those mountains?" Vladi almost cried. "They go on forever."

Father Alexi chuckled as he looked with love at his youngest son. All the boys had their mother's blond hair and blue eyes. Only his daughter had the dark skin and almond eyes of Alaska's Creoles.

"They look like they go on forever, but when you see range after range of snow-covered peaks in Alaska, you will see real mountains. In Alaska, we will travel by dogsled."

Kira muttered, "Having a sled and some dogs would be good." Then she smiled and said, "Bozhe has given us strong legs. We will use them."

Father Alexi took his baby girl from his wife's aching arms. The little one cried and coughed, and his heart ached that he had no medicine.

Father Alexi received hostile looks when he entered the village high in the mountains. The people clamped their lips together and turned away. No one made eye contact. He was dirty and trail-worn—a stranger, perhaps, a spy?

He found the church deserted; it had been ransacked, tapestries and icons destroyed, and everything of value stolen. There was no sign of the priest or his family. What to do? Who to trust?

Near the edge of the town, he called to a young woman, hardly more than a girl. She hurried away, clutching two loaves of black bread. A few minutes later, Father Alexi hailed another and pointed to the church. She tucked her bread tighter under her arm and wouldn't meet his eyes. "It's not safe here," she whispered, "the Reds have set up a district office. All strangers must report."

An older woman passed, also clutching bread. "They have taken our hand mills, so we can no longer grind our own flour."

"And they have confiscated all of the grain for taxes." The

younger woman glanced to the right and the left, then looked over her shoulder.

The old woman tucked a strand of gray hair under her head-scarf and spat on the ground. "They set up a bakery and decided how much bread we are allowed." She spat again, narrowly missing the priest's worn boots. "They will starve us."

"Don't say such things in front of this stranger, you foolish old woman," the younger bread carrier said.

"I mean you no harm," Father Alexi whispered a blessing and made the sign of the cross.

The old woman crossed herself and said, "May Bozhe protect you."

The younger one lifted her eyes to his for a brief moment. He cringed at the despair in her glance. "The Reds are right. There is no God."

Father Alexi hurried back to his family. The Reds were not supposed to be this far south. They must be entrenched if they had set up a district office to monitor and control these small mountain villages.

That evening when the younger boys had gone to bed, he asked Ilya to join the discussion. "You are sixteen, son, almost a man."

Ilya's chest expanded, and he sat up straighter as he wiped the sleep from his eyes.

"We will move our things deeper into the forest tomorrow, away from the trail. You will be in charge while I explore the area. I must know where the Reds are."

With a troubled face and a clenched jaw, Ilya said, "Perhaps you should look for the Whites. We can join them and fight."

"Many will die in our country's conflict. I choose life for you and your brothers."

"You say our country, but you are running away. I am old

enough to fight, brave enough."

"The Reds are too many, the Whites too few. Running seems cowardly, but it is what Bozhe commands."

"Russia is our home, my home; it's worth fighting for." His eyes were fierce, and his fists clenched and unclenched.

"Alaska will be a better place for us.'"

"I am Russian." Ilya swallowed, hung his head, and refused to argue further.

Father Alexi appreciated his son's efforts to respect him. "Sometimes son, it takes more courage to obey when everything within you wants to go your own way. Understand?"

The boy nodded, but his eyes showed no agreement.

"Keep watch while I am gone. Protect your mother and siblings."

TWENTY-SIX

Father Alexi returned six days later. During his absence, Ilya had spent most of his time foraging for food and building a temporary shelter. Father Alexi's heart swelled. The boy was responsible, a son to be proud of.

"The Reds and the Whites fight in the eastern steppes, close to these foothills."

Ilya shook his fist in that direction. "We should join them. The Whites must have a headquarters nearby."

"I have found a hidden valley a day's trek back up the mountain. There is an abandoned hut. It will be our refuge until spring when traveling is easier."

"The baby will get well if we stay out of the weather, and I am wearied by the travel." The frown lines on Kira's face eased.

"Father, you said I'm a man. I am going to join the Whites and fight."

Father Alexi slapped the boy's face. "You will stay with your family!" The father reached for his son, but Ilya turned away.

The sad little family trekked up the mountain in silence. That night Father Alexi wept in his wife's arms. The following morning, Father Alexi stoked the fire and sent the boys to the shed for more wood.

"Ilya, say a prayer. Boys, there is hot tea, a little sugar, and canned peaches. Eat."

They warmed themselves before the fire and ate. All except Ilya looked at each other and grinned. Sometimes they laughed out loud for no reason. They were fed, warm, and safe after many weeks of weariness and wariness.

The hut was well-stocked with food and firewood. After a few days, they had become used to the forest sounds, but a month later, they heard an unfamiliar noise.

"Was that a wolf?" Vladi tumbled off the bed and stood by his mother.

"Don't be daft. It's a dog." Andrei's habit of constantly correcting his younger brother was a source of contention between them.

"A wild dog," Vladi's lower lip trembled.

"Just a dog. Nothing to be afraid of," Andrei's voice tried to sound brave, but he, too, stood near his mother.

More barking and pawing. "Kira, you and the baby get on the bed. Boys, behind me."

"When we left St. Petersburg, I told you we needed a weapon." Ilya stood at his father's side. Andrei huddled behind his father, but Vladi, who had jumped into the bed, pulled the covers over his head and whispered, "It sounds like a wolf."

Ilya grabbed a piece of firewood. "This is my weapon." Jaw tight, eyes straight ahead, Ilya held the wood high and glared at the door. Father Alexi smiled and nodded, but the boy didn't see.

The latch clicked, and the door opened slowly to reveal an enormous dog and a larger man. The dog crouched low and growled. The man's eyes narrowed, and his staff was raised, ready to strike. "I am the shepherd. This is my hut."

He wore a sheepskin jacket with a hood, thick gloves, and stout boots. The dog beside him growled again. Cautiously the man stepped over the threshold. He had not lowered his weapon. The snowflakes clinging to his eyelashes and his black beard streaked with gray gave him the appearance of a gentle giant. Father Alexi kept his eyes on the shepherd and slowly tugged at the chain around his neck. The firelight glinted on the golden cross.

The shepherd leaned his staff against the doorframe, clasped the leather cord around his own neck, and pulled a small wooden cross from beneath his clothing. He whispered to the dog, which muffled his growl and wagged his tail instead.

"Sir, is your dog a wolf?" Vladi's head peeked out from the covers.

The shepherd smiled, "Sometimes I think so. You may take him out and play chase in the snow."

"Is he safe?"

"If you are kind to him, he will be kind to you."

Andrei and Vladi hollered and hooped and ran out the door. Andrei turned back, "What is his name?"

The shepherd laughed, "Wolf. His name is Wolf."

Ilya crouched near the kachelofen, a massive masonry fireplace with a small hearth. He poked it with a stick. Although he pretended to ignore them, Father Alexi knew he listened to everything. Kira stayed on the bed with the coughing baby. The two men sat at the table, and Father Alexi apologized for invading the shepherd's home and eating nearly all of his provisions.

"Your baby is ill. I will bring you a lamb. Good broth for her and meat for the rest of you."

"How can we ever repay you?"

His eyes misted, and he swallowed twice before answering, "Do you have His words?" He fingered his cross.

"His words? Do you mean a Bible?" Father Alexi reached into

his valise and placed it on the table.

The shepherd's hand hovered over it. "Tell me the words."

Father Alexi pushed the Bible across the table. The shepherd hung his head and whispered, "The Book does not speak to me. Please."

They were interrupted by the baby's violent coughing. The shepherd stood. "First, I will bring the lamb and bread, and then you will make the Book speak."

The foamy waves of Kodiak Harbor rolled in and splashed the shore as they had since creation. The sound of the sea and the smell of rotting seaweed seeped through the half-opened window. Much as he loved Alaska, Father Alexi thought about that Russian valley's sweet air and green pastures. As he filled the samovar with water and prepared more tea, he wondered how much to tell the Professor.

The silence was broken by the Professor's questions. "Who was this man? Did you stay in the mountains all winter? Did he betray you? Probably not; you both had crosses. Did the baby's cough get better?"

"No questions."

"Sorry, Father. I am in that mountain hut with you and need to know what happened next." The Professor shook his thermos. No more coffee. He sighed, held out his glass mug, and the Father filled it with strong black tea, almost as dark as the coffee he had just finished.

Evening approached, and the shepherd prepared to leave.

"Where are you going?" Father Alexi asked

"I have another hut a few miles away in the upper meadow. I do not wish to disturb your family."

"We are guests in your hut; you must stay."

The shepherd nodded his agreement. "The hut is small; I will prepare a place for myself in the woodshed."

"You will be frozen by morning," Kira wrung her hands.

He smiled, bowed slightly, and pointed to the wooden door beside the large masonry fireplace. "As you see, the woodshed is on the other side of the kachelofen and stays as warm as the hut. I built it to help the wood dry quickly, even in winter. I will be fine."

Vladi, always eager, always ready—even though the youngest—volunteered to be an apprentice shepherd and was welcomed. Andrei said, "I will also help you, Mr. Shepherd."

Still sullen and stubborn, Ilya did his best to ignore this gentle giant.

"Will you watch with me tonight? There is much danger for the sheep, and you look like a strong lad," the shepherd asked Ilya.

"I'll go with you. I'll help." Vladi jumped up and down around the shepherd, who never took his eyes off Ilya.

"My son is responsible, and he will surely be a help to you," Kira smiled.

Ilya glared at his mother but did not argue. Ilya spent his nights with the shepherd for the rest of the winter, often in a tent on the edge of the sheepfold. The boy endured the cold, lonely nights without complaint.

The shepherd supplied each of them with sheepskin coats, leggings, and fresh meat. And once a week, he provided black bread and beets. In exchange, Father Alexi taught him to read and planned to gift him the Bible when they left.

In a few weeks, the great snow drifts on the upper edges of the valley melted, and abundant grass soon appeared on the valley floor. The sheep thrived, as did the occupants of the little hut.

Calm, quiet, peaceful. It would have been perfect for Father Alexi, except it was not Alaska, his baby girl refused to get well, and Ilya's soul-sickness worsened.

"I cannot reach my son," Kira said, "I am afraid he will leave us and fight for Russia."

"He's just a boy longing for adventure. He will not abandon his family."

She tried to smile, but it did not reach her eyes. "I pray and pray, but in his heart, he is already gone."

Father Alexi hoped his eldest son listened as he read the Scriptures aloud to the shepherd after their evening meal. Father Alexi asked the shepherd how he knew about the Lord.

The gentle giant rubbed his beard, poked at the fire, and asked the boys to bring in more wood. Only when the fire blazed did he answer. "I have lived in these mountains my entire life. My mother taught me to love Bozhe and his Great Son, a shepherd. We are His sheep." He scratched his cheek, smoothed his beard, and laughed, "Sheep are stupid. If I do not care for my sheep, they will go their own way, become lost and die. The same is true for us, no?"

Vladi laughed, "Baa-baa-baa."

Ilya growled, "Do not be so stupid. You are not a little boy. Grow yourself up."

Kira shushed them with a look, and Father Alexi turned back to the shepherd. "You have never been to a church?"

He shook his head and said he occasionally went to one of the mountain villages on market day with his parents, and his mother pointed out the church's onion-shaped dome. Beautiful, but they did not welcome smelly shepherds.

He had not been in any village since their deaths many years ago. He preferred to meet people at the edge of the woods and barter for his needs.

In the depth of winter, in that isolated place, Father Alexi found a spiritual peace beyond anything he had ever known. No icons or tapestries, no church traditions or routines. Just a shepherd, an eager disciple who wanted to hear the Word. Perhaps the shepherd was the teacher. His care for the sheep, God's creation, and the gentle way he served Father Alexi's family was a wonder to the priest.

When the paths were entirely free of snow and ice, the shepherd traveled to the closest village. Upon his return, he said he had heard the fighting had moved north and west of the Urals. The family rejoiced, but their faces fell when he said, "The militia left behind a District Commissioner with a small but ruthless armed force. They are a law unto themselves."

"Perhaps we need to leave," Father Alexi said, "before this Commissioner discovers us."

Kira picked up the baby, "She is so thin and weak. It will not be good for her to travel."

"I want to be a shepherd," Vladi said.

"Let's stay here forever," Andrei added.

Father Alexi turned away from Kira's pleading eyes, smiled, and mussed Vladi's hair. Maybe they could. He must have said the words aloud, for the shepherd took him aside and said, "The District Commissioner saw me in the village and forced me to register. He requires half my flock as taxes. The greed in his eyes told me he won't be satisfied until he has taken everything. I fear he will discover this valley and you."

Father Alexi gazed around the hut that had become his sanctuary. He put his hand on the shepherd's shoulder, "Will you come with us?"

"The mountains are vast, but I know them well. There are more hidden valleys and other shepherds. I must bring them Bozhe's Word. But first, I will lead you away."

"Through the valley of the shadow of death," Father Alexi's eyes filled with tears, and he embraced this humble man who had saved them from a brutal Russian winter and unknowingly helped him hang on to his faltering faith.

The shepherd grabbed a piece of kindling from the woodbox, sharpened the stick, and drew a map on the hut's dirt floor. "You should be able to board the train at Omsk unless the Reds have taken that territory."

Kira's face lit up when she heard the word train. Father Alexi did not tell her how many miles it was to Omsk and that they would walk all the way. She hummed as she packed, and he felt no guilt for keeping the information from her.

The shepherd made a travois and loaded it with as many food-stuffs as Andrei and Vladi could pull. It was spring planting time, and there would be no gleaning.

"I will butcher a lamb." The shepherd headed to the valley floor.

The following morning Kira's cry broke the valley's stillness and echoed through the hills. "He's gone! My son is gone!"

The boys searched the nearby woods and stream. Father Alexi watched the shepherd leave the sheep and stride up the hill toward him. "The boy has gone to join the Whites." It was a statement from the shepherd, not a question.

"There's no note, no goodbye. His mother is beside herself," Father Alexi groaned.

"He left her this." The shepherd handed Father Alexi a carved wooden cross dangling from a leather cord. "Those nights you forced him to watch with me were silent until he finally spoke of his love for Mother Russia and his determination to join the Whites."

"Why didn't you tell me?"

He stood straight and looked at the priest with sad eyes. "You knew."

Father Alexi felt himself stiffen. "I guess I did."

"He was determined to go, so I taught him to defend himself with a club and a staff. We practiced nearly every night. I taught him to fight with his hands as well." The shepherd looked at his large, calloused, and scarred hands. "I once killed a wolf with these hands."

Father Alexi shivered. A club and a staff were no match for a gun or sword. "Thank you."

The shepherd smiled. "I made him bring the Book and read the words before we practiced. I also gave him my father's sword."

Father Alexi called Kira and the boys. They cried and grieved and then prayed. Kira handed the baby to her husband, "I must be alone. Watch the children."

Vladi's red eyes looked at his father and asked, "Why did he go?"

"He wants to fight! I hate him!" Andrei cried. "We will never see him again."

"Andrei, be silent!" Father Alexi yelled. Vladi burst into tears, wrapped his arms around his father's waist, and sobbed.

Kira returned from the creek three hours later. Her eyes were red-rimmed and puffy, but she managed a half-smile. "We leave him in the arms of Bozhe." She wiped her nose, looked heavenward, and kissed the little cross Ilya had carved.

"We left our refuge that afternoon. And so—I lost my firstborn." Father Alexi wiped his eyes with the back of his hand.

"I don't know what to say, Father. Have you tried to locate him?" The Professor pulled out a handkerchief and swiped at his own eyes.

"Even during the Second World War, when Russia was our ally, it was impossible to obtain accurate information." Father Alexi blew his nose and fiddled with the samovar to cover his emotions. "Ilya would have changed his name if he was smart—and he was a very intelligent boy. With the Cold War—" His eyes dimmed momentarily, then he sighed and said with forced cheerfulness, "I must rest now since we are going to Afognak tomorrow."

"Excuse me? Afognak?"

"We're going to the Selaviq."

"Selaviq?"

"No questions."

"Are we flying?" The Professor gulped.

"Miss Ruth will pick us up after breakfast. You may eat with me. Bring the pastries."

"I love your home, but you need a cat or perhaps a good Alaskan dog," Miss Ruth said.

"I'll get one as soon as you do," Haven Ray laughed.

"I'd have a retired sled dog if I didn't travel so much."

"When are you going to slow down? I'm in my sixties, and you run circles around me even though you're two decades older."

Miss Ruth laughed, "Believe me, I don't have the energy I used to."

"I've missed you, dear Miss Ruth. There is so much to talk about. I have found us a Selaviq, in a small village not far from town if you think your friend would rather not fly. I fear we must change our plans. There will be no Selavig on Afognak. I called the cleric at the Kodiak church, and he said they had no priest."

"Don't worry. We shall celebrate on Afognak."

"What do you mean?"

"As I told you, the Professor is here to interview Father Alexi, a retired priest from Sitka. He's frail but not ill, and I assume he'd love to lead the procession."

"I'm ashamed to say I've lost touch with my old schoolmates on Afognak. We were only there for a few years." Haven Ray frowned. "I don't have your writing capacity, Miss Ruth. It is all I can do to answer your letters promptly."

"Back in the day, all we had were letters and face-to-face visits. Now there are telephones and telegrams, and ham radios. So many modern ways to keep in touch. And that reminds me, I'd like to call and tell Father Alexi."

"Christmas on Afognak, I can hardly wait."

"It's January, my dear," Miss Ruth chuckled and pulled a small gift from her coat pocket.

Haven Ray opened the gaily wrapped present to reveal a Parker Brothers fountain pen and pencil set. "It's lovely. Your gift is coming later. When I was a little girl, I was convinced Russian Christmas was the real one. After my first Selaviq, I refused to open my presents in December. My mother was horrified, but she couldn't change my mind." Haven Ray put the kettle on and set the table with her best china. "Do you think your Professor friend would like to come?"

"We won't give him a choice, my dear. I'm sure he will enjoy it."

Haven Ray laughed, "I don't know if you could get him in Robbie's plane again? The weather forecast is not great for the next few days."

"Hopefully, he doesn't know Robbie will have to land on the beach when the tide's out."

"We could always hire a boat and spare the poor boy."

"Remember, there is no harbor. I always got drenched whenever I traveled to Afognak by steamer and was shuffled ashore in a canoe or kayak."

The hotel was old but clean. The mattress was hard, but the sheets were soft. Perhaps threadbare was a more apt description, but there were plenty of blankets. The wallpaper was faded, but the radiator kept the room warm. Its noisy clanking was a small price to pay for the comfort.

He should sleep. Instead, he stuffed both pillows behind his head, crawled under the covers, reread his notes, and listened to his tape recording before retiring. His dreams were full of images of the Russian Revolution, the snow-covered Ural Mountains, the Trans-Siberian Railway, and Chinese bandits. He woke in the midst of a treacherous sea voyage.

The Professor who began this project without enthusiasm was starting to believe everyone who settled in Sitka had a story. Stories worthy of Hollywood movies, like Marty, East of Eden, or Rebel Without a Cause. People who lived interesting lives. The Professor began to look at people differently. He did not think he could continue to hide in his books and classes. What had Miss Ruth done to him?

❦

"Are you sure this trip is necessary, Miss Ruth? Do we need to fly?"

"It's a beautiful day Professor, no need to be afraid."

"I'm not afraid, just not in favor of tiny airplanes." He helped Miss Ruth climb into Robbie's small plane. "Thank you, Miss Ruth, for choosing me for this project."

Her eyes twinkled as she raised her black skirt and stepped into the plane. "Father Alexi is a complicated but fascinating gentleman, isn't he?"

"Not just him, everyone."

"I can still hear, Miss Ruth." Father Alexi spoke from inside the cramped aircraft. "I am a simple man."

"So you would have everyone believe." She settled herself beside the aging priest and patted his arm. The Professor wedged in beside her and glanced at Haven Ray in the copilot's seat.

"Would you rather sit up here, Professor? The view is better."

The lilt in her voice suggested she was teasing. He swallowed and said, "I'd rather not see anything."

Afognak Island was a short twenty-five air miles from the small municipal airport on Kodiak. The sky was blue, the weather was clear, and the temperature hovered just below zero. The tide was out, and Robbie landed the single-engine plane on the snow-covered beach near the village. As was their custom, when any boat or small airplane came to Afognak, the entire population welcomed whoever arrived.

"Thank you, Robert. Nice flight," the Professor said and tried to mean it.

The pilot sniffed and pointed to the sky. "I don't like the look of those clouds or how the air smells. We might be in for it."

As the group exited the airplane, a few of Miss Ruth's former students, now village elders, exclaimed, "Is that Miss Ruth?"

"It is!"

"Welcome, teacher!"

The Professor shivered in the sub-zero air as he and Robert half-carried the bundled-up Father to where a sled and dog team waited.

"I could have walked," Father Alexi complained as he was strapped into the sled.

Miss Ruth laid his cane across his lap and whispered, "Hush now. It gives these men a chance to use their muscles. Life is so easy now they don't often get to show their manly strength."

The Father quirked his eyebrow but said nothing. He decided to enjoy himself. He hadn't ridden in a dogsled since he was a child. The adults and elders followed the sled to the village. The children and teenagers helped Robert roll the small plane above the tide line and secure the aircraft.

Robert had several things to arrange to keep the gas and oil from freezing. He selected two teenagers to help and sent the other kids to the schoolhouse. They went reluctantly until he told them they would have a contest later, and whoever won would have a ride in his airplane, provided Chief Mishka agreed. They scampered away, conferring on the best way to secure the Chief's permission.

At the entrance to the schoolhouse, a distinguished man, his face half-covered by his furs, stepped forward. "The years have been kind to you, Miss Ruth." He extended his hand. "You must be an elder in Sitka by now."

She laughed, shook her head, and held his gloved hand for a long moment rather than shaking it. "The years have been kind to you as well. I understand you are the Chief now."

"Of a very small village. So many of our younger people have left to find a better life, or at least an easier one."

Miss Ruth surveyed the crowd. "But I see you still have several younger families that have stayed to care for the elders."

"We are fortunate. Who have you brought with you?" Chief Mishka asked.

Haven Ray stepped forward, "Do you remember me, Little Bear?"

He studied her carefully, "You remembered Mishka means little bear, and I recognize the scrimshaw earrings my mother gave you when you left us so many years ago."

Haven Ray fingered the earrings she had worn since she was a child. "My mother refused permission to have my ears pierced."

He bowed slightly, and his eyes twinkled. "You borrowed her hat pin. Lethal."

"And I insisted you pierce my ears, Little Bear. If I remember correctly, I wanted to pierce yours, but you would not agree."

"Even the seals in Kupreanof Strait heard your cries. Perhaps I was not so brave." He pulled on his ear lobe and smiled. "You do not look the same without the freckles and long braids, but you are little Haven Ray who wanted to have a Selaviq every week," he said.

"I'm afraid my freckles and braids have been replaced by wrinkles and gray hair," She grinned and added, "but I still want a Selaviq."

Chief Mishka frowned, "We have no priest."

A deep voice came from the dog sled, "I came for a Selaviq, and I shall have one." Father Alexi threw off the straps that held him in the sled and tossed the blanket aside. The villagers saw his clerical clothes.

"It's a priest," one of the children yelled.

"Miss Ruth, You brought us a Father!"

"But is he the right kind of priest?" an elder asked.

"Who is he? Where does he come from?"

"We do not know this man," another grumbled.

The villagers murmured, and a few shouted. The Chief clapped his hands, and the crowd quieted. "Father, I hesitate to ask—"

Father Alexi gripped his cane tightly with one hand and, with the other, pulled out the cross he wore next to his skin and held it high. At the sight of the Old Believer's Byzantine Cross, the villagers clapped and shouted.

"Father, will you carry the star?"

The priest bowed. "I am Father Alexi, and I would be honored."

The kids ran into the crowd, full of questions. One little girl asked her mother, "What's going on?"

"Miss Ruth brought us a Father, and we shall have a Selaviq," the mother squeezed her hand.

"The pilot said he'd give us a ride into the sky," the Chief's grandson yelled.

"What?"

"Well, he's having some kind of contest, and the winner will ride with your permission."

Chief Mishka turned toward Miss Ruth, "We are delighted you have brought us the Father. Everyone go home, get food, and bring it to the school house. We shall feast and tell the little ones stories about when we were young, and Miss Ruth was our teacher. Tomorrow night under the stars, we shall have our Selavig."

"Looks like bad weather," one of the children said.

"The sky is full of clouds," said another.

"Do not fear. We shall have our Selaviq under clear skies and bright stars," Father Alexi promised.

Father Alexi's prediction came true. The star was brought forth and given to the frail clergyman. Chief Mishka motioned to his son to walk beside the Father and assist him if needed. Haven Ray stood at his other side.

"Is this your first Starring, Mrs. Turner?"

As giddy as she was all those years ago, Haven Ray laughed and touched the not-yet Spinning Star. "I walked beside this very star as a young child."

"Here in Afognak? You must come for tea tomorrow and tell me."

She nodded and said, 'Look at the children's faces, such joy."

Father Alexi tilted the star toward the closest boy and told him to give it a spin. He did not see the boy's face but saw his own sons, forever young, forever gone. Pain pierced his heart. He bit his lip and lifted the star even higher. "Let the Selaviq begin." He would embrace these children, these people as if they were his own.

Robbie had worked his way through the crowd to Miss Ruth's side. He shook his head. "Storm's coming, Miss Ruth. If we stay, we may be stranded here until it passes."

The storm rolled over Afognak Island at its leisure. The people used the schoolhouse as their meeting place for Haven Ray's clinic and evening socials.

On the third day, Miss Ruth questioned her friend, "Professor, why have you been staring out the window all afternoon?"

"The weather still looks bad. I am glad you told me to pack for a few days."

"The storm gave you time to tell the schoolchildren about your life in Fairbanks and the project we are working on."

"Not very adventurous. They were more interested in hearing about when you taught their parents."

"Grandparents, actually."

He glanced out the window again and poured them both tea. "I keep forgetting how old you are." The tea sloshed over the cup's rim, and he blushed; whether from his words or his clumsiness, he wasn't sure.

Miss Ruth laughed and wiped up the mess. "It has also allowed Haven Ray to run a clinic for the past few days. She has learned to take her medical kit wherever she goes."

"She's an interesting woman. Tell me more about her."

"I'd rather talk about Father Alexi. He has decided to stay here and minister to the villagers."

The Professor's cup rattled against his saucer. "He's not only frail, he's ill. Something to do with his heart, I think. He keeps a bottle of pills close."

"Hmmm. Still, it's the Father's choice."

The Professor paced then stood before Miss Ruth, his face mottled and his voice high-pitched. "The steamship only comes every couple of weeks. The village doesn't even have electricity. Who will take care of him? How will he survive? What if he runs out of medicine and gets sick?"

"You don't know too much about Native ways, do you? The hunters and fishers will share their food. The women will share their garden produce, dried fish, and berries. They will send their children to chop his wood and do whatever needs doing."

"It's criminal. He's too old. He won't last long."

"This place has given him a renewed interest in life, a purpose. He knows it will probably shorten his time, but it's a price he is willing to pay. We'll ask Haven Ray if she can get a good supply of his pills."

"Will you please talk some sense into him?"

"I think he is being very sensible. Life isn't always measured in the number of one's days."

The Professor stared out the window. "I'll talk to him."

"No."

"But, Miss Ruth."

"No."

❧

"May I talk to you, Father?" The Professor's voice cracked as he removed his gloves, boots, and heavy coat at the arctic entrance to the small cabin next to the church.

"I'm grateful the village women have cleaned the cabin and donated dishes and blankets until I can send for my things. The cupboards are full of food, and the children have filled the woodbox. When my books and vestments arrive, I will be a happy man. I've enjoyed having you and the pilot as my guests."

The Professor peeled off the scarf wound twice around his neck, a thick sweater, and a hat. "Yes, Robert and I have been comfortable sharing this cabin with you while we're here." The Professor looked at the small dwelling through the Father's eyes. It seemed adequate, even cozy. "Father, Miss Ruth says you plan to stay."

"Oh yes."

"But, Father—" the Professor swallowed several times, and his Adam's apple bobbed.

"Look out the window, my young friend. What do you see?" The two stood together and watched the large snowflakes fall slowly from the sky.

"I can't see anything. The snow is too heavy and thick."

Father Alexi chuckled, "Have you ever heard of soul snow?"

"Stormy Durand talked about it when I interviewed him, but I didn't get it."

Father Alexi stroked his beard, now white as the snow gathering on the windowsill. "Keep looking. There is a serenity, a purity in these soft flakes. The stillness filling the atmosphere is like heaven's angels speaking, although everything is silent."

The Professor scratched his head. "I still don't understand."

"I stood in the softly falling flakes and breathed heaven's air. I communed with the One who sent the snow. With His purity, He covered my past, cleansed my present, and enhanced my future. Soul snow hides the grime and dirt. It falls on everything equally, whether in the wilderness or the city. It shows me what my soul can look like with all the impurities covered or removed."

"I guess so." The conversation was not going the way the Professor thought it would.

"Do not be concerned for me. This soul snow has given me clarity. I will stay here, and these will be my people."

"But, Father."

"You know my story, how I began my life in a village much like this."

"Forgive me, but you are frail and ill. I say this out of concern for you. This life is too hard for you."

Father Alexi chuckled, put the kettle on the front of the wood-burning stove, and pulled a packet of sugar cubes from the cupboard. "Thank you, but I am centered in Bozhe and content. I will finish my life here."

The Professor slumped into the chair and sighed.

"Open your soul to the One who sent the snow," Father Alexi said as he filled the Professor's cup.

The Professor looked through the window and shivered; the snow looked like lacey shrouds draped over the trees.

The snow stopped falling sometime in the night. Robert checked and rechecked the condition of his airplane. When he arrived, the village children had collected every available fur and blanket, which Robert had piled onto the tarp-covered small plane. He had several small fires continually burning, which kept the air around the aircraft at an adequate level, although still well below zero. The gas and oil were at allowable temperatures, and all systems were ready.

"Visibility is good, Miss Ruth, and I will put the floaters on. There is too much snow, and the tide is too high for me to take off from the beach."

"I was hoping we could stay another day."

Robert glanced toward the sky. "I've been on the radio with the Weather Service and Coast Guard. The ceiling is acceptable, but another storm is moving in this direction."

"I'll tell Haven Ray to finish her clinic and say her goodbyes. Do I have time for a visit with the schoolchildren?"

"A short one and send the Mishka boy to me. I owe him a plane ride."

As Miss Ruth approached the schoolhouse, nearly a dozen truant children left their snowy games and followed her. She opened the door and saw three students at the front desks. Those behind her slithered in and sat at theirs.

"Children, take off your boots and outer garments. Hang them up properly. Don't come into my classroom in such a rude way. You've left snow over my nice clean floor," the teacher's face was pinched as she scowled at them.

Miss Ruth's heart broke for these beautiful children, and she remembered her early years in Alaska under the authority of a woman as grim as this one.

"Tell us a story, Miss Ruth."

"My grandfather said you were the best teacher in the world and even knew our language."

"Unacceptable! English only." The word was whispered by the sour woman who folded her arms and stood rigidly against the blackboard.

"Tell us about the Selaviq when the nurse-lady was a little girl."

"Superstitious nonsense!" Could the teacher's face have been more pinched?

"Hush, children," Miss Ruth whispered. Her tone was light, and her smile broad. "Let me talk to your teacher. She has come a long way to try to help you."

The two women moved to the back of the room where parkas, mukluks, hats, and gloves hung on wooden pegs.

"I didn't want to come here," the young teacher whispered.

"Neither did I, and I was just about your age," Miss Ruth answered.

"How did you survive? I hate the weather, and I don't have enough books or supplies."

"I can't do anything about the weather, but make a list of what you need and include things for Christmas and birthdays. Fun things for the children. It doesn't take much to bring them joy."

"I can't worry about that. I can barely get them into the schoolroom as it is. And who's going to bring me joy?"

"Why did you become a teacher?"

"I don't even know anymore."

Miss Ruth put her arms around this young woman. "It's because you care. But I think you have been deeply hurt."

The teacher stiffened, hiccupped, sniffed, and then the tears flowed. "I lost my husband in the war. We'd only been married a few months when he shipped out."

"And you threw yourself into your work and didn't allow yourself to grieve?"

"Not exactly, I was expecting, but the baby was stillborn. No husband, no baby. All I had were pitying looks from family and friends. I had to get as far away as possible."

"This is certainly far and away. Your heart is tight and constricted. You are holding on to the pain."

"It's all I have left."

"Look into the faces of these children. I can tell you a story about each of them."

"But you've only been here a few days.'

Miss Ruth nodded and said, "Those two are orphans raised by relatives. That one's mother died giving birth, and the baby did not survive either."

The teacher gasped and held her stomach.

"The fathers of the three in the back row never returned from hunting sea lions. There is much sadness here, and you have an opportunity to change that. If you focus on that, I believe your pain will lessen, your heart will ease, and you will have room for joy. Not the happiness you expected life to give you, but these children will comfort you if you let them."

"I don't know if I can. I don't know how."

"Bozhe will show you." Miss Ruth gave the weeping teacher a handkerchief and a bag of lemon drops. "Have a good cry among the boots and jackets while I tell your students about an amazing Irish woman and the magic of lemon drops."

Chief Mishka stood silent, staring over the Professor's shoulder, hearing the concerns about Father Alexi.

"I'm sure you understand. This is no life for such a frail old man. I mean, there are no medical facilities or regular contact with the outside world. What if he gets sick, falls, and breaks a bone?"

Still no answer. The Professor struggled to fill the silence with all the reasons Chief Mishkin should send the priest away. Finally, his words trailed away, and he shoved his hands in his jacket pockets, glaring and muttering about the barely civilized living in this isolated village.

Chief Mishkin pointed toward the beach. "Time for you to go."

The Professor stomped to the beach and was silent as he helped the two women into the airplane. He was wet up to his knees from a rogue wave. He bit his lip and swore under his breath.

"Sorry, Professor," Robert said, eyeing his drenched snow boots and pants. "Sit in the copilot's seat, and I'll get the heater on as soon as possible."

The Professor asked, "Are you sure the weather will hold?"

"It's Alaska. You're never sure," Robert grinned, "that's the fun of it."

The villagers shouted their farewells as the small plane ricocheted over the waves. Miss Ruth and Haven Ray pressed their faces to the window and waved.

During takeoff, the Professor thought they were bouncing on cement. He clamped his teeth together and vowed he would not complain about this short ride back to Kodiak, no matter how terrifying. He groaned when he remembered that soon there would be a long flight across the Gulf to Sitka.

He leaned and rested his forehead on the window for one last glance. The villagers had given Father Alexi a parka and mukluks of black fur, trimmed in ermine, making him easily recognizable. Robert waggled the wings in a final goodbye. The children ran down the beach until the little airplane disappeared in the low-hanging clouds.

The Professor squirmed in his seat and fought the urge to argue with Miss Ruth for leaving Father Alexi behind. He trembled and wondered if he was afraid of her. He sighed and leaned his head against the cold window. She wouldn't be able to hear him over the small plane's engine anyway.

The short flight to Kodiak was uneventful, and he was glad to be back at his hotel. He bought a sandwich and coffee, took them to his room, and pulled the notes from his briefcase. Agrefena Evans, Ade Bunderson, Stormy Durand, and Father Alexi—all their stories ended in Sitka, except for the Father's. The Professor wondered how many chapters the old man had left.

He picked up his sandwich, took a bite, and laid it on the plate. Guilt left him without an appetite. He drank his coffee and began to read about these people he had come to admire. *Will my life be a story anyone would want to read? Would anyone write it?*

Before he left Kodiak, the Professor telephoned Miss Ruth. "I have failed with Father Alexi."

"What do you mean? He is a content, happy man. Partly because you persuaded him to tell his story. You did well, Professor."

He held the handset away from him, stared into it, and then said, "There is so much of his story I don't know. How he evaded the Bolshivicks for months. His trek across a bandit-infested China. The time after the shipwreck. I don't even know the details that sent him to Sitka from Kodiak."

Miss Ruth cut him off. "The Bishop of Alaska sent him to St. Michaels. Father Alexi did his best, but his grief kept him from embracing the people as his own. He's better now."

"But his health, his medication?"

"Haven Ray has sent him several months' supply. He will be fine; if not, you've done your part. Leave the rest with Bozhe."

The Professor shook his head and frowned even though he knew Miss Ruth couldn't see him. The following day he took a steamship across the Gulf. If he ever flew again, he vowed it would be in a large prop job. Two hours into the voyage, he wasn't sure the steamer was a good idea. Getting from one place to another in Alaska was fraught with peril.

The waves were huge, and he hid in his cabin, praying to Miss Ruth's God and hoping he would not suffer a shipwreck as Father Alexi had so many years ago. He tried to focus on the bare lightbulb, but the pitch and roll of the ship made it swing wildly. It gave him a stomach ache. Closing his eyes didn't help. He pictured his tranquil life in Fairbanks, surrounded by books. If he wanted to travel, he went to the library. Books were the safest mode of transportation.

Now back in Sitka, he shrugged off the effects of his journey and typed his notes about Father Alexi while wondering how the older man fared. He also thought about Haven Ray and the Navy Jeep. There was a story there, and he aimed to find it. He looked forward to Miss Ruth's return to Sitka. He intended to get some answers about Haven Ray.

Miss Ruth visited with her Kodiak friends while Haven Ray worked but returned in time to ensure she had dinner in the oven each evening.

"How are you, dear?" Miss Ruth asked as Haven Ray shut the door behind her and shook the raindrops away. "You've seemed more tired since we returned from Afognak, and that cough is nasty."

"Just the winter darkness and cold, I think."

"I think it's more than that. Have you seen a doctor?"

"You are just as bad as the nurses I work with," Haven Ray grumbled. "I'm waiting for the results of several tests. In the meantime, I prefer not to think about it."

A knock at the door interrupted Miss Ruth's protest. Haven Ray returned with a small wicker basket she handed to Miss Ruth. "Your Christmas present."

A soft mew came from the basket. Miss Ruth dropped to her knees and lifted the tiny calico aloft. "I can't have a cat." She held the little feline to her heart.

"You have so many friends that can care for her when you travel, but she's not a sled dog. I can take her back," Haven Ray wrung her hands.

The kitten gave a soft kitty cry and licked Miss Ruth's fingers. "Nonsense. She's perfect."

Haven Ray set the table and answered the telephone's shrill ring while Miss Ruth poured a saucer of milk for the little feline.

"Thank you. Yes. Goodbye." All the color drained from her face as she turned toward Miss Ruth. "That's news I didn't want to hear. I feel like a little girl who wants her mother."

Miss Ruth led her to the chintz-covered couch and held her hand. "Tell me."

"Tuberculosis, although I feel fine, just a cough and fatigue." Haven Ray reached for a pitcher on the coffee table. She poured a glass of water. "When I was little, my mother feared every cough or cold was consumption. Our last winter in Afognak was brutal, blizzard after blizzard."

"I remember."

"My mother thought my constant cough was tuberculosis."

"I'm so glad it wasn't."

Haven Ray continued as if Miss Ruth had not spoken. "She stopped fretting over me when my father and his team were lost on their return from the Kenai Peninsula. The searchers never found a trace of my Dad or his crew."

"I remember some of the village men helped in that search. But then, one day, you and your mother were gone without saying goodbye."

"She moved us to Kodiak in order to check at the surveyor's office regularly. She struggled for three years and finally accepted that he had died. She washed her hands of Alaska, and we moved to my grandparent's place in California."

"I'm glad you wrote to me."

"I'm sure my childish letters were difficult to interpret, but writing them helped me, and your letters comforted me. After accepting Dad's death, Mom turned her focus back to me, worrying and fretting. It was difficult for the doctors to convince her my constant childhood congestion was due to bronchitis, not tuberculosis. The doctors said my body housed TB germs, but they were inactive."

"It must have been hard for her to accept that TB might flare up at any time."

Haven Ray smiled. "It did flare up in the late forties, remember. I'm sorry my mother lived in such fear for me."

"She loved you very much." Miss Ruth handed Haven Ray a handkerchief. "My dear, let me be your mother."

Haven Ray blew her nose, coughed, and attempted a wan smile. "The doctor has arranged for me to enter the sanitarium on Alice Island."

"That's perfect. Alice Island is less than ten miles from Sitka. I'll be able to visit often. Jake Steiner can take me in his skiff."

Haven Ray picked up the kitten who nestled at her feet. "Will you bring her and a large bag of lemon drops?"

Miss Ruth laughed and scratched the kitten behind the ears. "I can probably smuggle her in—but what will we name her?"

Haven Ray petted the little feline, and Miss Ruth saw the little girl with freckles and long braids she had come to love on Afognak Island so many years ago.

Haven Ray's eyes brightened, "Let's name her Selaviq, and we'll call her Selly."

"Purr—fect."

TWENTY-SEVEN

The Professor slid a bundle of rough drafts across the table at the Sitka Café. "I still don't like it that we left Father Alexi on Afognak." He stared over Miss Ruth's shoulder to the waters of Sitka Sound.

Agrefena placed their breakfast plates on the table and said, "Do not worry about Father Alexi, Professor. He is where he needs to be. Bozhe knows."

"Does everyone in this town know everybody's business, even their feelings?" The Professor frowned after the Native woman.

"Of course, it's part of small-town living." Miss Ruth picked up her fork and cut the reindeer steak.

"Have you heard from him?"

She shook her head. "The Old Believers on Afognak will take good care of him." She patted the young man's arm. "The Bishop of Alaska forced him to retire from the church here in Sitka. Men like Father Alexi need to be needed."

"Won't the Bishop remove him from the church in Afognak?"

Miss Ruth lifted her coffee cup to her lips and winked at the Professor. 'I'm sure they will never know he's there."

"But those people live in such a subsistence sort of way. No modern conveniences."

Miss Ruth laughed and punched his arm. "You forget, I lived for several years in Afognak. Believe me, it was much more primitive in the early 1900s."

The Professor tried to let go of his misgivings. "There are too many gaps in his story. I don't even know how he came to settle in Sitka, except that the church sent him. I know nothing of all the years he lived here."

"That's just it, Professor. Father Alexi never settled in Sitka."

The Professor nearly spilled his coffee, and the cup rattled in the saucer as he set it down. "Huh?"

"He lived here for years. He served the people but wasn't settled, not in his soul. Your interviews helped him to review his past and let go of his pain and grief. He's settled now. Well done, Professor."

"I'm afraid for him." He choked on his toast.

"No, Professor. You are afraid for yourself. You don't think you could live such a life."

Once again, Miss Ruth's words caused the Professor to look within. Such an annoying woman! He couldn't see himself in Afognak or anywhere like it. Adjusting to this small town was all he could handle. Fairbanks, by no means a city, had five times the population of Sitka's mere thousand.

What did he fear? He knew he was more comfortable with college life. That's probably why he had changed his major twice. That way, he could remain among his books and academic pursuits. He was no outdoorsman, an obvious disadvantage in the Territory of Alaska. The Professor tugged on his ear as these thoughts ran through his mind. He saw Miss Ruth look at him intently and wondered if his emotions flickered in his eyes? Were his feelings visible on his face?

She merely smiled and changed the subject. "I will need your help in the next few weeks. Haven Ray is in the sanitarium on Alice Island."

"TB?" The Professor gulped, and his coffee slid down the wrong way; he coughed. "How is she?"

"She had a bout in the 1940s and was treated with the new drug streptomycin. But she's had a relapse, and apparently, so have many others who were treated with that drug."

"How bad is it?"

"Visitation is restricted, but I'm going to force my way in tomorrow."

"I'm coming with you."

"You hardly know her."

"Miss Ruth, you have removed me from my classrooms and academic pursuits. By interviewing those who have settled in Sitka, you changed me. I care about people in a way I never have before."

"That doesn't surprise me. I saw that potential in you. "

Agrefena refilled their coffee cups and cleared their plates. Miss Ruth asked for the check.

"You said you needed my help?" The Professor snatched the check from her hand. "You never let me pay, but today it's my treat."

"You are a dear. I almost forgot."Miss Ruth snapped her fingers, reached into her handbag, and pulled out an invoice and a set of keys. "Haven Ray's Jeep is arriving by steamer this afternoon. She says you can use it while you are here."

"There's not a lot of roads in Sitka. Where would I go?"

"I think she feels better knowing you are babysitting her beloved vehicle. I'm leaving the day after tomorrow and will return in a few weeks. I'm off to a village near Bristol Bay."

"I'll keep an eye on Haven Ray for you. If she trusts me with her Jeep, maybe she'll trust me with her story."

"Be sure she tells you about evacuating the Aleutians during the war." Miss Ruth winked at the young man.

"You can't just drop things like that into the conversation, Miss Ruth!"

"Just stirring your curiosity, my dear friend."

"It doesn't need stirring. I want to return to all the people I've met and beg for more stories about their lives, loves, losses, hopes, and dreams." He looked at Agrefena wiping the counter. "Mrs. Evans is warming up to me. She wants to read my story and said she might add to it if she thinks I did a good job."

"Well done, Professor."

He shook his head and tugged on his other ear. "What have you done to me?"

"I leave Haven Ray in good hands. You can stay in my cabin and take care of my cat."

"That could work. I have dozens of pages of notes and reels of tape scattered around my hotel room. The maid will be glad to see me go. I've written several drafts, but I'm unhappy with them."

"I like what I've seen." She reached into her pocketbook again. "Here's the keys to my cabin, although I never bother locking it."

The Professor continued as if Miss Ruth had not spoken, "How I'm going to put it all together, I don't know."

"If you run into trouble, visit Sam Mitchelll, Jr. at the Sitka Sentinel. He'll help you."

"Why didn't you give the project to him?"

"Sam loves Alaska and its history. The committee has him searching through all the old newspapers in the state. He'll report on sourdoughs, gold seekers, federal appointees, and report on the corruption."

"Corruption?"

"Learn your history, boy. The settling of Alaska, especially after we bought it from the Russians and again when gold was discovered, was one of the most corrupt enterprises of the United States government. We want it read into the state's legislative minutes."

The Professor became a familiar sight as he drove Haven Ray's old Jeep through town. It pleased him when the locals raised their hands and shouted their greetings. He frequented the Sitka Café and eavesdropped on everyone's conversations. *I'm becoming a regular small-town fellow, minding everybody's business.* He told himself he was caring, not nosy.

Agrefena served him breakfast without asking him what he wanted. She even told him a couple of stories to add to his report. It made him feel accepted. His coffee cup was continually topped off. Everyone had opinions about the project, offering suggestions, ideas, and ways he *could get it right*—in their words. None had much merit, but he nodded and thanked them.

One morning, as he patted his stomach and tipped his chair back, balancing it on two legs, he listened to the men at the round table gripe. Government regulations on fishing and forestry production would ruin America's last wilderness. "Worse when statehood come." Ivan chewed on his mustache and stared into his coffee cup.

Ade scooted his chair closer to Jake's and hollered, "Professor, bring your chair over here and tell us what you think."

"Is too young to know," Ivan Mishkin muttered.

Agrefena tapped him on the shoulder with her wooden spoon

even as she topped off his coffee. "Quiet, old man. The Professor is young but smart. Come, Professor."

Heads turned, and coffee cups stopped halfway to their destination. Eyebrows rose, and a low rumbling was heard throughout the Café. The Professor was a pleasant fellow but inexperienced—an outsider. What was Ade thinking?

The men hid their surprise and waited as the amazed young man pulled his chair into their private domain. "Thanks, fellows, I think—"

"No think." Ivan chewed on his mustache. "Answer question."

"You haven't asked a question," the Professor stuttered.

"Then no talk. Listen." The old Russian pointed his pipe at Ade, who peppered the Professor with questions about his interviews, what his college professors in Fairbanks said about statehood, and what his fellow students thought. He also wanted to know the Professor's opinion about the future of Alaska's resources, Native rights, and the federal government's responsibility to the citizens of Alaska.

After several cups of coffee and some of Agrefena's French crullers, the Professor held up his hand and begged, "No more questions. I have no answers, and my opinions are grossly uninformed. I don't know what I think."

"You better get informed. Things are changing." Jake Steiner let the disgust show on his face.

"Sorry, Mr. Steiner. I haven't read a newspaper in months. I've been consumed with interviewing those on Miss Ruth's lists. My head has been in the past."

Ivan poked the Professor's chest with his pipe, "Past is future."

The sweet, pungent tobacco smoke filled the Professor's nostrils and gave him a headache. "I must finish my reports, but I will consider your questions. Perhaps, we can talk again? I think you are the ones with the answers."

"Good boy, not so dumb." Ivan waved him away with his pipe.

TWENTY-EIGHT

"I don't have time to talk to this so-called Professor. Why did you let him make an appointment, anyway?"

Margaret Mary refilled Sam's coffee and said, "You're just mad that Miss Ruth didn't give the project to you."

Sam grabbed the cup, and the too-hot liquid burned his lips. "How can you say that? You know how busy I am researching the Territory's newspapers," he growled.

"You think you can do everything, my boy; you always have." Margaret Mary carried her coffee back to the linotype machine, taking small sips along the way, and began her morning's work.

The Professor entered the chaos of the Sitka Sentenial. He saw stacks of old newspapers in a corner, the counter piled high with papers and flyers, and a wooden leg leaning against a file cabinet. What was that about? He reminded himself to stay focused. The older woman clanking away on an even older linotype machine raised her hand in greeting even though her back was to him. Uncanny. And just as Miss Ruth had described him, Sam Mitchell, Jr., the editor, sat behind a messy desk, chomping on an unlit cigar, talking on the phone, and scribbling notes on the back of an envelope.

"Uh-huh. Uh-huh. Yep. Good." Sam waved his cigar toward the chair facing the large oak desk. The chair's occupant, a large stack of newspapers, hindered the Professor from sitting. Sam pointed to the pile and motioned for the Professor to move them to the battered work table in the center of the room. He did, then sat on the edge of the chair and tried not to listen to the editor's phone call.

Sam grunted into the phone, let the handset fall back into its cradle, and turned his attention toward the young man. "So, Professor, why did you come to see me?" He laid the well-chewed cigar in the overflowing ashtray near his elbow—one of several on his desk.

"Yes, well, with Miss Ruth gone—"

"Where's she gone now?" Sam unwrapped the cellophane from a new cigar.

"She said you were working on the project. I thought she'd keep you up to date on her whereabouts."

Sam raised his eyebrows.

"Bristol Bay...she's gone to Bristol Bay," the Professor stammered.

Sam scratched his head and sighed. "I received a letter from the Committee's secretary, and I've been up to my eyeballs in research for them. That, and keeping the paper going single-handed, keeps me busy, but I could have done the Sitka interviews. She should have known that."

The Professor shifted in his chair, "She said I could come to you for help since you were an expert in Sitka history."

Margaret Mary, the aging linotype operator, held her hands high. "What about these hands, Sam? They do a lot of work getting the paper out."

Sam glared, and the Professor wondered how the woman heard anything over the clacking and clanging of the machine. Sam muttered, "You're right, MM. I couldn't do a thing without you."

"Mr. Mitchell?" The Professor wasn't sure why he had come.

"Call me, Sam. What can I do for you?"

"I majored in history, Ancient Near East mostly, then switched my major to the history of the Americas. But I'm not an archivist or a writer. I don't know what Miss Ruth was thinking."

"I don't know either," Sam mumbled as he shuffled through the papers on his desk and opened and slammed his desk drawers. He went to his filing cabinet. "Here it is." He handed the Professor a thin book. "I imagine you have one of these?"

"Strunk and White, Elements of Style. Yes, I've used that in writing research papers. It really helps with grammar, but these stories are different. I'm out of my depth."

"Pick one," Sam said as he tapped his well-chewed cigar on the edge of his overflowing ashtray.

"Pick what?"

"Pick one of the people on your list and tell me their story." Sam leaned back in his chair, propped his feet on his desk, and closed his eyes.

The Professor stared at the newspaper editor, who looked like he would doze off at any moment.

"You can start anytime, Professor."

Sam opened his eyes twenty minutes later, and his feet slammed to the floor. He threw his now-dead cigar into the wastebasket, noticed the ash on the front of his shirt, and brushed it away. "Do that."

"Excuse me," The Professor licked his dry lips. "Do what?"

"Write the story just the way you told it to me. Pretend you are telling the story to someone, your mother, a girlfriend, or me. Use punctuation to express your tone."

"It doesn't seem very professional." The Professor sighed, and his shoulders slumped.

Sam lit another of his beloved cigars and blew the smoke upward. It drifted toward the Professor, who resigned himself to the headache that was sure to come. He rubbed his forehead and the back of his neck and said, "I do have a friend at the University. She's a great listener."

"Write the story as if you were talking to her. You'll be fine. Come in for a chat anytime, but now I've got to follow up on a story. The news won't wait." He stubbed out his cigar, felt his breast pocket to make sure he had a fresh supply and grabbed his fedora. "You can use the worktable if you need a place, and Margaret Mary will get you whatever you need."

"Will you read my drafts? Give me some pointers."

"Sure, kid." The door banged shut behind him.

"Wait, Mr. Mitchelll. Do you know someone named Haven Ray Turner?"

Margaret Mary shut off the linotype and said, "Wasn't she involved in evacuating the Aleutians during the war? I seem to recall a story in the Anchorage paper some years ago. She worked with the Navy during the planning stages. What a messy business that was. Why do you ask?"

"Mrs. Turner is in the sanatarium on Alice Island. I'm going to see her tomorrow."

The trip to Alice Island didn't take long. The day was dank, dark, and drizzly. "No reason to worry, Professor. No storms on the horizon, and I'll be back in two hours. Be waiting for me at the dock."

"Thanks, Mr. Steiner."

Jake laughed, "You can't sit at the round table and call me Mr."

The Professor sat in an uncomfortable chair in one of the visitor's rooms. Haven Ray carefully kept her distance. "I've been warned to keep my germs to myself."

The Professor smiled, but it didn't reach his eyes. He shifted in his chair and said, "I'm sure I'll be fine."

"I have a letter from Miss Ruth and one from Father Alexi."

"He hasn't written to me."

Haven Ray laughed, "I bet you've been too busy to write to him."

The Professor felt the heat rush into his face. Haven Ray was right. He had not written to the old priest.

"Why don't you send him a copy of your interview and ask if you portrayed him accurately or if there was anything he'd like to add."

"I'll do that, but now I'd like to hear your story, especially the evacuation of the Aleutians and how you ended up with that Jeep."

"The Jeep is mine now, but the story belongs to Heaven."

"Heaven? What do you mean?"

"My daughter, Heaven Ray. You must talk to her, but she and her husband are currently in the Pribilof Islands."

"Can't you tell me her story?"

Haven Ray smiled and shook her head. "Heaven Ray owns her own story."

The Professor saw her weariness and knew his visit had ended. "But you own the Jeep."

"It's yours, Professor. Enjoy it."

TWENTY-NINE

She opened the door on the third knock but didn't speak. He cleared his throat and shuffled his feet. "Uh, your husband told you I was coming?"

The door inched open a little farther. "You're the Professor?"

He laughed and said, "I'm still in grad school, but Mr. Bunderson started calling me that, and now everyone does."

"My husband is not a Mr." She almost smiled.

"It seemed more polite, but he did tell me to call him Ade."

She stepped back and indicated he could set up his equipment on the oak table beneath the window while ignoring his small talk. She bustled about the kitchen making tea, poured the steaming black tea into a glass mug with a metal handle, and set a bowl of sugar cubes beside it.

She smiled slightly when he drank it the Russian way. "You know our customs?"

"Father Alexi taught me when Miss Ruth and I visited him on Kodiak Island."

"Ade didn't tell me you met the Father," Ollyanna said, "How is he—and Miss Ruth? She's been away from Sitka for a while." He noticed the smile reached her eyes this time.

She set a small plate of Russian Tea Cakes on the table. "Father Alexi always ate four."

The Professor ate one in a single bite, licked the powdered sugar from his lips, and said, "I bet I can beat the Father's record."

"The Father just took four," Ollyanna said without smiling.

He reached for another and mumbled, "I'll just match his record then."

He answered her questions about the elderly priest and Miss Ruth until Ollyanna reluctantly allowed him to begin the interview.

"Your husband said you grew up in Ninilchik. What was that like?"

She shrugged. "Like living in any small village, I suppose."

"Please, tell me about it. I need it for background."

She looked out of the window, eyes unfocused. Her fingers clenched and unclenched in her lap.

Following her gaze, he asked, "Swan Lake? You've always lived by the water?"

Swan Lake, with its lily pads and water birds, and the waters surrounding Baranoff Island, filled with dozens of tiny islands, was nothing like the big water of her childhood. She sank into the past.

Ollyanna Oskolkoff climbed the bluff to The Holy Transfiguration of our Lord Chapel overlooking Cook Inlet, a climb she made almost daily. The Russian Orthodox Church had crowned the ridge in 1901, nearly thirty years ago. The elders said the church had existed since 1846, although in another location. Ollyanna thought it couldn't have been more precious than this small white building.

At the hill's crest, the fifteen-year-old, already considered a woman, turned her back to the church and stared across Cook Inlet. Standing tall in the range across the water, Mount Redoubt, its volcanic dome snow-covered and majestic, gazed back at her. Behind her, the church stood as a sentinel over the village below. The water, the mountains, the church. From birth and baptism to death and burial—Ollyanna had always been comforted by Ninilchik's rhythm of life.

Today, a restlessness grabbed her and wouldn't let go. Her thoughts swirled as she reached the crest of the bluff:

Oh, to be a child again, seeing myself sitting in the oomiak with my father and the others, hunting seals or occasionally a whale—learning to fish from the beach with dipnets or traps—picking berries with my mother and grandmother, unmindful of the scratches on my arms or the sticky berry juice dripping down my chin and attracting tiny flying insects—Anna, swiping at the bugs until they turned on her—learning to handle the ulu and seeing the racks of salmon strips drying in the sun—all of it brought great satisfaction. However, I cut my own skin more than the fish's—grinning and eating fish jerky despite my missing front teeth—digging clams, mud crawling up my bare legs, then washing them both in the icy sea, unaware of my messy braids and grimy fingernails—playing chase with other dirty-faced children.

Oh, to be a child again, having no concept of time—living in endless summer under cloudless blue skies—enjoying eternal winter when the sun refused to visit—sitting near the fire and hearing tales of those who came before—walking the footpaths between the tiny houses of little Ninilchik I was unaware time would continue, and childhood would end.

Ollyanna told the Professor how her parents had been lost at sea, but her grandparents and various relatives were buried in the cemetery adjacent to the small church.

She often brought her lunch or a book which she left unread as she wandered among her people. The book, 'Little Women,' had belonged to Anna. Ollyanna often carried it with her, hoping it would ease the pain and anger about her sister leaving home. It never did.

She rambled among the small white picket fences enclosing her family's graves and read the names carved in stone. White wooden crosses in the Russian style pointed to heaven; some graves also had spirit houses sitting atop them.

Father Restov said the spirit houses promoted superstitions and were not holy, but the former priest had allowed it.

"We are true believers," Ollyanna told those in her family's plot. "We love Bozhe, and He tells us what is right."

Unlike other Native villages, Ninilchik had been founded by retired Russian fur traders and their Native wives nearly a hundred years ago. They were accompanied by an Orthodox priest. Russian beliefs and traditions remained strong. She was glad her relatives had only crosses and small fences surrounding their graves. Everyone she loved resided in the village or the graveyard, except her sister Anna, who had left years ago to attend the Sheldon Jackson School in Sitka.

Over six hundred miles across the Gulf of Alaska was too far for Ollyanna to picture. A bustling fishing town of almost a thousand people was also beyond her comprehension. She couldn't imagine her sister in distant Sitka. So far away with so many people.

Why did Anna want more? The government school in Ninilchik taught them all sorts of useless things. English. History. Geography.

Anna had lingered after school nearly every day. She asked the teacher many questions about faraway places and how others lived.

She borrowed every book the teacher had brought to their village. One Christmas, the teacher gifted 'Little Women" to Anna, who read it repeatedly, sometimes out loud, to Ollyanna.

After Anna left, Father Restov told Ollyanna the book was her sister's message to her, that Anna thought the world beyond Ninilchik was worth exploring. Ollyanna did not agree.

Attendance at the little one-room schoolhouse was sporadic due to hunting, fishing, and foraging. Food had to be gathered in summer if they were to eat in winter.

No matter what, Father Restov's children attended school every day, which meant Anna and Ollyanna did as well. Anna soaked up every word, every bit of knowledge. Ollyanna, six years younger than her sister, was not fond of school. More than half the time, she slipped away before lunch to play on the beach or in the woods.

Didn't Anna know she would lose her heritage if she embraced the white world? She would lose her past, her identity, and her sister.

Anna attended Sitka's school to learn "civilized" white ways. *Why, Anna?* Native practices were good enough for Ollyanna. She knew how to hunt the deer and moose deep in the Kenai. Every part was used for food, clothing, blankets, or rugs. Nothing of the animal was wasted. Ducks and geese were harder to kill, but she could do that, too. The same was true regarding fish and other creatures in the sea.

Her favorite duty, picking berries, continued as she grew into young womanhood. She often went alone or with the Restov's younger children. They gathered everything from salmonberries and nagoonberries to red currants and crowberries or the most popular—low-bush cranberries. Stored in a wooden barrel and covered with water, those vibrant cranberries lasted through the winter.

As a young girl with her mother and grandmother, she learned which berries were poisonous but edible once cooked and which were best for sauce or jam. She carried the memory of those long-ago days every time she picked up a berry basket.

THIRTY

Sweet little Ninilchik, isolated and unadorned, hard-working and uncomplicated. When the United States purchased Alaska in 1867 and put it under the control of the US Military, Ninilchik was too small to merit a military presence. There was no deep-water port for the Navy's large ships and no road linking Ninilchik to the outside world.

Left alone, the isolated community preserved its Russian language, culture, and Native traditions well into the twentieth century. As the salmon swam through their life cycle, so did the easy-going people of Ninilchik.

Little Ninilchik, altogether known and loved. Ollyanna had been ignorant of anything across the water or mountains until Anna talked of life beyond the village. On days like today, when she missed her sister so terribly, she wished Anna had been less adventurous.

Ollyanna recognized life in the village could be dangerous; there were many accidents on land and at sea. Father Restov took in any orphan without relatives, even though his wife was constantly with child. Ollyanna lost count after a dozen babies had been born to the priest's wife. She could no longer tell who was orphaned and who was born to the Restovs. All were family. The Oskolkoff sisters had lived with the Restovs for over half their childhoods.

The children slept on the tiny house's loft floor, tumbling together like sled dog puppies. Every morning, before dawn, Ollyanna dressed quietly and crept down the ladder to the lower floor's one room, careful not to awaken the priest and his wife. She stoked the fire in the woodstove, loaded the empty buckets and water baskets onto the wooden wagon, and dragged it to nearby Deep Creek. Pulling the full load back constantly strained her arms and made her sweat. She poured bucket after bucket into the big barrel on the porch. She helped wash and dress the younger children and assigned chores to the others.

The priest's wife, whom Ollyanna called Mother Restov, relied on her to help run the household and care for the children, more so after Anna left.

One morning when she dished up the oatmeal and blueberries, Mother Restov said, "Father wants to see you at the church."

"At the church, why?" Ollyanna wiped another sticky face and tied a bib around the baby.

"He has received a letter and wants to talk to you privately."

Ollyanna clutched her stomach and leaned against the table. She took a deep breath, steadied herself, and said, "Is Anna dead?"

"Drink." Mother Restov held out a dipper full of water. "The Father read it twice, folded it carefully, and put it in his pocket. He said for you to come as soon as you finish your chores."

"Chores?" Ollyanna's ashen face betrayed her emotions. "Of course, chores."

Mother Restov patted the girl's cheek. "Go now. The children and I will do the chores."

Ollyanna gazed across the dark water of Cook Inlet and pictured her younger years:

Oh, to be a child again with Anna sleeping beside me, sharing a pillow. Hand in hand, we walked on the beach and threw rocks into the water. Hers always went farther and skipped more.

We never went the long way to the church but always climbed the bluff. Anna said the road was for old people and babies. We stood for the three-hour services, sometimes holding one another up. Oh, to be a child again, listening to Anna tell stories of our ancestor, Gregorii Oskolkoff, from faraway Kaluga, Russia. He did not come to make a fortune in furs but to tell us of Bozhe and His Great Son. Oh, Anna, why didn't you stay in Ninilchik? Why couldn't you be satisfied with life here? Why did you have to go? And now you are dead! You were all the family I had. Now you're gone, and I have no one. This is all your fault. I hate you! I love you! Oh, Anna!

In her haste to scale the bluff, Ollyanna missed a foothold, slipped, and slid several yards, scraping her limbs. She spat on her hand and wiped her bloody elbows and knees.

When she reached Father Restov's tiny office in the church, her arms and legs were stained with dirty red blotches. Tears left trails down her dusty face.

"Olly, what happened? Are you alright?"

"Just tell me how she died?"

"Who died?"

"That's what you want to tell me."

"No one died."

"It's Anna."

"No, dear child." He pulled a large white handkerchief from a fold in his cassock and handed it to her.

She ignored it and wailed, "I know you don't want to say it out loud, but she's dead! She's dead!" Ollyanna fell to the floor and pounded her fists on the polished plank floor.

Father Restov knelt beside her. "Anna is indeed in trouble, but

250

she is not dead."

Ollyanna hiccuped, took the handkerchief from the Father, and swiped at her scrapes. She calmed herself and said, "Tell me."

⁂

Father Restov folded the letter carefully and pushed it into its envelope. "...and so, you must go to Sitka."

"Leave Ninilchik?"

"I admit it will be difficult, especially for my wife. You are such a help to her, and she loves you like her own."

Ollyanna grabbed onto his words like a lifeline. "You're right. I can't go. Mother Restov needs me." She brushed at her eyes.

Father Restov sputtered, "That is not what I said. We will make do."

"Bad things happened because Anna left. She is cursed." Ollyanna clutched the straight-backed chair's wooden arms and tried to push the fear away. "Bad things will happen to me."

"My dear, Anna is not cursed. Why would you think that?"

"Bozhe is punishing her. You bring her back, Father. Make her do what's right."

The priest paced the room and then sat behind his desk. He pulled several letters from the top drawer. "I have been corresponding with Father Alexi in Sitka. Anna refuses to return. He believes she is ashamed."

"Anna has never written asking for help."

"You know how unreliable and sporadic the mail service is. We don't even have a real post office, just a box in Michael Demidoff's living room."

"You have lots of letters." Ollyanna looked at the priest's cluttered desk.

Father Restov chuckled, "Father Alexi does not rely on the United States Postal Service. His letters travel from church to church, priest to priest, until they make their way to our little village, although they are sometimes delayed for weeks during the winter. But none of that matters. Your duty to your sister remains."

Ollyanna could not argue with the Father but knew she would never leave Ninilchik. "I must return to Mother Restov."

"We will talk again."

Ollyanna nodded but was determined to stay out of the Father's sight. She would make herself so useful that Mother Restov would never let her go.

Ollyanna ignored the bluff and walked the long way back to the village. She kicked at every rock in her way on the unpaved road. Anna could have written any time during the last few years but hadn't. Not even a card at Christmas. Anna didn't want her, didn't need her.

Father Restov stood at the church entrance watching the girl slowly drag herself down the road, shoulders slumped. How could two sisters be so different? Anna, older by half a dozen years, was intelligent, adventurous, and bold, sometimes reckless. Anna talked to anyone about anything. Ollyanna was wise in Native ways but reserved, timid, overly cautious, and almost suspicious of anything new or unknown.

Their physical appearance was also different. Anna was a natural beauty by anyone's standard: tall, slim, and doe-eyed with high cheekbones. He supposed Ollyanna was pleasant looking, with her round face and long braids, although slightly pudgy.

THIRTY-ONE

A sullen and sad Ollyanna stood at the ship's rail as it steamed down the peninsula and passed Afognak Island on the way to Kodiak.

She had seen large ships on their way to and from Anchorage. Occasionally one anchored offshore, and supplies or the sporadic mail deliveries were brought into Ninilchik by a small boat. Boarding the steamship was unnerving to this Native girl who had only been on the sea in kayaks or oomiaks.

Her tiny cabin was pleasant with its comfortable bed and the round window. She had never slept alone but amid all the children's night noises. Who would comfort them when they had nightmares? Who would comfort her?

Father Restov patted her hand. "Do not be afraid. The ship is loud, the belching smoke from the three smokestacks is unpleasant, and the sea choppy, but we are quite safe."

"It is not the water I fear." Her dark eyes were as dull as her voice.

"This is a good thing you are doing, Ollyanna. Love Bozhe and do what's right. Anna does not feel worthy after the choices she has made."

"I don't understand."

Father Restov guided her to a chair in the dining salon and bought two cups of tea and some pastries. He placed a sugar cube between his teeth and sucked the tea through it, then said, "From Father Alexi's letters, we know that Anna was, well...we know she had a child."

Ollyanna shuddered.

"This Miss Ruth person cared for her and the baby. When Anna recovered from childbirth, Miss Ruth asked her to help with cooking and cleaning. I suspect she did that so Anna wouldn't feel like a charity case."

"Then why didn't Anna stay?"

"She was always impulsive." Father Restov sighed and reached for a pastry. "I hoped she would outgrow her recklessness."

Ollyanna looked away from the sweets and picked up the teacup. The warmth from the liquid soothed her. "She constantly looked for more but never said what the more was."

"She met a man who promised to love her, and now she has another child and no man."

Ollyanna shivered. "Another? Maybe love was the more she wanted." The young teenager lifted teary eyes to the priest. "Didn't she know I loved her? Is it my fault she left?"

"Do not blame yourself. Anna simply wanted to go to school."

Ollyanna looked into her teacup and spoke without meeting the Father's eyes. "She's never listened to me, not when fishing or in the woods. Many times we almost didn't make it. She's careless, not at all cautious."

"Convince Anna she doesn't need to settle for any man that comes along," the priest directed.

"I could never convince Anna of anything. I still think it would be better if you went to Sitka, and if she refuses to return home, bring the little ones."

"I can't leave the people of Ninilchik for that long, and legally I cannot force her to return or take her children away."

"Come with me, help me."

"You know I can only go as far as Kodiak. Miss Ruth sent a ticket for your passage from Kodiak to Sitka. I will see you safely aboard, and she will meet you at the other end."

"But Father—"

"There is a worldwide economic crisis, and money is almost non-existent. Steamship tickets across the gulf are expensive." His voice quivered, and Ollyanna knew he hoped she would accept this excuse.

"Money has always been non-existent in Ninilchik. The sea and the forest are our markets—the animals our clothing store," Ollyanna then frowned, "Will I need money in Sitka?"

"Father Alexi says many women, Native and white, work in the fish cannery during the season. You might be able to clean houses for the whites. You and Anna will figure it out. Surely, this Miss Ruth will help."

Ollyanna shuddered. "You said Anna was ashamed. What if she refuses to see me?"

Father Restov looked at the young woman sitting across from him. "When fishing season is over, and her money runs out, Anna has often gone from man to man. I don't want to give you any gruesome details, my dear, but each man is worse than the last. Father Alexi suspects she has been drinking as well. For the children's sake, you must find a way. Always remember to love Bozhe and do what's right."

"I'll go to help the child, er, children." Ollyanna's heart thudded as she pictured Anna's little ones. What kind of life did they have? Their childhood didn't sound anything like hers and Anna's.

Oh, to be a child again, listening to the rain on the roof: Telling stories to the younger children, always with a happy ending, watching the storms over the ocean while snug in the little wooden house with moss chinking between the logs, a cheery fire in the wood stove. Sad that my parents were gone but happy knowing they were in Bozhe's land of endless summer, with His Great Son to watch over them.

I know Bozhe is watching over me, but does He see me, really know me?

"Mrs. Bunderson? Ollyanna?"

"Sorry, I was miles away." Ollyanna stood, holding the teapot. "I often get lost in my thoughts."

"Thoughts about the past?"

She nodded.

"Can you share them?"

She poured more tea.

The steamship arrived in Kodiak all too soon. Before they disembarked, Father Restov spoke to her in a quiet voice. "Dear Ollyanna, you have known everyone in little Ninilchik your whole life. Everyone in the village lived with the same values."

"Some people in Ninilchik—the white people, were not good." Ollyanna refused to meet his eyes.

"Look at me, child. Just like with the Creole, the Yupik, and the Russians, some people are good, and some are not. But in our own village, we know who is who, eh? It will not be so in Sitka. You will meet all kinds."

"You mean bad people?"

Father Restov patted her shoulder, "I don't want to cause you any distress, just be careful and reserve your trust for those who earn it."

Ollyanna shoved her hands in her pockets and looked at the passengers disembarking the ship. Most were white and from the big city of Anchorage. She had not spoken to them during the voyage. What kind of people were they? How could she tell? The dockworkers offloading the cargo spoke roughly, swearing at one another and then laughing. Were they trustworthy?

Father Restov said he didn't want her to be distressed, but the clenched fists in her pockets and the sweat on her upper lip told her she was full of fear.

She silently followed the Father to the home of Kodiak's priest. They stayed overnight with him and his wife. They were childless and begged Ollyanna for story after story of Ninilchik's children and how they foraged for their livelihood and played games on the beach. All the silly adventures of the village seemed to thrill and entertain them.

The reason for Ollyanna's journey to Sitka was not mentioned. But the looks exchanged between the Kodiak couple and Father Restov assured her they knew. Ollyanna gave no indication that she was aware of their knowledge.

As the hour grew late, she could not hide her yawns and was soon shown to her room, but she could not sleep. As she reviewed her life in quiet little Ninilchik, her anger against Anna stirred. She punched the pillow and wished she were returning home instead of sailing southeast to Sitka. She imagined Anna's children, the little ones who needed their Auntie Olly. She determined to do her best for them. She loved them already. As Ollyanna prayed for sleep to come quickly, she wondered if love could overcome fear.

❧

"We're at the point of no return, Miss." The burly seaman spoke to Ollyanna, who had been standing at the ship's rail for hours.

"What?"

"It's the halfway point, Miss. It's the same distance to the harbor we seek as the harbor we left. If we run into trouble, we will continue on."

"Will we run into trouble?" She shuddered, wrapped her arms around herself, and remembered her parents, who had been lost at sea.

"Aye, I think we will. The waves are still, but the air is silent and too warm. Look up." He pointed to the clouds scudding across the sky. "When the clouds have gathered together, the rains will come, and the waves will rise. You are from Cook Inlet. You know these things."

"My people are water people, and many have been lost in such storms. I have never been on the open water in a severe storm." She shuddered again and continued to hug herself.

The crewman looked at the massive steamship. "I bet you've never been on a ship this big. Return to your cabin now. This lull will be over soon, the sky will erupt, and the sea will explode. But do not worry. The ship is seaworthy, and the captain is capable. It will be a rough ride, but we'll make it."

Ollyanna did not return to her cabin but gathered with a few other hardy passengers in the ship's main salon. They stood near the windows, watching the weather with apprehension, hanging on to whatever they could to brace themselves from the shifting pitch and roll of the vessel.

Soon the swells rose, and although it was mid-afternoon, the sky turned as black as the sea. The cook staggered in with boxed lunches of egg sandwiches, Cornish meat pies, and cookies. He also provided coffee and tea in thermoses and juice in Mason jars. He secured them in a closed cupboard.

"I suggest you not eat unless your stomachs are steady. I'm going to lash myself into my bunk. I suggest you go to your cabins and do the same."

Most passengers felt queasy, ignored the boxed lunches, and went to their cabins, stumbling and lurching along the way. They were as eager to escape the smell of the egg salad as they were the storm.

Holding onto two boxed lunches and the Mason jar as the ship rolled was difficult. Halfway to her cabin, Ollyanna dropped the jar, which shattered, and the juice rolled with the ship as the shards scattered across the ship's narrow hallway.

The turbulent storm lasted a day and a night. Many passengers did not return topside until they reached port. The steamship had been driven slightly off course, delaying its arrival in Sitka by several hours.

The ship slowed as it chugged past the tip of Japonski Island and slipped into its berth. Once again, Ollyanna stood at the rail. She saw a tall white woman dressed in black and a Russian Orthodox priest clad in the same dark color. They must be her welcoming committee, although if she could find a way to avoid them, she would.

They were calm and polite as they led her to the Russian Bishop's house. Over tea, Miss Ruth reached for Ollyanna's hand.

"There are some difficult things I need to share with you, my dear."

Ollyanna pulled her hand away. She bowed her head and waited.

Miss Ruth took a deep breath and looked toward Father Alexi. He nodded, refilled their teacups, then sat back and fiddled with his prayer book.

"Your sister is not in Sitka."

The color drained from Ollyanna's brown face, and she looked as pale as a seagull. "I want to go home."

"We think we know where she is, and plans are underway to rescue her."

"Please let me go home—what? Rescue?"

Miss Ruth knelt before the girl and took her hands. "Ollyanna, can you hear me? Listen. A friend of mine saw a Native woman with three children hustled aboard a small boat leaving Sitka."

Ollyanna shook her head and whispered, "Anna only has two babies."

The priest and the older woman exchanged a look. Ollyanna shuddered. "Three? It can't be her—can it?"

"She looked fearful—as if she didn't want to be there. Unobserved, my friend Ade Bunderson followed the boat nearly eighty miles down the coast, almost to Port Alexander. He saw the skipper slip into Secret Cove, where several other fishing vessels were anchored. Ade knew this secluded cove was a hideout used to offload illegally caught fish."

"But what has that to do with Anna?"

"Perhaps they needed a cook and someone to do their laundry," Father Alexi spoke softly.

There was another look between the two adults, and Ollyanna

knew those fishermen wanted Anna for other things. "Poor Anna, she is so stupid!" Ollyanna hid her face in her hands and wailed.

She remembered Father Restov's warnings about dangerous people and not being too quick to trust.

"Do you mind if I use the word nefarious," the Professor asked.

Ollyanna jerked as she was brought back to the present by his question. "What does that word—nefarious—mean?"

The Professor squirmed in his chair. "Well, er, it means dangerous."

She gave him a look he didn't wish to interpret and said, "Use whatever word you want, Professor. It is difficult to speak of the past, and when you stop me, I do not want to begin again."

The Professor nodded and left the word dangerous in his notes. Ollyanna focused on the conversation at the Russian Bishop's house so many years ago, and her story unfolded in her mind like a movie playing in Budnikov's theater.

Oh, to be a child again... Oh, to be a child again...

Ollyanna's thoughts were interrupted by the memory of Miss Ruth's voice. "My friend Ade, the police chief, Stormy Durand, and several men from town are on their way to Secret Cove. They will find Anna and bring her home."

"Our home is in Ninilchik."

"They will bring her back to Sitka."

"And then what?"

"Then you and Anna and I will have a meeting. I have a plan. But for now, you are coming home with me. A hot bath and a good meal are what you need."

"What is a hot bath?"

When Miss Ruth explained, Ollyanna said, "I have always

bathed in Deep Creek. I do not know if I will like this hot bath."

"Trust me, my dear, you will."

Ollyanna clutched her small deerskin pack and followed Miss Ruth from the Russian Bishop's House to the woman's cabin on Indian River. She tried not to stare at all the people. She had never seen an automobile, a horse, or a bicycle.

In Ninilchik, there were only footpaths and trails between the dwellings, which now looked like mere shacks compared to what she saw in Sitka. There were long wooden platforms from the edge of the road to the door of the houses. Miss Ruth called them sidewalks. Large poles were spaced along the edge of the streets, with ropes stretched from pole to pole along the top. Miss Ruth said it was not rope but wire, and it brought light to the houses. What kind of world had she come to?

Ollyanna's head hurt. Everyone knew the sun brought light by day, and the moon and stars shone at night, although they burned seal oil for light in the dark winter months. Her steps slowed, and her heartbeats increased.

Light was not supposed to come from poles looped together with what looked like a rope made from sea lion intestines. People should not walk on wooden boards but on dusty footpaths in dry weather and muddy trails when it rains. Noisy black monsters jerked and jostled along, spewing smoke and honking like the geese she hunted in the Kenai. Ollyanna jumped out of the way and clung to Miss Ruth.

"You will get used to all this noise and nonsense, my dear."

Ollyanna trudged behind Miss Ruth, hearing her voice, but the thoughts swirling through her mind crowded out the flow of talk from the older woman.

Finally, Miss Ruth stopped before a small cabin. "I know this has been difficult, and everything is new and strange. I felt the same way the first time I visited a Yupik village. So, a bath, food, and a bed will clear your mind and allow you to absorb everything you've seen and heard."

⁂

"The weather is shifting. We need to get this done as soon as possible." Ade gripped the steering wheel of the boat until his hands ached. He held her steady in the choppy water and dropped anchor outside Secret Cove.

"The barometer dropped this morning; we knew it was going to be a harrowing ride," Jake Steiner spat tobacco juice over the side.

"Steady, Bull." Stormy Durand grabbed the mastiff's collar as Ade's small trawler rolled in the swells. The lawman lifted his bullhorn and addressed the two boats approaching. "Bring us the woman and her children, and we will let you go about your business," Stormy yelled.

The surly captain of the faster of the two boats threw his cigar in the water, "And if we refuse?"

The police chief of Sitka smiled, "Name's Stormy Durand."

One of the crewmen spoke to his captain, "I know him. He's an easy-going cuss unless you cross him."

"He's a sly one, always has a plan," another said.

"That so? He don't look so smart to me," the captain sneered.

Bull growled, and Stormy chuckled, "Ade, here—" Stormy gestured toward Ade, who held the microphone of his newly installed radio high above his head "—has a Revenue Cutter on the radio.

It's just a few miles away. We can tell them we suspect illegal fishing here or direct them to Crawfish Inlet, Yamani Cove, or even up north to Icy Strait."

"How do we know you won't squeal anyway?" The captain lit another cigar.

"Well, now," Stormy tilted his hat back and drawled into the bullhorn, "That would involve a lot of paperwork for me, and I'm averse to that."

"C'mon, Capt, that woman and her brats ain't worth it."

"She ain't that good a cook anyway," another complained.

"Ain't her cooking I'm interested in," the captain slurred and pulled a flask from his hip pocket.

When negotiations between Sitka's lawman and the captain of the illegal fisherman had begun, the smaller of the illegal boaters had backed into Secret Cove. It now returned with Anna and her children. "We got 'em, sir," The seaman addressed his words to Stormy and lashed his boat to Ade's trawler.

"You can take the brats; I'll keep the woman," the captain roared.

Anna huddled in the back of the boat, arms wrapped around her frightened children, screamed and spoke rapidly in a mixture of Russian, English, and Alituig.

Stormy laughed and yelled through his bullhorn, "I suggest you relocate your business to another hidden cove."

Stormy and Jake helped them aboard, then Ade gunned the engine and headed north, pushing his vessel to its limit. The clouds unloaded, and the trip up the coast was unpleasant as they tried and failed to outrun the storm. Anna tended to her seasick children, who clutched their upset stomachs and retched.

Three days had passed since Anna and her children were delivered to Miss Ruth's cabin—dirty, wet, and hungry. Miss Ruth took charge of their physical needs first. The emotional and spiritual healing would be long in coming.

Ollyanna hurried to answer Miss Ruth's summons. She instantly fell in love with her nephew and nieces, squatting on the floor and playing with them. The youngest, Elizaveta, was barely walking. Anna huddled in a corner and did not speak or meet anyone's eyes.

Ollyanna didn't know how to approach her sister, so she did nothing. Miss Ruth watched and prayed and hoped a solution would present itself. A week passed, and then two, and there was no progress between the sisters.

"I don't know what to say to her," Ollyanna whispered to Miss Ruth.

"She feels great shame, and I assume she thinks you are also ashamed of her."

Ollyanna bit her lip and looked toward the corner where Anna huddled. Elizaveta had crawled into her mother's lap and fallen asleep. Anna idly stroked the toddler's hair. Henry and Firy played outside the open cabin door. "I love her children, but Anna should have stayed in Ninilchik."

"You blame her for seeking an education, a better life?"

"This is not better. Bozhe has cursed her."

"That is a vile thing to say." Miss Ruth shook the girl's shoulders. "I will hear no more of such talk."

Tears slipped from Ollyanna's eyes, and Miss Ruth enveloped her in a fierce hug. "I'm sorry. I shouldn't have attacked you like that. Bozhe loves your sister as He loves you. His heart is breaking over the things she has suffered and the choices she has made."

Ollyanna pressed her face into Miss Ruth's shoulder and sobbed. "I can't bear to imagine what she's gone through."

Miss Ruth patted the girl's back. "Do you know how unworthy she thinks she is?"

"I love my sister, but I hate her for leaving me."

"Bozhe has much to do in both of your lives, and I wish I could be here to help you."

"What? Where are you going?"

"I'll be in Haines for several weeks. Father Alexi will come by as often as possible to check on both of you, and so will my fisherman friend, Ade Bunderson."

"The white man who rescued Anna?"

"Do not be wary of him. He is all that is good in the whites and none that is evil."

Ollyanna bit her lower lip. If she was lucky, this fisherman would be too busy to stop by. "I can cook and care for the children, but I don't know what to do about Anna. She sits in the corner, barely eats, and will not speak."

"It will be difficult, Ollyanna, but I trust you. I'm sure you will do the right thing. Ade will visit the grocer and bring you what you need, and I will settle with him when I return, so don't worry about food."

"Everything I need is in your garden or the nearby forest. Tell the white man he doesn't need to come."

Miss Ruth patted her cheek. "I know I will find all is well when I return."

The weeks passed slowly for Ollyanna, and all had not gone well. On the day Miss Ruth was due to return, Ollyanna glanced toward the cabin door repeatedly. Before Miss Ruth opened the gate and stepped onto the wooden sidewalk, Ollyanna burst through the door and flung herself into the older woman's arms. "Gone! They're gone!"

Miss Ruth dropped her valise and held the distraught girl as the story tumbled out. She led Ollyanna into the cabin and made tea. As the soothing liquid did its job, Ollyanna calmed down, and Miss Ruth said, "Tell me again from the beginning."

"Ade Bunderson came every day and usually brought a fish or clams, sometimes sea celery or halibut cheeks; usually the whites throw that part away. So stupid. Strange food from the grocer until I told him to stop. He brought something called a French cruller from the Sitka Café. So tasty. One day, the silly man even brought flowers."

Miss Ruth glanced at the wilted Sitka Rose and Forget-Me-Nots in the Mason jar on the corner windowsill. "Hmmm, not bad for a white man."

"I have forgotten that he is white. Isn't that strange, Miss Ruth?" Ollyanna smiled, and a faint tinge of pink stained her cheeks.

"Why do you think he brought those particular flowers?" Miss Ruth refilled the teacups.

"What do you mean?"

"The Sitka Rose is the marriage of a flower from Sitka and one from across the waters—Japan, I think. The blue ones are called Forget-Me-Nots. I believe Ade is sending you a message through the flowers."

Ollyanna's teacup clattered against the saucer, and she closed her eyes. Miss Ruth saw the girl's embarrassment and bewilderment and said, "But about your sister?"

Ollyanna's eyes filled, "Father Alexi came every day. He prayed with us and told us we must love Bozhe and do what's right. Anna never looked up, but I could tell she listened. She always looked toward the door when the Father was due to arrive. She even began to eat a little more and talk. Not about anything important. Just the weather and such."

"Very good, but what happened to drive her away?"

"It's all my fault. I should have never come here."

"Nonsense! I'm sure whatever you did, it was with the best intentions."

Ollyanna shrugged. She wasn't sure her motivations were pure. "Little Elizaveta started to call me Mama. I confess I didn't stop her. She didn't know better, but Anna raged and slapped her across the face."

"I snatched Elizaveta and yelled at Anna, told her she was a horrible mother, and the children would be better off with me. I told her how stupid she was to shack up with those men who were no better than wolves." Ollyanna left and sat on the cabin's front porch.

Miss Ruth bit her lip and put the kettle on again. After a few moments, she stood in the doorway and whispered, "Olly, tell me the rest."

Ollyanna shuddered, took a deep breath, and continued. "Anna shrank back into the corner. She didn't say anything or lift her eyes for the rest of the day. The children were quiet as well. I bathed them, read a story, and put them to bed early. When I got up the following morning, they were gone."

"We will find her again."

Ollyanna shook her head and sighed, "When Father Alexi saw that Anna was gone, he said perhaps we need to let her come to the end of herself, that she must come back on her own."

Miss Ruth stirred a little honey into her tea. "The Father is wise. It may do more harm than good if we keep rescuing her."

"I will never forgive myself."

"Yes, you will. The Lord is sovereign even over this. He knows where she is, and we will pray for her."

Elbows on the table, chin in her hands, Ollyanna stared into her tea cup. "I should go home."

Miss Ruth put her arm around the girls' shoulders. "That is exactly what you should not do. When Anna comes to her senses, she will need you more than ever."

Ollyanna sniffed and accepted the handkerchief from Miss Ruth, who said, "Now, let's get organized." She picked up the jar of dead flowers.

"Please don't throw them away." Ollyanna turned away and mumbled, "It's just that no one has given me flowers before."

"No one or a special someone?"

"Both." Ollyanna took the wilted flowers, wrapped them in an old scarf, and put them under her pillow. "I don't know what to do."

"I'd be grateful for your company for the next few weeks, then I'm off to Skagway. You can care for my garden while I'm gone."

Ollyanna cleaned houses for two white schoolteachers and the bachelor police chief, Stormy Durand. Even as she cleaned, she continually asked Bozhe to care for Anna and the children.

Ade Bunderson continued his daily visits to the cabin, bringing food and flowers. Miss Ruth ignored Ollyanna's pink cheeks and nervous laughter and winked at Ade as she bustled about the place.

After Miss Ruth left for Skagway, Ade continued his visits but would not enter the cabin since Ollyanna was alone. They sat on the porch, or he knelt in the dirt and helped her weed the garden. One day he stammered, "I, I have news. It took a while, but I found out Anna worked at the fish cannery during the season and stayed with the Bravebird family. They are good people, Ollyanna. The grandmother took care of the kids."

"Take me to her."

"She's not there anymore. She's with a man named John," Ade swore and mumbled, "not a very nice man."

"What can we do?"

"I kept my eye on the place, barged in, and talked to her when I saw John passed out on the porch." He raised sad eyes to Ollyanna. "She refused to leave, said she wouldn't take charity."

Ollyanna wrung her hands and then banged her fist on the doorpost. "She is too proud, always thinking she can do everything herself."

"I pleaded with her. She said as long as John left the children alone, she could handle him. I'm sorry, Ollyanna, I didn't know what else to do." Ade's face was ashen.

"Show me where this awful person's house is."

"It's better if I don't."

"Show me."

"I will show you when Miss Ruth returns."

Ollyanna glared at him and bit her lip, but Ade would not change his mind.

❦

The Professor had drunk more tea than he wanted and excused himself to use the bathroom. When he returned, Ollyanna apologized. "I'm sorry, Professor. You wanted to know why I came to Sitka, and I have dragged you into my family's problems. Please don't put any of that into your report."

"It's your family story, nothing to be ashamed of."

"I've spent much time with Miss Ruth and Father Alexi. I've visited other churches in town. They all spoke about compassion and forgiveness. I learned much."

He nodded and said, "Tell me about that."

She leaned forward and said, "I try to honor everyone with honesty and mercy." She laughed, grinned, and lifted her teacup, "Everyone except Ade. I like to give him a little trouble now and then."

The Professor dropped his pencil. Was this very reserved Yupik from Ninilchik teasing him? Her eyes sparkled, and her cheeks dimpled. Yes, he thought she was. He laughed, turned the tape recorder on, and said, "What happened to Anna?"

"I'll not tell you anymore except she left that horrible John person, and Bill Wall found her on the beach."

"Ade told me some about Bill, interesting fellow."

"Mmmm." Ollyanna's eyes were glazed. She put her chin in her hand and rested her elbow on the table.

"I'll turn off my tape recorder and put my pencil in my pocket if you continue. Please. My curiosity is giving me a headache."

Ollyanna gave him a sideways glance and, with a *pfft*, continued, "Anna and the kids were huddled between several massive driftwood logs when Bill found her. She was fearful of him but even more afraid of John, who was coming down the beach, threatening what he would do when he got his hands on her and the kids." Ollyanna shuddered at the memory. "All I know is Bill took care of that awful man. I don't know what he did, and I don't want to. Bill wanted to take Anna to his house, feed the kids, and let them get warm, but she insisted he take her to Indiantown. The fishing season was coming, and she could earn her keep."

"And then what?"

"Then I nearly ruined her life. I don't want to talk about it." She stood and put her apron on. Then untied it, hung it on the back of the chair, and sat down again.

The Professor did not speak. He merely softened his face and looked at her as Ollyanna picked up her teacup and put it in the sink. She laid the cookie jar's lid on the counter and held the jar out to him. He shook his head. She sighed and sat down, hugging the ceramic jar.

"Much like Ade visiting me at Miss Ruth's cabin every day, Bill frequently showed up in Indiantown. He became friends with Petrov Bravebird. Soon Anna looked forward to his visits." Ollyanna shrugged her shoulders and gave the Professor an intense stare. "Bill is a reserved man, sparse with his words. But somehow, his quiet acceptance and kindness toward Anna helped heal her. But I didn't know that. I thought Anna was ready to shack up with another scoundrel."

"I can't imagine Bill Wall as a scoundrel."

Tears came to Ollyanna's eyes. "I shouldn't have done it."

"Done what?" The Professor kept his voice as gentle as possible.

"I often visited the children while Anna was working. I told them not to tell, but of course, they did. Anna never said anything to the Bravebirds, so they allowed me to come whenever I wanted. When I learned about Bill—that he was interested in Anna, I took

272

the kids and didn't bring them back. Anna came running to Miss Ruth's cabin, and we argued. I was fierce and shouted at her. In three languages." She almost laughed but then choked on her tea. "Anna insisted Bill was not like the others, and he wanted to marry her."

"I told her rather forcefully how I felt about that." Ollyanna leaned closer and whispered, "Even as we argued, I could tell Anna was more like her old self. She was fearful and upset because I took her children, but she was not angry in a hateful way. Still, I was not convinced Bill Wall was a worthy man."

The Professor reached out to pat her hand, then drew it back."When I interviewed Ade, he had nothing but good things to say about him."

"Ade was furious that I distrusted Bill. He avoided me for a week. He told me he wouldn't see me until I agreed to go with him to Bill's house."

"Did you go?"

"My husband is a stubborn man, Professor—more stubborn than me, it turns out. The yard was tidy, unlike some others on Biorka Street, and the house was clean. Bill didn't say much; he just showed me the room he had prepared for the kids. Pink bedspreads and curtains. And he had built a bed for Henry. It was beautifully crafted."

"So, pink curtains convinced you this man was good enough for your sister?" The Professor's left eyebrow disappeared under a lock of hair that had fallen forward.

"Bill's dog, Popeye, was devoted to him." Ollyanna grinned. "The dog was a mutt and not nearly as smart as sled dogs, but I could tell he trusted his master and was devoted to him."

The Professor chuckled, shook his head, and wished he had left his tape recorder running.

"Even though Bill was not religious, I think Bozhe used him to break through Anna's shame." Ollyanna stared at the icon on the Beautiful Corner.

The Professor followed her gaze, shifted in his chair, and rubbed his jaw. "Yes, er, what about you and Ade? How did you, er, fall in love?"

Ollyanna laughed, "That is none of your business."

"But it's part of your story."

"I can't believe the Alaska State Legislature needs to know our love story, although it is a good one. That's where your interviews are going to be filed, right?"

"I'm curious."

"You seem to have a lot of curiosity. Never mind."

"I'll ask Ade," the Professor laughed. "I'll tell him he can regale me with several fish stories if he tells me how you fell in love."

"But we didn't. At least, I didn't." Ollyanna looked directly at him, almost daring him to question her further.

"You didn't love him, but you married him?"

"I fell in love with Anna's children and wanted my own."

"So you married a man you didn't love in order to have children? I find that hard to believe."

"Not so hard. Natives marry to strengthen the clan, the family. Ade Bunderson rescued my sister. He went out of his way to help her more than once. He was a good and loyal friend to Bill Wall. He brought me flowers. I liked that."

"But still, Mrs. Bunderson, er, Ollyanna—"

"Anna's children called him Uncle, and Popeye adored him."

The Professor scratched his chin. "The dog again? I give up."

Ollyanna laughed, "Don't worry, Professor. It wasn't too long after our wedding that I knew I loved that man. It's worth several of Ade's fish stories, so you must ask him," Ollyanna laughed again.

The Professor groaned and asked, "Can I have more tea cakes?"

"Before you make this interview official, will you show it to Miss Ruth? She will know what parts are not necessary to share. I may have been too free with Anna's story; may she rest in peace."

The Professor nodded. "You came to Sitka against your will. Why didn't you return to Ninilchik once you were reconciled to Anna or after you married? Was it Ade? Did he refuse to go?"

Ollyanna took a deep breath, closed her eyes, and folded her hands in her lap.

Oh, to be a child again when our parents were still alive. Summer bonfires on the beach with large pots of steaming clams, not caring that the acrid woodsmoke enveloped our hair and stung our eyes.

Oh, to be a child again...

Ollyanna shook her head and told herself she was not a child. She could cherish her sweet memories, but life was to be lived here and now.

"It's true, Professor; I never wanted to leave Ninilchik. Never planned to settle in Sitka. But Bozhe had other ideas. He gave me a safe and secure childhood in the tiny village of my ancestors. His purpose for me was to reestablish my relationship with my sister, love Bozhe, and do what's right here in Sitka. He brought the man I was destined to marry to this place. Ninilchik was my firm foundation, my past. Sitka is my present and my future."

The Professor walked down Lake Street toward town. The cross on the spire of St. Michael's glistened in the sun. Behind him, frogs sat on the lake's lilypads and croaked in Sitka's ubiquitous drizzle. He saw Ade Bunderson walking toward him with a salmon on a line.

"Where's the Jeep?"

"Getting its oil changed."

"When's the book coming out. I always fancied myself in a book. Even thought about writing one."

"It's not a book, Ade. It's going to be read into the State record."

"Statehood, bah. You'd reach more people if it was a book."

"That's quite an idea. I was thinking I could use some of what I learned for my thesis, for my master's."

Ade scratched his head and regretted he hadn't gone to high school. "Write a book, Professor."

"That all you catch?"

Ade laughed and tried to sound gruff, "Shut your mouth, boy. The rest are at the cannery. This is my—rather—your supper." He slung the fish over the Professor's shoulder.

The slimy fish rubbed against the Professor's jacket, and he grimaced.

"I could see you had your hands full with all your writing materials," Ade chuckled.

The fishy smell worked its way into the Professor's nostrils, and he turned his head. "How about you and Ollyanna come for dinner?"

"In that case, I'll take the salmon back, and you come to our house." Ade clapped him on the back. "I can hardly wait to ask Ollie what she told you."

"Your wife is quite the woman. Fascinating."

Ade's grin was as big as the salmon. He rocked back on his heels and laughed aloud. "The next time you come to the Café, sit with me."

"You mean?"

"Yeah, the round table."

The Professor watched Ade amble home, marveling as he remembered Ade's story. Maybe someday he would help this rugged Alaskan tell his fish tales. He continued on his way, a little bit taller, a little bit prouder. He had been accepted by those who settled in Sitka.

The drizzle became a biting rain as he dashed into the filling station. He looked forward to seeing that salmon on a dinner plate.

EPILOGUE
Fairbanks, Alaska 1962

She met him on the tarmac. He went into her arms quickly and lay his head on her shoulder. She smelled of wild honey and cloudberries. She must have been making jam. The sun was hot as it often was in the interior in the summer months.

"Was it a bad flight?" she asked.

He shook his head and nestled closer. A muffled sob escaped, and his shoulders shook.

"It's alright," she said, rubbing his back, "she had a long, adventurous life and knew where she was going."

"Oh, Mary, I thought she'd live forever." He slapped the back of his neck. "Darn bugs," he muttered.

She led him out of the airport and chattered about unimportant things to give him a chance to regain his composure. He would tell her everything when he was ready.

"Where's our girl?"

"At my sister's. You know she loves to babysit. Now that little Cindy is walking, I can't have her underfoot while making jam. We'll pick her up on the way home."

Once they arrived, she prepared dinner, and their young daughter took over the chattering. Later, Cindy begged for an extra story when he tucked the little girl into bed. He came into the kitchen, still drained, and sat at the table.

"Did Cindy notice how sad you were?" his wife asked as she finished drying the dishes.

"I managed to fake a bit of cheerfulness and even do the voices for the stories."

"You didn't eat much, hungry?" She wiped her hands on the damp dish towel and poured him a cup of tea. "Are you ready to talk?"

"The mosquitoes are bad this year. Those few minutes on the tarmac were enough for them to dive bomb and attack." He scratched his arms and the back of his neck.

"It's summer in Fairbanks. The bugs are no worse than usual, though a few folks have said they look bigger." She set a bottle of calamine lotion and a few cotton balls beside him. "But that's not what you want to talk about."

He sipped the tea and grimaced, "Coffee would be better if it's not too much trouble."

She filled the percolator, measured the grounds, then said, "Talk."

He shook the bottle and then set it down, unopened. "I thought she would live forever. Everybody did."

"Honey, she was in her nineties."

"She didn't seem that old."

"Do you remember how she flew into town for our wedding, barely making it to the ceremony in time? I was surprised she came. She didn't know me, and you had just worked on that project for her," Mary said.

"Those few years working with her changed me. I've never known anyone like her." He took a deep breath and said, "They told me Robert's plane went down suddenly, but he's okay. I wonder what Miss Ruth's last thoughts were?" He shuddered, remembering his near panic on each of today's flights. Even now, his heart raced. He grabbed the table's edge, slowed his breathing, and calmed himself. He did not want to alarm his wife.

"She looked weary at our wedding. When I mentioned it, she patted my arm and told me not to worry; she would soon leave the land of the dying for the land of the living."

"Our wedding? That was several years ago." He reached for a biscuit and the jar of cloudberry jam. "She always looked the same to me. What did she mean?"

"We were interrupted and never finished our conversation. I'd forgotten about it until just now."

"Do you think she meant earth and heaven?"

"Honestly, I thought she meant she was going to the lower forty-eight. You know how dead everything is around here in winter. But now, I think you're right." She picked up the bottle of anti-inch lotion.

"It was a long service, and afterward, there was an even longer gathering at the Sitka Café. So many people told stories about Miss Ruth. Most I had never heard before. I swear I could write another book."

"Why don't you?" She dabbed lotion on his swollen welts.

He laughed and splashed a bit of milk into his coffee. "No, thank you! Writing is not for me. Besides, that book is really yours. You took my interviews and put them into story form."

"You did all the work. I just arranged it."

"We're a good team." He kissed her hand. "I think Sam Mitchell, the editor of Sitka's newspaper, might be the man to write about Miss Ruth's life. He kept scribbling in his notebook, asking people to repeat things. Finally, Agrefena took his pencil and told him this was a time to honor Miss Ruth."

"Miss Ruth thought you were a good writer. Isn't that why she chose you for the project?"

The Professor, transfixed by the milky swirls, stared into his cup. He raised his head and looked into his wife's eyes. After a long moment, he sipped the hot drink and said, "I don't think that's why. She saw a lack in me and decided to fix it."

"I don't understand, dear. Nothing is lacking in you. Why would she do such a thing?"

"My history professor sent me for the interview. Maybe he saw the lack, or they conspired together. I'm a bit unclear about the details. Miss Ruth never mentioned anything negative. She just pushed me into her project."

"I'm so glad you flew down to Sitka for the funeral." She clasped his hand across the table. "And back the same day, I'm so proud of you."

He felt the heat crawl up his neck. His wife was one of the few who knew he hated flying, how an unreasonable fear grabbed him as soon as the propellers groaned and revved up. It made him feel less than manly. "If it were anyone other than Miss Ruth, I would not have gone, but it wasn't a rough flight. The weather was good. But my imagination attacked me several times. I imagined Miss Ruth and Robert as their plane went down and wondered if my plane would do the same."

"You mustn't think such things, dear one. You must trust the pilot and the plane." To distract him, she pulled his book from the shelf and handed it to him. He brushed his fingers over the title.

"I'm glad I didn't use my name, but I wish you would have let me put yours on the cover; you did all the editing and rewriting to make it what it is."

She turned to the dedication page and said, "Read it."

He sighed, swallowed, and read:

For Miss Ruth

You touched many lives
in Sitka, the Southeast, and beyond,
by simply being who you were.
People felt charmed, amazed, and sometimes harassed,
in a loving way, of course.
You altered the course of my life,
and I will be forever grateful.

He closed the book and laid his hand on the cover. "I don't know what I am feeling."

"She was like a grandmother to you." She stood behind him and rubbed his shoulders.

"More than that, I think." He gulped his now lukewarm coffee. "But I have something we need to think about. It doesn't make sense, and I'm unsure what to do." He held out his cup.

She poured more coffee and made egg salad sandwiches. He often took a while to get to the main topic of discussion, and his dithering always increased his appetite. And hers.

"Sitka is a beautiful little town. I met many people when I worked on Miss Ruth's project."

"Hmmm. It rains a lot there. I don't like the rain." She set the plate of sandwiches on the table and took one.

"The rain makes everything green and lush. It snows, but there are no blizzards, not like here."

"But still—rain."

"Mr. Armstrong, Sheldon Jackson's President, wants me to come and teach."

"That's a Native School, not a college, and you're a college professor."

"Assistant professor. Anyway, they recently added a Junior College with thirty-seven students. I would be a full professor."

"That was always your goal, but thirty-seven students? And a move to Sitka, away from my sister? I don't know."

"It's more complicated than that. The Junior College is not yet accredited."

"Not accredited? How will that affect your career? Our future? I have so many questions." She patted his arm. "It's been a long day; we're both tired. Let's think about it tomorrow."

"I don't think I can sleep until I figure this out—until we figure it out."

She yawned, stretched, and said, "I don't have any words of advice for you, but I know you will do what's right."

"Miss Ruth said many who settled in Sitka felt they had found a place and a person."

She kissed the top of his head. "Miss Ruth won't be there, dear."

"I know, but something is drawing me."

"Or someone. What did Miss Ruth always say—Love Bozhe and do what's right,"

He smiled at her, "I don't know."

"You will. I'm going to bed." She stifled a yawn and kissed the top of his head again.

He watched her leave. His Mary—her serenity anchored him. Flipping through the pages, he sat quietly through the night, remembering all the people he had met because of Miss Ruth, all the hours he had listened to their stories, how he had come to care for each of them, how it changed his view of history and of himself.

He chuckled as he put his cup and saucer in the sink. He suspected Miss Ruth knew how this project would affect him. As he turned off the lights and climbed the stairs, he regretted she always refused to be interviewed.

MY MAMA'S MAMA: BOOK 5

HEAVEN'S RAY

CHAPTER 1
Kodiak Island
Territory of Alaska

"Who was that?" Ensign Mark Lawson IV slapped a stack of reports on the battered metal desk, but his eyes were on the pretty woman who breezed past him without a glance. He wasn't used to it. Women always gave him a second look and usually a third. Older women, young women. Pretty ones and those not-so-pretty. It didn't matter. They all looked. What was wrong with this one?

"She's not for you."

"What's her name?"

The short, thin, and non-descript clerk arranged Commander Lawson's schedule and organized the multiple copies of the paperwork the Navy seemed to favor. Nothing happened on the base that he couldn't sort out and control. Nothing except the Commander's son. "Let it go, Ensign."

Mark Lawson sat on the edge of the large metal desk. "Come on, Elly, what's her name?"

"In case you have forgotten my name—it's Elwood A. Richardson, Yeoman 1st Class, United States Navy. I'll thank you to remember that."

"You've known me since I was three. I'm harmless. Tell me her name."

"You are not harmless, and this girl is different." The Yeoman tapped the Bible on the edge of his desk. "You need to do some serious thinking, young man."

"There's a war on Elly, and a lot of us aren't going to make it. We have to live it up while we can."

"And if you don't make it, what then?" He tapped the book again.

Ensign Lawson shrugged. "My mother dragged me to her elegant Washington, D.C. church. People were concerned with how they looked and who had the ear of the most powerful congressman. It was more like a country club than anything religious."

"You know I'm not talking about religion or church. I'm talking about the Creator of the universe, a Holy Being. He's holy, and you're not. What would you say to Him if you didn't make it?"

Ensign Lawson shook the serious thought away. "All I'm thinking about right now is that girl. I need someone different. I'm so tired of—just tired of it all." Ensign Lawson's shoulders sagged, and he fiddled with the yeoman's stapler.

Elwood Richardson studied the Ensign for a long minute. He saw a dull red creep up the young man's face. Richardson looked toward the Commander's door, then whispered, "Heaven Ray Turner, but you didn't hear that from me."

"Heaven? She's the feisty civilian nurse that took on the Old Man last month, right?" The Ensign exchanged the stapler for a chocolate from the open box on Richardson's desk. "Not everyone has the guts to do that."

"A little respect for Captain Mark Lawson III, your father, remember?" Yeoman Richardson removed the candy box from the Ensign's reach. "Your party boy attitude is not something he approves of."

"By the way, is the Old—the Commander in?"

Hearing his son's voice, Commander Lawson came to the doorway of his office and frowned, "Stay away from that girl. She and her mother are the finest nurses I've ever seen. Until more Navy nurses arrive, I need these civilians. Don't distract them."

"It's not my intention to distract anyone, Sir."

Commander Lawson snorted his disbelief and said, "Those two recently returned from assessing the Station Hospitals in Cold Bay, Naknek, Adak, Unalaska, and Umnak. I'm sure they are both exhausted. Nurse Turner doesn't need you filling her head with—whatever it is you fill women's heads with."

Ensign Mark Lawson stood at attention and gave his father a precise salute, although his eyes twinkled, "Yes, Sir."

The Commander returned to his office as he muttered, "If I hadn't promised your mother... I'd put you on a battleship ASAP."

Ensign Lawson spoke aloud, "I wish he would."

"Your father wishes he were on a ship as well."

"He's always been behind a desk. He loves pushing papers around."

"You don't know him as well as you think. After World War I, the Navy discovered your father's organizational talent and put him behind a desk."

"So what did he do in the war? He always refused to talk about it."

The yeoman shrugged, "That's his story, not mine."

Mark looked through the window. Bulldozers pushed dirt from one side of the compound to the other. He had heard his father curse Kodiak's lousy ground, muskeg or rock, covered with a layer of volcanic ash ranging from three inches to eight feet in depth. Sometimes crews encountered drifts up to twenty feet, stopping construction until it could be hauled away. Trucks loaded with volcanic ash or men and supplies drove everywhere on the un-paved roads, throwing up dust in Kodiak's fierce wind when it was dry and stalling in thick mud during rainy weather. Cranes hauled timbers into place. Men yelled orders to each other but couldn't be heard over the machines.

"This base is chaotic, hardly functioning," Ensign Lawson sputtered.

"That's why the Navy assigned your father here. The civilian construction crews brought up from the States are overworked, and there are not enough of them. As you know, the seaplane and submarine bases must be on a war footing as soon as possible."

"It's a mess."

"The Commander is trying to get some Seabees posted up here. As you know, Europe and the Pacific get the first crack at them."

"That's where the action is, and I am stuck on this rock," Ensign Lawson moaned.

"We arrived here a year sooner than our contract specified be-cause Japanese interest turned to the north. But you didn't hear that from me." The Yeoman 1st Class closed his eyes and pursed his lips. He glanced at the Commander's door and said, "It was just a SNAFU that you ended up here."

"I thought the Old Man arranged it."

The irritated clerk stared at the closed door with the gold let-tering: Captain Mark Lawson III, Commander, USN Kodiak. He sighed and chose a dark chocolate cream. "Your mother put the idea into a certain senator's ear at a cocktail party in DC. A senator that had influence with the Department of the Navy."

"Why so nervous, Elly, sneaking all those looks at the Com-mander's door. He can't hear you."

"I wouldn't be too sure," Yeoman Richardson shrugged, "but you didn't hear that from me."

"I don't hear much from you, Elly, and I love it." The six-foot-two Ensign stretched, snagged another chocolate, and wondered if he would have joined the Navy given a choice. Expectations ran high for the fourth-generation son of a prominent Naval family. His family's political influence in the nation's capital increased everyone's expectations of him. Ensign Mark Lawson IV felt the presence and pressure of many eyes focused on him even though he was stationed in faraway Alaska.

Yeoman Richardson shoved the candy box into a drawer, gave the Ensign another long look, then whispered, "Heaven Ray's mother was supposed to pick her up but has been delayed. It's a long walk to the girl's home."

"Thanks, Elly, you're the best." Grinning, Ensign Lawson opened the drawer, grabbed the box of chocolates, and dashed out. A moment later, the commander's Jeep threw dusty little tornadoes from the back tires as it roared away.

Before the yeoman returned to his paperwork, he peered out of the window and stared after the vehicle. "Heaven Ray, you just might be the making of that boy—please God."

He unlocked the metal filing cabinet and pulled out another box of chocolates while wondering what consequences the ensign would suffer for taking the Old Man's Jeep.

The Jeep slowed next to Heaven Ray. Eyes straight ahead, she kept walking.

"Hop in. I'll give you a ride."

"It's a nice day. I'll walk."

"It's a long way to wherever you are going."

"My legs are strong."

"And lovely."

"Move along, Ensign. I'm not interested."

"In what? A ride?"

"In you. I've heard about your way with the ladies."

The Ensign gunned the engine and sped away. A few yards ahead, he executed a perfect U-turn and blocked her way. She quietly waited for him to speak. He seemed to be at a loss for words. She tapped her foot. He focused on it.

"Didn't your mother tell you it's rude to stare?" she asked.

"I have chocolate."

"No, thank you."

"How can you turn down chocolate?"

She threw a half-grin in his direction. "I admit it's harder to turn down the chocolate than you."

"I am deeply hurt." He placed his hand over his heart and sighed but couldn't keep the twinkle from his eyes.

"I imagine women succumb to your charms all the time."

He removed his cover—military cap—ran his hand through his black wavy hair and winked. "So, you admit I am charming. That's progress."

"I admit nothing."

He looked toward the sky. "Those dark clouds tell me it's going to rain soon."

She glanced upwards. "I don't think it will rain for an hour or so, but on the off chance you're right, I'll accept a ride and only a ride." She climbed into the Jeep, sat at attention, and once again kept her face forward.

"Nothing else is on offer, ma'am."

"Not even the chocolate?"

"No, ma'am," He laughed and stuffed the box under his seat.

The petite auburn-haired nurse with the classic profile remained silent as they crossed the base and headed toward Kodiak. He asked about her parents, what had brought them to Alaska, why she became a nurse, what readiness the Station Hospitals were in, and what kind of music, movies, books, and food she liked. Her refusal to answer confused him, and he kept glancing her way. He drove slowly even though the dark clouds seemed ready to release their rain.

"You can drop me there." She pointed to a square white cement building at the end of the town's main road. Several local girls were clustered on the wooden sidewalk. He groaned. He had dated all of them at least twice. They whistled and waved and soon crowded around the Jeep.

"Thank you, Ensign," Heaven Ray murmured politely.

"Wait, don't you want coffee, tea, a sandwich, something?" He spoke to her back. She was already halfway into the building.

A tall brunette leaned against the Jeep and laughed, "Torpedoed, Mark. You've been hit."

"What's with her anyway, Delores?"

"Mark, you're all fun and games, which is good since there is a war on, and we'll all probably die."

"Yeah?"

"She's not like that. In fact, Heaven is a good name for her. Even when we were kids, she always talked about God and heaven.

Despite that, we still like her."

Mark shook his head and wondered if Heaven Ray was a religious fanatic. She was pretty, no doubt about that. He decided she was worth the risk. "What are you all doing here?"

"In an hour, the mayor is giving a talk on civil defense at city hall." She pointed to a small building across the unpaved street. "We knew Heaven would be interested."

"But how did you know she'd be here now?"

Delores laughed. "Mail plane flew over thirty minutes ago. Everybody stops by the post office sooner rather than later."

"Small towns," Mark muttered.

Delores slugged him on the arm. "Don't disparage our ways, City Boy."

He grinned sheepishly and changed the subject. "I heard she barged into the Commander's office last month, demanding to tour the Station Hospitals. Elly—Yeoman Richardson—wouldn't give me any details."

Delores laughed and leaned against the Jeep. "She made an appointment and had an answer to all of the Commander's questions. Besides, her mother works for the Territorial Government and has been taking Heaven to the Aleutians for years—unofficially."

"Seems to me a lot of things are done unofficially in Alaska."

Delores winked at the Ensign. "It didn't sit well with Heaven Ray that she was not allowed to go when she had the necessary qualifications and experience."

"She's not Navy."

Delores shrugged. "A technicality. None of us are Navy, yet Barbara and I work at the dispensary and will work at the base hospital."

"If they ever finish the construction."

Delores continued, "Rita is one of Kodiak's best bush pilots and airline mechanics. She's shown your Navy pilots how to scrounge for parts and jerry-rig a thing or two when they couldn't get anything through official channels."

"Rumors are Heaven Ray was aggressive, even feisty." Mark stared at the building, hoping to see the lovely nurse emerge.

Delores crossed her arms and studied the Comander's son. "And how would your father have responded to that?"

Mark shook his head, then grinned. "Not well, but you'd think Nurse Turner would want to dispel the rumors."

"She doesn't pay any attention to gossip. She's out of your league, Marky-boy. Best back off." The woman's red lipstick shimmered in the sun, and her mouth formed a pouty bow.

The girls around the Jeep all talked at once. After dating, he remained friends with all of them. He believed himself to be honest and likable, and everyone, male or female, seemed to agree. "Girls, you're the best. Are you going to help with my heavenly campaign?"

An attractive blonde named Louise said, "She's a goody-two-shoes, Mark. You'd be better off with a real woman."

"Like you?" The green-eyed redhead asked.

"Better than you!"

"Now girls—you lovely girls," Mark pleaded. "I adore you all. You know I do."

Del looked toward the entrance of the post office. "Don't look now, but she's peeking through the glass door."

"That's a good sign, isn't it, girls?" Mark pulled the box from under the seat and handed it to Del. Distracted, the girls giggled and gobbled the candy. A few minutes later, Mark asked, "How long does it take to pick up the mail anyway?"

"You weren't paying attention, Mark. Heaven Ray's left the building and hurried around the corner."

An elderly woman walking by with her mail stopped. "Heaven Ray? She received a letter from her father. She said the mayor would understand she needed to hurry home."

"I thought Heaven Ray's mother was a widow." Mark flashed his dashing smile.

The old woman patted the gray hair that escaped from her headscarf and gave Mark a second look. "Her father is a doctor, and we were sad to lose him. He signed up after the war started and is on a ship."

"The Lexington," Delores added, "Apparently, aircraft carriers need doctors too, and Doc Turner's an excellent surgeon and GP."

The following day, an embarrassed Seaman Recruit delivered a box of chocolates to Heaven Ray at the Fort Abercrombie Dispensary near Miller's Point.

"Why are you giving me this?" Heaven Ray tapped her foot and tried to keep the irritation from her voice. She was confident Ensign Lawson had forced this lowly sailor to do his bidding.

"Ensign's orders, ma'am. I'll be swabbing the decks if you refuse his gift."

"I see." Heaven Ray felt sorry for the pimple-faced boy and took the box from him as the other nurses and office staff gathered around. "There, I have accepted." She opened the box, and in a few seconds, it was empty.

"Yes, ma'am." He turned to go.

"Wait." She handed the empty chocolate box to the uncomfortable sailor and said, "Tell the Ensign the nurses were thankful for the candy. It was delicious."

"But, ma'am, you didn't have any."

"You can tell him that, too."

Everyone laughed, and Delores said, "I don't think our Mark has ever been rebuffed."

"Do I have to, ma'am?" The Seaman Recruit gulped and looked at the giggling women. Heaven Ray was nowhere to be seen.

Delores flung her arm across the flustered seaman's shoulder and escorted him out of the building. "You tell Mark that Nurse Turner is as stubborn as he is. Do you understand me, sailor?"

He shook her arm off his shoulder. "I understand." As he walked away, he tossed the empty candy box into a nearby trash can, muttering, "She's just a nurse. I don't have to obey her. I enlisted to fight, not to be a delivery boy."

Mark Lawson sent chocolates daily, sometimes with a single wildflower, whatever he found growing around the base. The Seaman Recruit felt like a yo-yo delivering the candy boxes, always returning with a negative report. Heaven Ray gave the chocolates to nurses, patients, even the janitor. She took the wildflowers home to her mother, who delighted in them.

Finally, the Seaman Recruit checked Heaven Ray's schedule and left the candy at the nurses' station when Nurse Turner was not on duty. On her next day off, Heaven Ray met him outside of his barracks. She thrust several empty candy boxes in his direction. He stood at attention and let them fall at his feet.

❧

"You can toss me in the brig, Sir. You can keelhaul me or throw me overboard. I will not take any more chocolate to that—that nurse."

"I thought everyone loved that nurse."

The lowly sailor lowered his eyes and gnawed on his lip. "She's polite, but—but—she feels you should do your own courting."

"Courting? What an old-fashioned word." The Ensign rubbed his chin. "Is that what she said? Courting?"

The unfortunate seaman shuffled his feet, swallowed, and with a red face, mumbled, "Umm, Sure, I mean, y-yes, Sir."

"Hmmm, Dismissed!"

www.ingramcontent.com/pod-product-compliance
Lightning Source LLC
Chambersburg PA
CBHW061639190726
48289CB00006B/1670